the
bright
forever

Also by Lee Martin

~~~

Turning Bones
Quakertown
From Our House
The Least You Need to Know

the
bright
forever

a novel

LEE MARTIN

Shaye Areheart Books

NEW YORK

Published in the United States by Shaye Areheart Books, an imprint of the
Crown Publishing Group, a division of Random House, Inc., New York.
www.crownpublishing.com

Shaye Areheart Books and colophon are trademarks of Random House, Inc.

Library of Congress Cataloging-in-Publication Data
Martin, Lee, 1955–
The bright forever : a novel / Lee Martin.—1st ed.
1. Girls—Crimes against—Fiction.   2. Loss (Psychology)—Fiction.
3. Missing children—Fiction.   4. Kidnapping—Fiction.
5. Illinois—Fiction   6. Revenge—Fiction.   I. Title.
PS3563.A724927B75   2005
813'.54—dc22   2004023758

ISBN 1-4000-9791-6

Printed in the United States of America

Design by Lynne Amft

10 9 8 7 6 5 4 3 2 1

First Edition

To Deb

Thank you for asking the right questions

On the banks beyond the river
We shall meet, no more to sever;
In the bright, the bright forever,
In the summer land of song.

—Fanny J. Crosby, "The Bright Forever"

the
bright
forever

Raymond R.

I'M NOT saying I didn't do it. I don't know.

Mr. Dees

On the night it happened—July 5—the sun didn't set until
8:33. I went back later and checked the weather cartoon on the
Evening Register's front page: a smiling face on a fiercely bright sun.
I checked because it was the heart of summer, and I couldn't stop
thinking about that long light and all the people who were out in it;
I'd seen them sitting on porches, drinking Pepsis and listening to
WTHO's Top Fifty Countdown on transistor radios. I knew they
were getting a laugh out of *Peanuts* or *Hi and Lois* in the newspaper,
thrilling to the adventures of *Steve Canyon*. Cars were driving along
High Street—Trans-Ams and GTOs, Mustangs and Road Runners,
Chargers and Barracudas. Some of them were on their way to the
drive-in theater east of town—a twin bill, *Summer of '42* and *Bless
the Beasts and Children*. Others went downtown. Teenage boys were
ducking into the Rexall or the new Super Foodliner to pick up a
pack of Marlboros or Kools. Couples were strolling around the
courthouse square, lollygagging after supper at the Coach House
or a steak and a cold beer at the Top Hat Inn. They were window-
shopping, the ladies admiring the new knee-high boots at Bogan's

Shoe Store, high school girls looking at the first wire-rim glasses at Blank's Optical, the flared-leg pantsuits at Helene's Dress Shop, the friendship bracelets and engagement sets at Lett's Jewelry.

Enough time and opportunity, and yet no one could stop what was going to happen.

We were just an itty-bitty town in Indiana, on the flat plain beyond the rolling hills of the Hoosier National Forest—a glassworks town near the White River, which twisted and turned to the southwest before emptying into the Wabash and running down to the Ohio. That day, a Wednesday, the temperature had gotten up to ninety-three and the humidity had settled in and left everyone limp with trying. The air held in the smell of heat from the furnaces at the glassworks, the dead fish stink from the river, the sounds of people's living: ice cubes clinking in glasses, car mufflers rattling, screen doors creaking, mothers calling children to come in.

In the evening, when the breeze picked up enough to stir the leaves on the courthouse lawn's giant oaks and dusk started to fall, the air cooled just enough to make us forget how hot and unforgiving the day had been. After the hours spent working at the glassworks or the stone quarry or the gravel pit, people were glad to be moving about at their own pace, taking their time, letting the coming dark and the rustle of air convince them that soon there might be rain and then the heat would break. I was content to sit at the kitchen table, noodling around with the story problems I planned to use the next day with my summer students, one of whom was Katie Mackey.

Later, there would be a few folks who would step up and say they had something maybe the police ought to know. Their names would be in the newspapers—papers as far away as St. Louis and

Chicago—and on the Terre Haute and Indianapolis television sta-
tions, people who would be in the notebooks of all the magazine
writers who'd come—slick-talking out-of-towners with questions.
Newshounds from *Inside Detective, Police Gazette.* They'd want to
know how to find so-and-so.

I've never been able to tell this story and my part in it until now,
but listen, I'll say it true: a man can live with something like this
only so long before he has to make it known. My name is Henry
Dees, and I was a teacher then—a teacher of mathematics and a
summer tutor for the children like Katie who needed such a thing.
I'm an old man now, and even though more than thirty years have
gone by, I still remember that summer and its secrets, and the way
the heat was and how the light stretched on into evening like it
would never leave. If you want to listen, you'll have to trust me. Or
close the book; go back to your lives. I warn you: this is a story as
hard to hear as it is for me to tell.

Gilley

We were eating supper. That's what I remember, the four of us sitting at the table: Mom and Dad and me and Katie. It was just a night like that, a summer night, and pretty soon Katie would finish her lemon sherbet and ask to be excused and then run up the street to find her friend Renée Cherry. That's what would have happened. I've known it all these years. Renée and Katie would have made up, said they were sorry about the quarrel they'd had that morning, and played until dark, when Mom would have called my sister in.

But before any of that could happen, I said, "Katie didn't take back her library books."

I was still mad at her because sometime that afternoon she had gone into my room and listened to my Carole King album, *Tapestry*, and left a scratch on the "It's Too Late" track so it stuck on the chorus—"Too late, too late, too late"—and I wanted to pay her back. I wanted to see her get in Dutch with Dad, who had warned her about keeping library books past the due date. "Good golly, Little Miss Katie," he'd told her at breakfast. "If you're not careful, you'll be living a life of crime." We knew we were a family that people noticed, envied even, for our wealth and my father's influence in our town. Our family had owned Mackey Glass for years, and my father always told us we had to be careful not to screw up, not to give anyone a reason to think less of us. "If the police come looking for you," he said to Katie, "I'll tell them we tried our best to bring you up right, but you wouldn't listen. Now, I mean it, Katie. Take those books back today."

But she didn't. She and Renée spent all morning on the front porch. They were there when I was getting ready for work. I was seventeen that summer, and I was a clerk and stock boy at the J. C. Penney store downtown. I was standing in front of my dresser mirror, knotting my necktie, and I could hear Katie and Renée in the porch swing. The chains creaked as the swing moved back and forth. Katie and Renée were playing their favorite game—It's Gotta Go—where they made choices between things that they dearly loved. Pepsi or Coke, spaghetti or macaroni, Little Dot or Little Lulu, puppies or kittens, Barbie or Skipper, "You Can't Roller Skate in a Buffalo Herd" or "Hello Muddah, Hello Fadduh," Christmas or your birthday. Making a choice was heartbreaking and took hours. Often they'd end up bawling. They'd hug each other and agree that it was necessary. If it wasn't hard, it wouldn't matter. It proved how much they really loved the things they said they'd let go.

Renée's mother, Margot, claimed to have ESP. The sixth sense, she called it. A sign in front of her house said, WILL TELL YOU YOUR ENTIRE LIFE WITHOUT ASKING A SINGLE QUESTION. I'd gone to her earlier that summer. Just for a kick. She held my hands, turned them over, and traced the lines in my palms. "You will be chosen," she told me. "Soon a light will find you. Don't look away."

On the porch, Katie and Renée were trying to decide between

The Partridge Family and *The Brady Bunch*: one of them had to go. Katie said that Keith Partridge was dreamier than Greg Brady, but she'd much rather be friends with Marcia than with Laurie Partridge. Marcia was just so cute, and her hair was perfect; Laurie was too skinny, and Katie was fairly certain that she didn't really know how to play that electric piano. Renée, who usually took her cues from Katie, said yes, that was true, but who wouldn't choose Peter Brady over Danny Partridge?

"Maybe I wouldn't," Katie said.

The swing's chains stopped creaking; someone, maybe Renée, dragged her feet over the porch floor. "You can't mean that," she said, and she sounded very serious, like a grown-up. "You've got to be kidding. Danny instead of Peter? No way. Danny isn't nice."

I finished knotting my tie and went over to look out the window. A robin was parading around the lawn. The grass, still wet from the sprinkler, sparkled in the sunlight. The petunias in my mother's flower bed smelled sweet; their pink and red and white petals ruffled in the breeze.

"I think he's funny," Katie said.

"He's not funny," said Renée. "He's retarded."

"What about me?" Katie was getting worked up, the way she did sometimes. She could be a drama queen, in love with the spotlight. The day before, she'd worn sunglasses and posed on the stone bench in our backyard so I could take her picture with my Polaroid camera. I knew her eyes were wide open now as she faced Renée, and her cheeks were filled with air. When she got like that, I told her she looked like Porky Pig. "I'm funny," she said to Renée. "I always make you laugh when I do my Donald Duck voice. Isn't that funny?"

"No, it's retarded."

"You're the retarded one," Katie said.

For a good while neither of them said anything. The only sound was the wind through the trees. Then Renée said, "Maybe I should just go home now."

Katie agreed. "Maybe you should."

"Do you want me to go?"

"If that's what you want."

"All right. I guess you want me to go."

So Renée left, and Katie ran into the house bawling, and she never got around to taking her books back to the library. She ruined my new record instead, and even though I wanted to feel sorry for her because she'd had that fight with Renée, I couldn't, and I said what I did, and Dad blew his top.

"Katie." He leaned across the table and shook a finger at her. "What did I tell you?"

She jumped up from her chair. "I'm going to take them back right now." She was wearing a pair of orange shorts and a black T-shirt. Her brown hair, lightened from the sun, was combed off her forehead and pinned with gold barrettes. "The library's open until seven o'clock. I've got plenty of time."

She never even stopped to put on sandals. They were right there at the back door, but she didn't put them on. I thought about stopping her. I thought about saying, "Katie, your sandals." But I didn't. She was barefoot, and she swung open the screen door. She threw her library books into her bicycle basket and I watched her stand up on the pedals until she reached the top of the hill. Then she sat down and bent over her handlebars, and her long hair flew out behind her, and I watched her until she was gone.

Clare

THE IDEA was to build a porch on the front of the house. Ray said he could put it up in a whipstitch. He'd build it out of cement blocks so it'd never rot. He'd put a shingle roof over it and hang a swing from the rafters so we could sit out there of an evening, the two of us—Ray and me, just like folks do. Maybe then, he said, the high-and-mighty neighbors would come to visit and we'd all gab as the sun went down. When the mosquitoes came out and the lightning bugs, Ray would say, "How about a game of cards?" Everyone would come into the house, and we'd play a few hands of pinochle at the kitchen table. Ray would turn on the radio; I'd serve strawberry shortcake because it was that time of year, June, when the strawberries were ripe. "How'd that be?" he asked me. Pinochle and music and strawberry shortcake—and I told him I believed that'd suit me just fine.

He wasn't always my life. That's what I want you to know. My first husband, Bill, he died when he took sick in the heart. He died on a January afternoon. He was in our bedroom, hanging up his coat, and he went down. I can't get the noise out of my head—

mercy—the way a man's body sounds when it collapses and hits the floor. The house shook. The storm windows rattled in their frames. Outside, the wind rocked the power lines, chased snakes of powdery snow across the street. Two girls walked past on their way home from school. They wore corduroy coats, and they'd pulled their hoods up over their heads. I could hear them chitter-chattering: *Cinderella dressed in yellow, went upstairs to kiss a fellow.* Then the wind swallowed up their bright voices.

Don't ask me what it was about Ray. We just hit it off. What good does it do to wonder over such things now?

We lived together in my house, lived there even before we married. I'll admit that. Yes, it's true. But even now, when I'm eighty-two, it doesn't seem like all that bad of a sin, just one come from being lonely, and won't God surely forgive that?

I keep thinking about the first time I saw Ray. Raymond Royal Wright. Raymond R. "You just keep saying my name," he told me.

We were uptown at the Top Hat Inn, where I went sometimes with my neighbors Leo and Lottie Marks. They were dancing to jukebox songs. This time it was Charley Pride singing that number that always made me wish I was forty years younger, just starting out, all my life ahead of me. I wanted to close my eyes and listen to Charley's molasses voice telling men to kiss an angel good morning and then love her like the devil when they got back home. Back in the corner, where I sat with Ray, the light was dim. He had on too much aftershave—that lime-scented Hai Karate that was so popular then. His cheeks were red, and he was grinning. He wasn't a looker, and I knew right away I had at least ten years on him, but oh, that grin, and the way his eyes sparkled like there was something exciting just around the corner. I don't mind saying it was cozy with him there at the table, and that song . . . well, I've already made it plain what that did to me.

"Raymond R.," he said again. He just had that way about him, and I did what he asked. I kept saying his name, and he filled in the rest.

"Raymond R."

"Magnificent."

"Raymond R."

"Strong."

"Raymond R."

"King of the mountain, as true as the day is long, all dressed up and no place to go."

I couldn't help but laugh then. Giggled like a girl. He took my hand, raised it to his lips, and kissed it. An old dame like me. Imagine.

"You must be out of your head," I told him, and then before I'd even known that it was going to happen, I was crying. It's funny how someone can come along and slice open your life, show you just exactly what's inside. Me? I was a widow storing up tears for all the lonely days and nights I feared lay in wait for me. Then Ray kissed my hand, and I knew I'd tell him anything, tell him about Bill and how toward the end he went inside himself and brooded over his sick heart. We forgot love, forgot what had brought us together in the first place. It all came back to me that day when he fell to the floor. I called the ambulance. I covered him with a quilt from the bed, the wedding-ring quilt Mama had made for us, and I sat there rubbing my hand over his face, letting my fingers remember what he'd looked like all those years back when he was black-haired and smooth-skinned.

"Darlin'." Ray patted my hand, held it between the two of his like he'd never let go, and I didn't want him to. That's how lonely I was. I want you to remember that. I'm not a smart woman. Never claimed to be. But I know how to love folks. Even now after all that's gone on. "Don't cry," he told me while Leo and Lottie were dancing. "I'm Raymond R. Darlin', I'm Mister Wright."

Mr. Dees

LIKE I SAID, it was a Wednesday, and I was at the kitchen table with my yellow legal pad and my fountain pen, the Parker 51 my parents gave me when I graduated from high school, valedictorian of the class of '49. It was a well-balanced pen with a Vacuumatic filler, a simple slip cap, and a hooded, extra-fine nib. My father paid twelve dollars and fifty cents for it at Orr's Stationery Shop. It was nearly ten o'clock when I heard footsteps on the front porch and then a knock at the door.

I switched on the porch light and peeked out between the curtain panels. On the porch, a police officer shaded his eyes with his hand, leaned over, and tried to peek in through the door glass. He wore a navy-blue uniform. I opened the door, and he straightened up, the leather of his gun belt and holster creaking as he took a step back. He was a tall, burly man, and his light-blue necktie came only halfway down his big belly.

He needed to ask me some questions, he said. I was Henry Dees, wasn't I, the one who taught at the high school?

"Yes," I told him. "That's me."

Was it true that I gave lessons to kids in the summer, school lessons? Was it true that one of my pupils was Katie Mackey? Had I been with her at her home that afternoon?

He had a pocket-size steno pad and a number 2 Faber-Castell pencil. The lead was dull, and he had tried to sharpen it with a pocketknife. It was a worn-down stub of a pencil, and it was painful for me to watch his thick fingers close around it. I offered him the use of my fountain pen, but he said no, he only had a few more questions, but it was a handsome pen, he could certainly see that. A Parker 51, wasn't it? Yes, sir, a fine pen.

"I spent an hour and a half at the Mackeys'," I said. "I'm teaching Katie how to solve story problems."

"Have you seen her since?"

"No."

"Have you been out of the house tonight?"

"No, I've been here. Is it something with Katie? Is that why you ask?"

June bugs batted their heads against the porch light's globe. A freight train took the curve into town and blasted its whistle. Wheels whined against the rails. The box cars creaked and groaned in their couplings.

"That's right," the officer said. "It's Katie. She left home after supper to return some library books, and now no one can find her. We were hoping she might be here."

"Why in the world would she be with me?"

"We're just checking things out, Mister Dees. You understand."

"I taught her story problems," I said, "and then I came home."

I had walked home from the Mackeys' even though it was too hot for walking, particularly once I got out of the shade of the giant oaks that lined the cobblestone streets in Katie's neighborhood. I loved it there, in the Heights, where the grand Victorian homes sat back from the sidewalks and the lawns were lush and landscaped with flower beds. Who hadn't gone past the Mackeys' house at one time or another and tried to imagine the majestic life that surely went on in such a home? My own neighborhood, Gooseneck, was a scatter of bungalows west of town on the Tenth Street spur, the cracked macadam road that branched off from Route 59 and angled past Mackey Glass. The burned smell was always in the air, and the stacks from the furnaces at the glassworks were wreathed with smoke. Each time I went to the Heights, I loved coming up onto the Mackeys' wraparound porch and hearing Katie bounding down the stairs. "Mama, it's Mister Dees," she'd call out, and my heart would fill with her bright voice.

I'll tell you this now. Yes, I loved Katie. I loved her pug nose, the sheen of her brown hair and the way it smelled of strawberries. Sometimes we sat in the porch swing, and she scooted over close to me so I could help her with her story problems. I can still feel the tickle of her hair on my arm as she bent over her tablet. The first time it happened I felt something I didn't have a name for, an odd mix of delight and fear. I could barely finish the lesson. I made errors, had to scratch out numbers with my pen until the tablet page was ink-stained and wrinkled. My fingers trembled. "Is it my fault?" she asked, and I told her no. I say it to her even now: "No, Katie. It was never, never your fault." How were you to know about the dark corners of a man's heart, a man like me, who had never married, who knew he would have no child of his own? Your surprised laugh when I told you that you had solved a problem correctly—the way you clapped your hands together and said, "Holy moly, Mister

Dees"—was more than I could wish. The sheer joy of you, my pupil—dare I say it?—my child.

The police officer closed his steno pad. "You'll let us know," he said, "if you think of anything that might help us?" He started down the porch steps, stopped, and turned back to me. "Oh, and you don't have any out-of-town trips planned, do you?"

"Me?" I said. "Where would I go?"

"Good. I'm sure the chief will want to talk to you. So stick close."

Little by little, the story would unfold. Everything would become public knowledge, verifiable facts that anyone could retrieve from newspaper articles, court documents, eyewitness accounts. But all that anyone knew that night was that Katie had gone to return books to the library and hadn't come home.

At the kitchen table, I sketched out this story problem, the one that still haunts me: "If a girl leaves home, pedaling her bicycle at a speed of 5 miles per hour, bound for the public library, which is 1.4 miles away, how long will it take her to arrive?"

Gilley

AFTER SUPPER, I went out into the backyard to practice chip shots. I was on the golf team at school, and in the summer, I tried to keep my game sharp. I had a tendency to scull my chips, short-arming my swing and catching only the top of the ball. That's what I was working on that night, brushing the grass with the blade of my wedge instead of chopping at the ball. I tried to make my mind quiet, to see only the ball, to live in that moment of backswing and follow-through. Weight on my front foot, my hands ahead of the ball, sweeping it off the grass. I kept at it for well over an hour. I hit shot after shot and watched the balls arc and drop in the gathering dusk. The fireflies came out, hovering and flickering, and I expected, at any minute, to see Katie and Renée Cherry chasing after them with Mason jars. "Got one," Renée would say, and Katie would answer, "Got two."

Then our patio lights came on, and my mother stepped outside. The screen door slapped against its frame. "Gilley." She had a loud voice. She and Katie. They were the talkers. "Gilley," she said again. She leaned over to snap a dried-up bloom off a geranium. "I want you to help Dad look for your sister."

We didn't think anything was wrong, not then. We thought Katie was just being Katie—scatterbrained—just doing what nine-year-old kids did. She'd probably stopped off at Renée Cherry's on her way back from the library, or ridden over to the city park to go down the curlicue slide. Any minute we'd hear her bike, chain rattling against its guard, coming up our drive.

"Let's check uptown," my father said when we were in the car. "Trace her route. Okay? Then, if we don't find her, we'll split up, go to her friends' houses. You know. Like that."

Here's what I didn't know: my father was a dangerous man. I'm not sure he knew that himself, but I can't say that I blame him. He was doing what we all do—I'm sure of this now—living blind. He thought he had his life right where he wanted it, thought he knew who he was—Junior Mackey, civil and gracious even if given to being quiet and brooding from time to time. He liked corny jokes. Here's one: *Two men walk into a bar. The third man ducks.* Don't feel bad if you don't get it. I didn't either the first time my father told it. He had to explain it to me. "Two men," he said. "A bar. Think iron. Think steel. Doink. Right in the noggin. The third man ducks."

We drove up High Street toward the courthouse square. "Keep your eyes open," my father told me, and I remember thinking with satisfaction, Well, now she's done it. Now she'll get it good, and that'll serve her right for scratching my album.

Even when I think back on it now, I remember the way the night air felt coming in through our open windows and how my father turned on the car radio so he could keep up with the Cardinals game in St. Louis. It was pleasant, really, being in that car, and listening to Harry Caray doing the play-by-play from Busch Stadium. At the Christian Church, a bride and groom were coming down the steps while the wedding guests showered them with rice. I could see the grains flash and sparkle as they slanted down. Uptown, some kids I knew from school had parked their cars in the Super Foodliner lot and were sitting on their hoods, boys and girls flirting and laughing, just killing time, really, because that's what we all thought we had in a small town in summer. Long hours of light. Lots and lots of time.

I thought I knew what this all meant, this coming and going. It was just life moving the way it did and yet seeming to stand still. That's how it felt when I was seventeen, satisfied with the long summer days and my senior year stretching out ahead of me, but at the same time eager for it all to pass so my real life, the one I would live in earnest, could begin. I was, like all seventeen-year-olds, sure of too many things. I thought I knew what it meant to be a family, but really I had no idea, not until that night when my father turned onto Fourteenth Street, along the west side of the courthouse, and we saw Katie's bicycle.

It was leaning against a parking meter in front of the J. C. Penney store. The front wheel was cockeyed, turned sharply to the right, and the bike had slid down the meter pole just enough to make it seem that at any second it might fall.

My father pulled into the parking spot so the headlights were fully on the bike, and I saw that the wire basket was empty.

"That's it, isn't it?" he said, and his voice was a different voice than I had ever heard from him: tight and too loud with what I now know was fear. "That's Katie's."

That afternoon, I'd crouched on the platform behind the store's front window, arranging a display of women's summer shoes: red vinyl sandals, black canvas sling-backs, white Keds sneakers. I'd watched the people passing on the sidewalk: clerks who worked in the courthouse offices, window-shopping on their afternoon coffee breaks; lawyers carrying briefcases, their suit coats hooked on a finger and draped over their shoulders; farm families who'd come to town on business, their faces scrubbed and bright. So when I saw Katie's bike, I got the queerest feeling to think that all night, since the time she had left it there and gone off wherever she had gone, people had walked by and never once thought that anything might be wrong.

My father and I got out of the car and stepped up onto the sidewalk. He took the bicycle by its handlebars, straightened it, and put down the kickstand. By this time, shortly after eight o'clock, there was little traffic downtown, but from time to time a car drove past, and I saw the people inside looking our way, wondering, I suppose, what we were doing there with that bicycle.

When I was arranging the shoe display that afternoon, a woman stopped to watch me and I was embarrassed to be handling the sandals and sling-backs and sneakers, the way I often turned shy when I had to help someone press her foot into a pump or buckle a sandal strap around her heel. To this day, I can't watch a woman slip her foot into a shoe without feeling that I'm seeing something I hadn't ought to see. Call me crazy, but you don't know my story yet, not all of it.

That night I didn't either, but as I stood there with my father, I sensed that I was moving into something—something hard. We all were: my father and I, and my mother, who waited for us at home. I wanted to be the third man from my father's joke. I wanted to duck under whatever we were walking into, and just keep moving through that summer—working at Penney's, going to church on

Sunday mornings, and then out to the country club for a round of golf. I wanted to go home and listen to Katie coming down the stairs from her bath, her bare feet hopping from the second step to the floor, her Josie and the Pussycats nightshirt billowing out around her when she threw her arms around my waist and I told her good night, good night, don't let the Heffalumps and Woozles bite. "Heffalumps and Woozles," she'd say, marching off to bed. "Oh, my. What a terrible sight."

Raymond R.

THEY SAY I kidnapped a girl in broad daylight off a street corner in Tower Hill.

Mr. Dees

I WAS WATCHING—I was always watching—and you, you people who now can't even remember my name, you thought you knew exactly who I was.

Gooseneck

No one in Gooseneck knew why Clare Mains had taken up with that Raymond Wright, that peckerwood no one could bring themselves to tolerate. No one but Mr. Dees, who lived down the road in a bungalow going to ruin. He knew it was two folks coming together so they wouldn't have to be alone. If anyone had asked, he would have told them. It was as simple as that.

Mr. Dees taught mathematics at the high school, and summers he offered tutoring for little pay, sometimes none at all if the parents were down on their luck. Although folks were pleasant to him—after all, he was a kind and patient teacher, always eager to lend a hand—he had no real friends since it was commonly assumed that he preferred to keep to himself. "Anything for a quiet life," his high school *Hilltopper* quote read, and, as if fulfilling this prophecy, he had lived alone without incident or scandal in Gooseneck, this curved road set off from the rest of the town, this grass widow of houses, twenty-three of them, that survived when the Mackey Glass Company bought land for its factory and lots back in the twenties. No one went to Gooseneck, folks said, unless they lived there or they were lost or they had a boy or girl who needed Mr. Dees.

Teach, Ray called him. "Hey, Teach," he said that first time. "Do you mind a little friendly advice?"

Mr. Dees was patching cracks in his concrete steps. It was a Saturday afternoon in April, and he liked the way the sky opened up, high and blue above him. A single-engine plane, its prop humming, flew over, and Mr. Dees, kneeling on the grass, tipped back his head. The sun was warm on his face. He shaded his eyes with his hand and wondered who was in the plane and where he was going. How magnificent to be flying on this day when there were no clouds, no wind, looking down on the town where trees were leafing out and the yellow daffodils were in bloom—looking down on him, Mr. Dees thought. For a moment he wondered what he looked like to whoever was in that plane. Surely, from that height, no one could see that he had cut his own hair that morning— he'd rather rag it up than have to make conversation at the barber- shop—or that his ears were too big and stuck out too far from his narrow head. No one in that plane could tell that his poplin jacket had a tear in the shoulder that he had very carefully mended with an iron-on patch, and no one could see how his eyeglasses sat crookedly on his nose because he dreaded having to walk into Blank's Optical and ask for an adjustment. He'd do it eventually. He'd go in and say in his teacher's voice what he wanted, but for now he was happy not to have to do that. The plane soared high above him and above the glassworks and its furnaces and smoke. Magnificent.

"I'm Henry Dees," he said to Ray, who was squatting down be- side him now, weight balanced easily on the balls of his feet, rear end hanging over his heels. "How do you know I'm a teacher?"

Ray touched a finger to the corner of each eye. "Keep the peep- ers open." He tugged on his earlobes. "Hear what you can hear.

Easy." He laid his hand on Mr. Dees's wrist. "Friend, I'm handy with these sorts of things. Now watch how I spread this mud."

Mr. Dees let Ray take the trowel from his hand. It was all too much for him, the upkeep of the house. Too much he was worthless to do: caulking, painting, electrical wiring; repairs to the furnace, the plumbing, the roof. He'd never listened when his father had tried to teach him how to do those things. What was the use? He didn't have the knack. His head was full of numbers, equations, problems. He liked to chase the unknown, find the answer, or noodle around with theorems, starting with the assertion of truth and then offering up the proof. That was how the world made sense to him. Doing away with mystery. But home repairs? It was always one problem on top of another. He understood them in theory—how to patch the cracked concrete, for example—but when it came time to do it, he was clumsy and inept, and he was glad now for Ray to have the trowel.

"Work the point in deep." Ray was talking to him in a soft, patient voice, the sort Mr. Dees used with his students. "Don't be shy. Tamp that mud in there. You got to fill that crack all the way up or else the damp gets in and then winter comes and the concrete freezes and heaves. Fill it all the way. Then when the mud starts to set, smooth it out with the back of your trowel. That's all there is to it."

He said all this without passing judgment on Mr. Dees and the slapdash way he'd been slopping on the mortar. Ray showed him how to patch the concrete without embarrassing him, and for that Mr. Dees was grateful.

So a few days later, when Ray asked him why it was that the folks in Gooseneck, neighbors Clare had known for years, suddenly had their noses out of joint ("Won't so much as give us the time of day"), he patiently explained that these people had known Bill Mains, had thought well of him, and now they were put off by the way Ray, so soon after Bill died, had moved in and set up shop.

Then, because he didn't know how to hold back the truth when it was there, clear and irrefutable, he told Ray that folks in Gooseneck had no patience with someone nosing around in their business—someone they considered an outsider, a gabby Gus who didn't mince words. They didn't want him, as he was prone to do, offering them advice on how to keep their houses in tip-top shape. He knocked on their doors and told them straight-out that they ought to do this or that—said it all with a big smile, of course, but still, there it was.

Mr. Dees knew all this because he watched and listened. In the Super Foodliner, the Rexall, the City Newsstand, he heard his neighbors talking, and what they said was *That Raymond Wright, that Johnny-come-lately, that know-it-all.* They rolled their eyes. *Raymond R.,* someone always said with a smirk, and someone else answered, *Raymond R. Wrong.*

In their houses, where Mr. Dees often went to tutor their children, they sometimes said these things to him. It was easy to tell him what they thought because they trusted him. They said these things to him, and he took them in, not knowing how to respond because the truth was he liked Raymond R., felt sorry for him, even, because Mr. Dees could see that he was trying so hard to make his neighbors like him. He remembered how Ray had taught him to patch the concrete steps. He was the only one of his neighbors who had ever come to offer a hand instead of asking him to please, please, do what he could to help their sons and daughters learn their numbers. *Please, Mister Dees. Can you teach them?*

These were people who worked hard hours, many of them at Mackey Glass. People like Leo and Lottie Marks, Tubby and Thelma Carl—all of them working. They came home in the evenings bone tired, and sometimes it was hard for them to keep up with what needed doing around their homes. They didn't want Raymond R. to point out curled roof shingles to them, or a bum paint job, or windows that weren't airtight, and it was hard for them to forgive him for being forward.

That's what Mr. Dees explained when Ray asked him for the story. He said it the way he always said something when he was trying to be encouraging—in a voice that was just a little sad, but also kind, the voice he used with his students, the one that said, *I'm disappointed in you, but don't worry. I know you'll do better.*

He and Ray were in Mr. Dees's garage. A strong wind had toppled one of the purple martin houses that Mr. Dees, a few years back, had paid a carpenter to build, and Ray was repairing it. He had brought down his miter saw and cut a new piece of wood to replace the side of the martin house that had splintered, and now he was tacking it into place.

"I just want to be a help," he said.

"I know you do," Mr. Dees told him.

"You didn't seem to mind when I showed you how to patch that concrete."

"Me?" Mr. Dees swallowed hard. He looked away, out the garage window to where the surprise lilies—the naked ladies—were just sending up their long, leafless stalks. He was embarrassed to say what he had been about to, that he had no friends, that he was thankful for Ray's company. "My house is old," he said instead. He cleared his throat. "All these houses in Gooseneck are old."

Ray laid his hammer down on the workbench. He ran his fingers over the bare wood. "You call me when you got something needs getting done." He kept his head down, and it touched Mr. Dees to hear his shy voice. "Any time. I mean it. Don't be afraid. You come get me."

So that was how their friendship began, with this moment in the garage when they both admitted, without saying as much, that they were less than satisfied with the way their lives had turned out. They never said the words. They never said "lonely." They never said "afraid." They never spoke of yearning or the wrong turns they'd taken over the years and the hard places they'd come to, but it was all plain in what they did say, which was, Mr. Dees knew, as much as they could risk because they were just starting to know each other and how much could anyone stand to feel pulsing in another person's heart?

He painted the new wood on the martin house, and when it was dry, he asked Raymond R. if he would be willing—that is, if he had the time—to help set the house back atop its pole.

They did the chore one evening at twilight when lights were coming on in houses up and down Gooseneck. Somewhere behind Mr. Dees's bungalow, where fields stretched back to wetlands, spring peepers sang. The wind was from the north, and it brought the scents of freshly plowed earth and wild onions growing in the fencerows. Martins swooped down from the darkening sky, some of them coming to roost in the row of houses, each of them with eight compartments—four over four.

"They like close quarters, don't they?" Ray said.

"They don't shy away from one another," Mr. Dees told him. "And they like to be near where people are living. It makes them feel safe. In fact, they'll only nest in these houses that people put up."

"Well, then," Ray said. "I guess we better put this one back up."

They set twelve-foot stepladders next to each other and to-gether, Mr. Dees to the right and Ray to the left, they carried the martin house to the point where they could set it on its pole. The wooden ladders creaked with their weight, the legs wobbling just a bit, sinking some in the damp grass. Mr. Dees steadied the house while Ray anchored it to its shelf with wood screws.

"There," he said when he was finished. "Good as new."

"That's a good job," Mr. Dees said.

"Yes, sir," said Ray. "That's all right."

Then they reached across the space between the ladders and shook hands.

It was then that an almost imperceptible shadow passed over them, just the slightest alteration in the dimming light, and Mr. Dees let his eyes follow that shadow to the catalpa tree along the side of his garage. He saw it then, the Cooper's hawk—he saw its white undertails and its white breast stained with thin red lines—and he knew that the hawk had come to ambush the martins.

It happened from time to time. A Cooper's hawk or a sharpie hid in the catalpa tree early in the morning or, like now, when dusk was falling and the martins were flying into their nests. Some morn-ings, Mr. Dees came out to the houses and found a scatter of black feathers, iridescent with purple, lying on the ground. The martins were so confident about their aerial skills that they thought they could always escape danger, and sometimes that faith cost them. They were ferocious at high altitudes. There they mobbed any hawk that swooped down on them. They called a loud, raspy *accck* as they dived on the hawk, coming within inches but not striking it, relying on their number and their noise to drive it away. But now, as they came to roost, they were stupid, blind to the Cooper's hawk, who waited for his chance.

Mr. Dees wouldn't come down from his ladder, not even after Ray had let go of his hand and said, "Almost dark, Teach."

"Over there." Mr. Dees pointed. "In that catalpa tree. A Cooper's hawk."

A martin gliding down to roost suddenly streaked upward. It shrieked an alarm call. The Cooper's hawk, its wings popping, burst from the tree, but it was too late. The martin was still rising, gone. Other martins dived at the hawk. Their mob calls filled the air.

Mr. Dees was shouting, but only later would he understand that he had done this. He was waving his arms. "You, you, you." He clapped his hands together. "You, shoo."

Finally, the hawk rose higher and banked off toward the woodlands. The martins swirled in a black mass, their calls gradually fading.

Mr. Dees realized then that Ray's hand was gripping his bicep. He felt the ladder wobble. "Easy, Teach. Easy." Ray's voice was steady. "I've got you. Don't worry. I won't let you fall."

It embarrassed Mr. Dees for Ray to see the secret he kept: how much the martins mattered to him. He couldn't begin to say what it did to him mornings when he heard their song. The first time, each spring, it was always a lone male, a scout, gliding and swooping through the sky, which was just beginning to brighten. He warbled and chittered, high above the martin houses that Mr. Dees had made ready. This was the dawnsong, the one that touched him the most—a sign of spring, a call to other martins that here, here, here was home.

He couldn't tell Ray that. He couldn't call it what it was, love.

But, and this was what amazed him, Ray knew it without anything having to be said, and, what's more, he understood.

"I hear those martins singing," he said, "and I think, It's not so bad, this world. It's not so bad as we'd have it. No, sir. Not at all."

CLARE LIKED to wake early and listen to the martins singing. Such a happy, bubbling sound, the song of babies babbling and cooing. She liked to lie in bed, close to Ray, and think how lucky she was. Spring had come, and the martins were singing, and she was in love. Who would have thought it, particularly back in January when Bill had died and left her alone? But here she was, almost sixty years old, with another chance at happiness, and who cared what the neighbors thought? Her life was hers, and if someone didn't like the fact that she had set up house with Raymond Royal Wright, then they could lump it.

He wasn't particularly handsome. Clare could say that without feeling ashamed; it was as much a fact as her own plain looks. He was a stocky man with a round, sunburned face, and his red hair had already thinned. Because he knew he wasn't, in his own words, "easy on the peepers," he tried hard to make up for it by being friendly.

One evening—Ray had gone down the road to help Mr. Dees with his birdhouse—Clare looked out the front window and saw Thelma and Tubby Carl coming out of Lottie and Leo Marks's house across the street. Thelma was carrying an empty pie tin. Tubby was smoking his pipe. Lottie and Leo stepped out onto their porch, Lottie with her hair curled and piled up on top of her head, Leo still holding a hand of playing cards. Clare knew they'd all been playing euchre or pinochle. They'd been cracking jokes. Even now they were laughing. Tubby had to take his pipe away from his mouth, he was laughing so hard, and Lottie's elaborate hairdo was wobbling. "Now, that's rich." Thelma beat the pie tin against her leg. "Did you hear that, Tubby? My God."

It hadn't been so long ago that Clare and Bill had been a part of their neighbors' card games and ice cream suppers, but after Bill died, Clare knew that what she had long suspected was indeed true. It had always been Bill's company that people like Thelma and Tubby, Lottie and Leo had valued, not hers. Before he got sick, Bill had an easy way about him. He liked good food and good jokes. He had a tattoo of a mermaid on his right bicep, and often when they were over at a neighbor's house, he rolled up his shirtsleeve, flexed his muscle, and made that mermaid wiggle and dance. "That's Clare, dancing the hootchy-kootchy," he said, and it made her face burn when everyone laughed as if they thought dancing the hootchy-kootchy was the last thing in the world skinny old plain-faced Clare would do. There she was, her chest caved in, her shoulders slumped, and there was the mermaid, all breasts and hips, all curves and long, flowing hair. When Clare heard everyone hoot and laugh, she wanted to go home and never come back. "Honestly," she told Bill one night. "I wish I never had to set foot in those people's houses again."

Now she had her wish. For a while after Bill died, neighbors like Thelma and Lottie stopped in to bring her a recipe from the *Evening Register* or to ask her if she'd like to come along to a Rebekkahs lodge meeting or to the Top Hat Inn for a bottle of beer and some songs on the jukebox, but she was shy without Bill to ease the way for her, and more often than not she said she had sewing to do or a TV program she wanted to watch, and then she took up with Ray, and soon the invitations stopped.

She was thinking about the purple martins that evening and how they came each spring to Mr. Dees's apartment houses as she watched the Carls and the Markses and listened to their cackles and guffaws. "Oh, God," Thelma kept saying. "Oh, God. Stop, stop. You'll make me pee my pants." Folks needed to be together. As much as she hated hearing Thelma—as much as she hated seeing her and Lottie and Tubby and Leo having so much fun—she also longed to be a part of it the way she did when she was a schoolgirl and harbored secret crushes on the girls with bright, pretty faces. She loved the way they called to one another in the hallways, their voices gay and confident: "Hey, Flo. Hey, Teep. What's the dope?" She knew she would never be one of those girls. She was too timid, too ordinary. But that didn't stop her from wanting their company.

Ray came down the road carrying his stepladder. Clare heard the ladder, toted at his side, dragging now and then over the macadam road. She felt the weight of the ladder in her own arms and how difficult it would be, if someone was bone tired, to keep it balanced so the tip of a leg wouldn't dip and scrape. She knew Ray was worn out. He'd come home that evening and said, "I'm give in." He was working concrete on a new hospital construction in Jasper. Some days, after work, he drove over to Patoka Lake and fished for bluegill, but on this night he had come straight home—"all used up," he'd said, "and no place to throw me away."

When Mr. Dees came to ask him to help with the birdhouse, Clare tried to convince Ray to let it go for another time when he wasn't so tired—"You take it easy, hon," she told him—but he said he didn't reckon it'd kill him to do Mr. Dees a good turn. "I can't help but feel sorry for him," he said, keeping his voice low so Mr.

Dees, who waited in the yard, wouldn't hear. "He's all alone. He can use a friend."

Now Ray was coming home, and as he got closer, the laughter that had been coming from Lottie and Leo Marks's front porch went dead, and then the noise of the ladder dragging was a miserable thing to hear. Clare's hand moved to her throat, her fingers feeling the flutter of pulse there. She hadn't thought to make this motion, but an overwhelming ache had surprised her, a sadness and longing that rose from her chest and filled her throat. She opened the door and stepped out into the night. She went hurrying up the road to meet Ray, not caring that Lottie and Leo and Thelma and Tubby were watching.

"Darlin'," Ray said with a sigh.

She didn't say a word. She just touched her fingers to his face. He took her hand, brought it to his lips, and kissed it. Then she picked up the end of that ladder, and together they carried it home.

Mr. Dees saw it all from where he was still standing by the martin houses. It was nearly dark, but he could see Ray struggling with the ladder. Then he heard the scraping stop, and the faraway sound of those people laughing stop, and there was enough light for him to make out Clare's slight figure coming up the road. He looked away. It wasn't his to see. A woman coming out to meet the man who loved her. It wasn't anything he knew. He knew instead the steps of children coming to their dining room tables for their lessons and the shy way they hesitated at their first meetings, their hair brushed and shining, their faces scrubbed and smelling of soap. "I'm Mister Dees," he told them. He held out his hand and waited until they touched their warm palms to his. "Good," he said. "Now we can begin."

~~~

CLARE'S FRONT DOOR opened right out into the yard, without even a single concrete step. That wasn't right, Ray said that night after he stowed the stepladder in the tool shed. That wasn't any way for someone to have to walk into a house. He'd build a porch, he told her, build it out of cement blocks, and then when he was done he'd build a garage out back. Make it big enough so he could have a workshop. Once he got going, why stop?

"A porch?" Clare said. "*And* a garage? Goodness, won't we be moving up in the world!"

Maybe, she thought, Ray wanted the porch and the garage because he intended to do something to the house to make it his, make it seem as if he had always lived in it with her. Maybe he wanted her to forget what it had felt like to live there with Bill. Ray, after all, was a man who had never been married. He'd had his fill, he told her, of bouncing around the country bird-dogging construction jobs, living in motor courts and trailer parks, taking his meals out or cooking on a hot plate. He wanted to make a home with her, wanted to stay in it through the winter instead of loading up and heading south, as had always been his habit. He was working on that hospital in Jasper, a job that would last the summer. He'd save his money, he told her. Then, when winter came and the work dried up, they'd be all right.

She wanted to trust in that. "My folks had a porch on their house," she told him. "They'd sit out on it after supper, and neighbors would stop by just to shoot the breeze. We'd have iced tea, and sometimes we'd have pie."

"Sure," he said. "Darlin', that's the way it should be."

If they had a porch, he explained, and they were out there night after night, neighbors like Lottie and Leo Marks—sure, he'd seen them out there with Thelma and Tubby Carl, had taken note of how they all shut their yaps when they saw him coming up the road—wouldn't be able to ignore them. Sooner or later, some of them would feel ashamed and they'd come over to say howdy-do. Then they'd find out how friendly he could be, and they'd be happy for Clare and life would get back to normal.

She imagined that he was eager to lay claim to a home, even that square frame house with its ugly brown asphalt shingle siding.

So the idea was to build a porch and then, little by little, win the neighbors over. They'd have the life he'd always dreamed of: a wife and a home and friends to fill it. "I've never had that," he told Clare. He said it with a quiet simplicity—merely stating the fact—and it broke her heart to know that it was so.

One evening in June, he came home when it was well past dark. Clare was outside taking clothes off the line. Earlier, she had walked home from Brookstone Manor, the nursing home where she worked—sometimes in the laundry, sometimes in housecleaning, and sometimes in the kitchen. She had scrubbed out her white uniform dress, her cook's apron, and three of the sleeveless T-shirts that Ray wore and had hung them to dry. Now she was taking down the clothes, folding them, and laying them in her laundry basket. Around her, faint voices drifted out through her neighbors' open windows, and from time to time a murmur of laughter rose up from a television program. A screen door's spring creaked. An oscillating fan whirred. She had left the clothes out as long as she could so she wouldn't have to stand in the light and have her neighbors pass by, talking in low voices—harping, so she would believe, about her and Ray and what a fool she was to take up with the likes of him. Soon the dew would start falling; already the air smelled of it, cool and damp, and she was hurrying to gather the clothes.

Ray drove his pickup into the yard. The tailpipe scraped over the gravel driveway. That's how low the rear end was riding. The headlight beams came to rest on her, and she shielded her eyes with her hand.

He cut off the engine. The truck backfired once and then was still. He opened the door, the hinges squealing, and the dome light's glow fell over him. He bent forward and touched his forehead to the steering wheel. Then he pulled his shoulders back, lifted his head, and ran a hand over his face, starting with his brow and then wiping straight down, over his eyes, nose, mouth, and chin.

Clare came across the yard and rested her clothes basket on the truck's fender. It was a 1958 Ford that he'd bought for a song from an excavating company, and instead of leaving TRI-STATE BACKHOE on the green doors, he'd painted a large black circle over each one. "Now that's sporty," he told Clare. Then, in the middle of each black circle, with white paint, he stenciled the truck's empty weight and the name of the city and state.

EW: 3900
Tower Hill, Ind.

Just below the windows, he painted his name in a small, elegant script: R. R. WRIGHT. "Raymond Royal Wright," he said when he finished. "Now folks know who they're dealing with."

Generally, he kept some tools and his fishing gear in the bed of the truck, but tonight the tools and the tackle were in the cab because the truck was loaded down with cement blocks—a gray-faced wall of them, squared and neat against the sideboards. Clare balanced the clothes basket against her hip, reached out her free hand, and laid it flat against the cement, which was rough and cool.

"You had me worried, Ray." She pulled her hand back from the blocks. "It got dark, and I kept thinking something had happened to you. Did you pass out again? Did you get sick from the sun?"

He had always been sensitive to the sun. From time to time on the job, the heat got to him and he keeled over. The men humped him down from the scaffold and laid him in the shade. They threw water in his face, took off their shirts and fanned him. Sometimes he pissed himself, and, of course, after he had his senses back they gave him a hard time, and he couldn't help but hate them. He sat in the shade with a cold drink, and sometimes he had to turn his head and gag up what was in his stomach, and he hated the men even more because they were out there in the sun, some of them bare-chested, calling out to one another. *Hot enough for you? Jesus, yes. Hot. Damn straight, it's hot. Hotter than a firecracker. Hotter than a billy goat in a pepper patch. Hotter than a naked dog in hell.*

"No, I didn't get sick." He slammed the truck's door, and his voice was sharp. For a good while, he didn't say anything, and when he finally spoke it was with a gentle tone. "I didn't get sick, darlin'. I had to wait for dark to load up these blocks. You should see the stack we've got up there at that hospital site. I just took a few. Not enough for anyone to miss."

From time to time, Clare caught a glimpse of his temper, but it wasn't anything that worried her. It was what she knew from men— their clenched jaw muscles, their bunched brows, their narrowed eyes. She knew the heat in their voices, their bluster. They were all little boys who'd never been loved enough, and now their big bodies couldn't hold all the hurt they carried. Sometimes, when Ray was sleeping, she ran her finger lightly over his scars—the ridge low on his belly where the doctors had opened him to operate for rupture, the small white line at the corner of his lip where a knife had cut him, the mark on his ankle where doctors had set the fractured bone with a steel pin—and she loved him for all he wouldn't tell her, all the stories behind those scars. She loved him for thinking he had to keep all that to himself.

"Ray," she said now. "You hadn't ought to have taken these blocks. What if someone finds out?"

"Ah, darlin'." He put his arm across her back and gave her a squeeze. "Don't you know I'm a lucky man?"

She thought of his scarred body. "Not that lucky."

"Why, sure I am. I got you, didn't I?"

"You're a nut. Sometimes I think you're off your rocker."

"Oh, I'm crazy all right. Crazy in love."

"Well, if you're crazy, I guess I am, too."

"That's right. You and me. We're head over heels. Tell me. Has any man ever treated you better?"

"No," she said. "Never."

Later, while she was sleeping, she woke to the sound of Ray moving through the house. At first she was confused. She thought she was still married to Bill. Then, when she had everything straight in her head, shame washed over her because she had denied her first husband when she had told Ray that no man had ever been as good to her as he had. But it was true, wasn't it? She lay in bed, listening to him opening cabinets, and she knew it was impossible to say what was between people, and the longer you were with someone, the harder it was to even come close. All she knew was that once she had been with Bill and now she was with Ray. She had come out of her old life and into a new one, and even if she wished for it, which she didn't—not really, she didn't, not in her heart of hearts—she couldn't go back.

"Ray?" she called to him. "Hon, are you hungry?"

She heard the refrigerator door open, heard the jangling of bottles. She called his name again, and when he didn't answer, she swung her legs over the side of the bed, got up, and walked out into the kitchen.

He was at the sink, pouring milk into a glass. He hadn't turned on a light, and because it was the night of the new moon—June 11—the kitchen was so dark that Clare wouldn't have been sure that it was Ray, that he was pouring milk, if not for the fact that he was whistling what had become his favorite song that summer, "Candy Man" ("Who can take a sunrise / Sprinkle it with dew?"), and she could smell the wax-coated milk carton.

She asked him what he was doing, and he told her, in a quiet, matter-of-fact voice, that he was going to have a glass of milky-wilky. She thought he was making a joke, and she laughed, but he didn't laugh along with her or say anything else.

"How can you see?" she asked. "You'll pour too much and make a mess."

No, he wouldn't make a mess, he said. He'd be just fine. He'd be scrumdiddlyumptious.

She'd never heard him use a silly word like that or speak with that sort of giggle leaping into his voice, the way it must have when he was a child.

No, Papa, he said. Not a mess. He'd be careful. He'd be a good boy.

"Ray," she said. "What's wrong? You're talking out of your head."

He was drinking now. She heard him gulping down the milk. She felt along the wall for the light switch, and when she turned it on and the harsh glare filled the kitchen, Ray set the glass on the counter and turned to look at her. His eyes were open, but he wasn't focusing on anything. She could tell that. He was asleep.

She didn't want to startle him. "Was it good?" She kept her voice even. "The milky-wilky?" It made her feel silly to say the word, but close to Ray, too, as if they shared a private language. "Did you like it?"

Yes, he told her. It was good.

"Are you ready to go back to bed?"

He shook his head. No, he was afraid.

"You don't have to be afraid. I'm here. I won't let anything bad happen to you."

Mom? he said.

"No, hon. I'm Clare. Here, give me your hand."

She tried to take his hand, but he wouldn't let her. He tossed his arms about as if he were trying to fight his way out of something. Goddamn it, he said. Goddamn.

"Shh, Ray. Shh."

She moved closer. His flailing arm knocked against her face. His knuckles caught her mouth. She felt blood come to her lip, heard herself whimper.

Ray went down on his knees. He went down, and he pulled his fists in close to his chest. He bowed his head, and his torso rocked back and forth. Clare knew he hadn't meant to hurt her. He had come up from a dream and carried it with him. He was caught in some twilight, part of him awake and part of him asleep. She got down on her knees and covered his fists with her hands. When he finally raised his head, his eyes opened wide, and she could tell that he saw her, understood who she was. She felt overwhelmed with love because he was back now. He was Ray, her Ray.

"Darlin'." He lifted up the hem of his T-shirt and gently dabbed at the bloody corner of her lip. "Clare?" he said, and she started to explain.

WELL, JESUS. Good Christ. He didn't know what to say. "You ought to shoot me," he told her. They were in the bathroom, where she was washing blood from her face. "Jesus Christ in a basket."

"You were asleep, Ray." She leaned over the sink, looking at her face in the medicine cabinet mirror. Her upper lip was red and puffy. "You didn't mean to hit me. I know that. You must have been having a bad dream."

In the mirror, she could see him behind her, sitting on the edge of the tub. He was looking down at the floor, and he shook his head. "I don't remember," he said. "Honest to God, Clare. I don't remember a thing."

They went back to bed, and he held her. "Go to sleep, hon," she told him. Soon the martins would start singing, the sky would light up, and then it would be time for them both to get ready for work. "You need your rest."

"I'm going to be better, Clare." She could feel him trembling. "I'm going to stop."

She was nodding off to sleep, and she didn't have the energy to ask him what he meant. She figured he was talking about the beer. Sometimes he drank more than he should, but that was one of the other things that she knew about men: from time to time, the world got too big for them, and they had to find a way to try to match it. Besides, he wasn't a mean drunk. He got sad instead, and sometimes he told her stories about hurtful things he'd carried with him since he was a boy in Minnesota.

The story she always remembered was the one about how his

parents couldn't afford for him to buy a hot lunch at school, so his mother packed him a sack lunch each day, always a fried-egg sandwich, nothing more. He and the other kids who couldn't buy a lunch had to sit at a folding table in the dark hallway just outside the cafeteria. He sat under the dim light of a twenty-five-watt bulb hanging from a rusty steam pipe. Sometimes water dripped down onto his head. He sat there and listened to the children chattering and laughing inside the cafeteria, the slap of trays on the tables, the jangle of silverware. He smelled the hot food: the hamburgs, the chicken and noodles, the Hungarian goulash, the vegetable soup. The kids who came from the cafeteria carried the aromas on their clothes, their skin. Ray smelled them when he walked down the hallway and when he sat in his classroom, breathing in the lingering spice and broth of hot food.

Clare had been a young woman during the Depression. She had eaten lard sandwiches, groundhog, and possum, and picked wild mustard and sour dock and boiled the leaves with soup beans. She knew what it meant to be hungry, and that was what Ray was, he told her. Starved. Whenever he drank too much beer and got all down in the mouth, or brought home a truckload of stolen blocks, she always thought of that little boy sitting under the steam pipe, water dripping on his head, so close to all that hot food that would never be his, and she forgave him for having such an emptiness and all the ways he tried to fill it. If that was the worst thing there was about him, this gluttony, she wouldn't complain about a Saturday-night drunk now and then. She'd drive down to the jail and bring him home. She'd listen to his sad stories. She'd put him to bed and lie beside him, as she was now, until he was quiet and they both could sleep.

~~~

MR. DEES was awake long before the martins began to sing. He often rose before dawn and prepared his breakfast—eggs (scrambled), potatoes (fried), sausage patties (also fried), wheat toast (with butter), coffee (black), orange juice (fresh squeezed), and, if he was feeling particularly peckish, a waffle (with butter and chocolate syrup). He was, to his own delight, a hearty eater. He took great pleasure in this secret that he had; he was a chowhound. It thrilled him to know that none of his neighbors—and certainly none of his pupils or their parents—suspected that he could eat like a thresher, and despite his appetite he stayed thin. His mother had always been thin. His father, too. All their lives. Nothing went to fat.

This morning, as he raked the eggs out onto his plate, lifted the sausage from the cooking grease, he couldn't help but chuckle, certain that his neighbors, if any of them happened to see the small rectangle of light through his kitchen window, would imagine that he was sitting down to a bowl of bran flakes, a piece of dry toast, a cup of tea. *Poor Mister Dees*, they would mutter. *What sort of life?*

But probably—and this thought sobered him—they didn't think of him at all. He was easy to forget until the time came that little Johnny and little Sally needed help with their numbers. Sure, folks knew who he was then, and how to find him, but without that place in their lives, he knew he would be one of those people, never married, who would show up in an obituary one day, and folks would say, *Oh, yes. Henry Dees.*

He played records while he ate. He had a portable phonograph, and he could put on a stack of 45s, the ones he drove to Bloomington to buy instead of walking into the Record Bin uptown and having the word get out that he was buying the same junk the kids were buying—some lovesick ballad by Donny Osmond, Bread, the Carpenters, or one of those Christian rock songs like "Put Your Hand in the Hand" or "My Sweet Lord," or worse yet those novelty records like "Chick-a-Boom," "They're Coming to Take Me Away, Ha-Haaa!" or "Yo-Yo." What would his neighbors think, he wondered, if they were to see him wolfing down eggs and sausage, stopping now and then to sing along, closing his eyes and crooning the words to "Baby I'm-A Want You," or "Sweet and Innocent," or "We've Only Just Begun"? Well, that was his secret, and he liked having secrets. It made him feel that he had one up on the people who thought they knew exactly who he was when really they didn't know anything at all.

No one knew about his appetite or the records, and no one knew that on certain evenings that summer he walked across town to the Heights, and there, from an alley that ran behind the Mackeys' house, he waited, hidden in darkness. Some nights, he saw the boy, Gilley, standing on the patio, lit by Chinese lanterns, practicing his golf swing, or Mr. Mackey dousing the coals on the barbecue, or Mrs. Mackey arranging freshly cut roses in a vase. Sooner or later, if luck would have it, he'd catch a glimpse of Katie. Maybe she'd come running across the lawn, trying to catch fireflies in a jar, and he'd hear her bare feet padding over the grass and her breath coming fast. Or she'd dance around on the patio, singing "Chick-a-Boom" in a loud voice. Or she'd sit quietly on a chaise longue, letting her mother braid her hair before sending her inside to take her bath and get ready for bed.

Some nights, Mr. Mackey said, "Well, how about it?" And that was enough to start everyone gabbing, calling out, all at once, the Dairy Queen ice cream treats they favored on that particular evening. A Peanut Buster Parfait for Gilley. A Mister Misty for Mrs. Mackey.

"A butterscotch Dilly Bar," Katie said one evening, "*and* a Hot Fudge Brownie Delight."

Mr. Mackey laughed. "You'll bust, Katie Delicious. You'll absolutely bust."

Once they were gone—loaded into the family car and off to the Dairy Queen—Mr. Dees walked across the grass to the patio. The golf club's grip was still warm from Gilley's hands; heat still lingered around the barbecue. The air smelled of its charcoal and the roses— ah, the freshly cut roses—red and pink, that Mrs. Mackey had left in the vase.

Mr. Dees tore a single petal from the bouquet and slipped it into his shirt pocket so later he could enjoy its scent and its sleek velvet. Katie's hairbrush was on the table. It was a Sleeping Beauty brush, and there was a nest of brown hair in its bristles. He took just a bit, no bigger than a cotton ball, but it was enough. He took it home, and before he went to sleep he raised it to his face and rubbed it across his cheek, and that was something else that no one knew.

The martins were singing by the time Mr. Dees finished his breakfast, and he turned off the phonograph so he could listen. It was then, in the presence of the martins' dawnsong—this call to the new day—that he felt ashamed. He was a glutton and a voyeur, and he wished with all his might that there were people in his life who could keep him from loving the world so much while at the same time feeling so far away from it. How would he ever explain this to the Mackeys if they happened to find out that he watched them, that he handled the things they touched, took a single rose petal, a fluff of hair? How would he say that he loved them?

He was thinking all this when he heard the shotgun blast. It rattled the coffee cup on its saucer, and the martins rose up from their houses, blackening the sky.

Mr. Dees ran outside, and there he saw Raymond R. coming around the corner of the garage, a single-barrel shotgun open and cradled in the crook of his right arm. The air was singed with cordite. In his left hand, he carried the Cooper's hawk. He carried it by its legs so that its wings, no life left to hold them folded, fanned open, and the hawk's head jounced against Raymond R.'s knee.

He tossed the hawk onto the dew-slicked grass at Mr. Dees's feet. "Teach," he said. "There's your hawk." He loaded another shell into the chamber and snapped the shotgun shut.

LATER THAT morning at the Mackeys', Mr. Dees couldn't forget the hawk or the way Raymond R. had asked him straight-out for money.

"I'm not a rich man," he'd said. "I got debts. I got to look after Clare. You . . . well, I figure you might have some money put back."

The truth was that Mr. Dees did have a few certificates of deposit at the savings and loan. They didn't add up to an extravagant sum—just enough for a rainy day.

"I patched those steps for you, Teach." Raymond R. gave him a grin. "I helped you with that birdhouse. I was wore out that night, brother. Bone tired."

The sun was up on the horizon now, red and fiery. It would be a hot day with locusts chirring and the air heavy and still. Mr. Dees felt the weight of all that heat, all that humid air. Raymond R. was right: He had done those repairs and never asked for a dime. He had treated Mr. Dees kindly and with respect.

"How much do you need?" Mr. Dees's voice sounded strange to him, as if it came from someone else. He knew business transactions—his services exchanged for whatever sum parents could pay, for nothing if that turned out to be the case. He didn't strike such agreements to be charitable, as everyone assumed, but because he was selfish, because he would have paid for the pleasure of walking into people's homes, sitting in their rooms, taking note, as he did when he watched the Mackeys, of everything in their lives. It embarrassed him to talk about need, especially with Raymond R., who knew too much about his own want. "A hundred?" Mr. Dees said.

"A thousand," Raymond R. told him. "Two if you've got it. I told you, Teach. I got debts."

Once at an assembly in high school, a physics teacher asked Mr. Dees to come up onstage and turn a gyroscope. Mr. Dees was no dope; he knew he was going to be the butt of the joke, but he went anyway, aware that when he tried to turn the gyroscope, it would keep spinning, resisting all his efforts. He could have told all those guffawing boneheads in the auditorium that a spinning object like the gyroscope resists changes to its axis of rotation because an applied force moves along with the object itself. The axis would always be perpendicular to the spinning object as long as it kept spinning fast enough. When he stood on that stage and tried to turn the gyroscope, he applied force to both the top and the bottom. The force balanced out, and the gyroscope kept spinning on its axis, no matter how hard he tried to turn it. He could have cited Newton's first law of motion, as he often did to his pupils when explaining the way yo-yos worked: "A body in motion continues to move at a constant speed along a straight line unless acted upon by an unbalanced force." But he played along that day on the stage. He gave the physics teacher exactly what he wanted—a stooge—just as he would be willing, most of his life, to do his best to deliver when someone asked him for a favor.

"A thousand?" Mr. Dees said to Raymond R. "That's a lot of money."

Raymond R. nudged the Cooper's hawk with his boot. "Teach," he said. "I thought we were friends. I swear I don't know anyone else to turn to. I thought I could count on you. That's what folks say: You can always count on Henry Dees."

"It's against the law to kill a hawk." A car drove past, and Mr. Dees wondered whether the driver had caught a glimpse of him and Raymond R. "That Cooper's hawk. It's protected."

"Didn't you want it gone?" Raymond R. squinted at Mr. Dees the way boys did when they were trying to figure out a math problem. "Jesus in a basket. I thought you'd be glad. You want something gone, by God, you go get it. Isn't that the way?"

"You shouldn't have shot it."

"It's just the two of us." Raymond R. laid a hand on Mr. Dees's shoulder. He leaned in close and whispered, "We're the only ones who have to know."

At the Mackeys', Katie sat on the edge of a dining room chair, her bare feet curled over the bottom rung. She had red polish on her toenails. Mr. Dees had noticed that right away when she came downstairs for her lesson, and even now he could smell the polish. He didn't approve. Nail polish for a nine-year-old. What sense did that make? He wondered whether he should say something to Mrs. Mackey, then thought better of it, understanding that he was there to teach arithmetic and not to offer advice on parenting. Him, the bachelor. Him, the odd duck. Oh, he knew how people talked. What in the world could he possibly know about raising a child?

He uncapped his fountain pen and tapped the nib beside the problem he had neatly written on a tablet page. He took great pride in his penmanship. It looked, so the teller at the savings and loan had remarked yesterday, like something out of a handwriting instruction book. "A careful man writes a careful hand," his mother had taught him, and he had practiced the Palmer Method until each letter was perfect. "Just look at your signature on this deposit slip," the teller had said. "You'd think a woman signed it. Not many men have pretty writing like that."

If a herd has fifty-six zebras, and someone wants to separate a fourth of them from the herd, how many will he have to move?

A story problem requiring work with fractions. Solving story problems, Mr. Dees told Katie, was a matter of translating a word sentence into a number sentence: $\frac{56}{1} \times \frac{1}{4}$ in this instance. "You see, we have fifty-six zebras." His pen scratched over the pad as he wrote the equation. Katie was fascinated with the pen. Could she hold it? she wanted to know. Could she use it to work out the problem? "If you get this problem right," Mr. Dees said, "I'll let you use the pen. In fact, if you get this right, I'll buy you one of your own. Now, fifty-six zebras, and we have to take a fourth of them away." He held his eyeglasses at the left temple, straightening them. His hair—he had again let it grow too long—flopped over his forehead, and he had to lay his pen down and use his fingers to comb the hair out of his eyes. The air around him smelled of ink and paper and Katie's shampoo—the delightful scent of strawberries—and that nail polish that Mr. Dees couldn't get out of his head.

Katie tapped her teeth with her pencil's eraser. "Fifty-six zebras," she said. "Holy moly, that's a lot of stripes."

"Katie." Mr. Dees gently closed his fingers around her wrist and moved her hand away from her mouth. "Concentrate. How would you multiply fifty-six by one-fourth?"

"I'd times the top numbers and the bottom numbers."

"What do we call the top numbers?"

"The numerators."

"Good. And the bottom?"

"The nominators."

"De-nominators," Mr. Dees said.

"De-nominators." Katie drew an equal sign at the right of the equation and then wrote the fraction $\frac{56}{4}$. "Fifty-six times one," she said, "equals fifty-six, and one times four equals four."

"Yes. Good. Now what do you have to do?"

"Simplify."

"Right. And how do you do that?"

"Divide fifty-six by four." Katie leaned over the tablet, her hair falling down across her arm as she worked the problem. "Four goes into five once with one left over. Bring down the six. Four goes into sixteen four times." She slapped her pencil down on the tablet and grabbed Mr. Dees around his arm. "Fourteen zebras," she said. "Holy moly, Mr. Dees. Fourteen."

The look on her face—a look of unexpected pleasure—over-whelmed him. What delight there was in her eyes, in her open mouth, in the way her warm fingers curled across his arm. Had fractions ever blessed a child to this degree? It was as if she had been lost in darkness and now had come out into the light, saved. Holy moly. What could he do, but take her hand in his and lift her arm and declare her "Katie, Champion of Fractions," and to hand over his pen to her, as he had promised, so she could use it to figure out the next problem.

"You said you'd buy one for me, Mister Dees."

He told her he would. He surely would.

Even as he celebrated this joy, he felt a pang of sadness creep over him. He knew he would rise soon and go back to Gooseneck, and Katie's life—the one with her family—would go on without him. He imagined the voices sounding in this house, the bodies in motion, while in Gooseneck he played his records, prepared his lessons, and gorged himself on food that never made him fat. Years from now, when Katie was a grown woman, she might vaguely remember the summer he taught her fractions, but his brief presence would be an insignificant part of the whole. He was a shadow thrown briefly on a wall. He could never have the substance or worth that her mother and father did, her brother, the boys who would love her, the children she would have.

Mrs. Mackey came into the room, drying her hands on a dish towel. "My word," she said. "What's all the to-do?"

It was nothing, Mr. Dees told her. It was just Katie learning fractions.

"Mama, look at this pen," Katie said. "Mister Dees is going to buy one for me."

Before Patsy Mackey could answer, Mr. Mackey, home for lunch, was at the back door calling. "Patsy, Katie, come quick."

The air stirred about Mr. Dees as Katie let the fountain pen drop to the table, and she and her mother rushed out of the dining room. He capped his pen and gathered up his tablet. What was it, he wondered, that made someone necessary, never to be forgotten? Wasn't it the loving? Wasn't it people looking out for one another? Wasn't it family? Husband/wife, sister/brother, parent/child. "Come quick," Mr. Mackey had said, and Katie and her mother had run to him. But what if one's life—choices made, circumstances accrued—had rendered such a scene impossible, left someone, as in the case of Mr. Dees, standing to the side, separated from the clan?

He had been the only child born to parents already past the middle of their lives: his mother nearly fifty, his father the same. A miracle it was, people said, this child. But to Mr. Dees, when he thought back on the way life had been with his parents, it always seemed that he was more of an intruder than a miracle. As he grew older, he realized two things: his parents had never intended to have children and, once they did, they didn't know what to do with him. He remembered one time, when he was around the age that Katie was now, walking into Helene's Dress Shop downtown with his mother and hearing the saleslady say, "My, my. Isn't your grandson a sweetheart?" His mother offered no word of correction. "I need a pair of new white gloves," she said. (Whenever she went out, she wore white gloves and a broad-brimmed hat covered with artificial flowers.) He understood from the way she squeezed his hand that he, too, was to keep quiet. What he knew about family was this: his wasn't normal. He had come to his parents too late in their lives, and they had little patience with him. "Shh, shh, shh," his mother was always cautioning. The words of wise men, she said, were heard in quiet. It said so in the Bible. The meek shall inherit the earth. She taught him scripture. "It is good," he repeated, "that a man should both hope and quietly wait for the salvation of the Lord." He learned to think before he spoke, to be careful, respectful, not knowing that at the same time he was learning to love by leaving people alone.

Outside, in the Mackeys' driveway, Katie was squealing. She was jumping up and down and clapping her hands together and shrieking as her father lifted a bicycle from the bed of his pickup truck. Mr. Dees watched from the back door. Just a moment, he thought. He would stay just a moment and then let himself out the front door and leave the Mackeys to their excitement. The bicycle was one of those Sting-Ray bikes that Mr. Dees had seen the boys and girls riding that summer. They sat low and had long banana seats. He had lingered in the Western Auto Store one afternoon, listening to the salesclerk explain the features. He had picked up the names of all the parts: the banana seat, the sissy bar that rose up behind it, the high butterfly handlebars, the sparkly silver streamers flowing out from the handgrips. A Sting-Ray. A twenty-inch Sting-Ray. Katie was riding hers in a circle in the driveway, and Mr. Mackey was standing by his truck, his hands on his hips, a grin on his face. Mr. Dees understood that Junior Mackey was pleased that he had been able to give Katie that bike. Mrs. Mackey turned back to the house—perhaps she had thought to run in and grab the Polaroid or the movie camera—and Mr. Dees was sorry for her to have to see him there, watching from behind the door. He stepped back, meaning to move quickly through the house, to make his escape, but the tablet slipped from his hand, fell to the floor. He stooped to retrieve it, and he heard the back door open, and then Mrs. Mackey was there, saying, "My goodness, we forgot all about you." He thought for a moment that she meant to invite him to come out to the driveway and watch Katie ride her new bike. Then she said, "Here, let me write you a check. I think we owe you for three sessions this week. Yes?"

Before he could stop himself, he said what had been on his mind all the time he had been coming to the Mackeys'. "She's a pretty girl, your Katie. A precious, pretty girl."

The look on Mrs. Mackey's face changed. Her smile faded. Her eyebrows came together as she squinted at him. He understood that if anyone else had said what he had it would have been an innocent compliment, the kind parents make about other people's children all the time, but from him it sounded wrong. It sounded like what it was, an expression of love from someone who had no right to make it. He tried to say something else, something that would assure Mrs. Mackey that his interest in Katie was merely that of a teacher, a teacher who was concerned about the way young boys and girls grew up and became responsible adults. "That nail polish," he said. "Isn't she too young?"

But that only made matters worse. "Little girls play with makeup," Mrs. Mackey said. "They play dress-up. They put on their mother's nail polish." She said all this in a way that made it clear that she thought she shouldn't have to say it. Mr. Dees should know as much. "I don't know what you think—"

He cut her off before she could finish. He didn't want to hear what she was about to tell him. "Yes, three," he said. "You're right, but don't worry. You can pay me another time." He looked back out to the driveway where Katie was still riding her new bike. "I don't want to keep you from your family," he said. "Go on. I'll let myself out the front."

When he stepped out onto the porch, he could still hear Katie's excited squeals, and he heard them as he turned toward home and for a good ways up the street, and he hated himself for not being able to tell Mrs. Mackey, or Raymond R. earlier, what he had really wanted to say. *I don't want to hurt anyone. I don't. Please help me.*

Mr. Dees

I BOUGHT THAT pen for Katie, and when I gave it to her, she hugged me around my waist. I dreamed of her. I won't deny it.

Raymond R.

MAYBE I STOLE those cement blocks. Sure, I'll own up to that. But, brother, that's all. You can ask my wife.

Clare

So he built that porch. Night after night, he was out there lay-ing blocks, and I was pulling weeds from the flower beds, the two of us talking back and forth to each other the way married folks do, and the only one who ever stopped to visit was Henry Dees.

He came one evening just after supper. I was sitting on a kitchen chair in the yard snapping beans, a mess of Kentucky Wonders one of the girls who worked at Brookstone Manor had brought me from her mother's garden. There were people there, you see, who cared for me—high school girls who called me Gram. They didn't live in Gooseneck. For the most part they were girls from the Heights, holding down summer jobs, making a little spending money work-ing at the nursing home. They had long hair that they had to tie back in ponytails or put up in hairnets if they worked in the kitchen, and they had tans from going to the swimming pool on their days off. Their boyfriends came by to get them after work, and I saw the way they flirted. They wrote the boys' names on their paycheck en-velopes and drew hearts around them. In the laundry, they played the radio, and I went home with their tunes in my head. I caught myself singing their words, and when I did, I felt the way I did that night at the Top Hat Inn when Ray kissed my hand. I was, as the girls at Brookstone Manor said about themselves, in L-U-V.

I was humming one of those songs to myself the evening Henry Dees came to see Ray. It was a song the girls sang over and over that summer, "Betcha by Golly, Wow," a song about being in love forever. Oh, I know it sounds silly. An old dame like me. But that was the truth of my life then.

You have to know how wonderful it can be in summer in that part of Indiana. Early summer, I mean, before the heat comes and the muggy air. Bobwhites call from the meadows, and mourning doves coo. Chicory blooms on roadsides—patches of blue—and the brown-eyed susans put on their yellow pinwheels. The monarch butterflies come to feed on the milkweed, and hummingbirds hover over the orange-red bells of the trumpet creeper. It's enough, my mother used to say, to make you sing at the kitchen pans. "That's from a poem," she told me. "I learned it in school." Summer, she said—the heart of summer—it was enough to make you shout all over God's Heaven.

Henry Dees spooked me. My head was full of that song, and I was bent over those beans, snapping them one, two, three, and he said my name. "Clare," he said, and I near jumped out of my skin.

He was fiddling with his eyeglasses, trying to get them to set right on his face. He took them off and messed with the left temple. Then he gave up and put the glasses back on and left them to sag.

"You ought to go into Blank's," I told him. "Get those glasses straightened up. They'll do it for free."

"Screw's loose." He put a finger under that left temple and jiggled it up and down, showing me the play. "I thought maybe Ray had a screwdriver."

"Itty-bitty screwdriver?" I said. "Well, I expect he might."

Behind us, Ray hefted a block into place and then tamped it down with the butt of his trowel handle. He was laying a low wall that would front the porch. He'd set the leads at each end and then stretched a line tight between them. The secret, he'd told me, was to plan the wall out ahead of time, to see exactly how the blocks would fit, and then to lay them in plumb and level. "It takes a world of patience," he'd said. He swung the trowel around and used the point to scrape away the mud that had oozed out. Then he slapped that mud back onto the mound on his mortarboard.

"Is that the professor?" he called over his shoulder. "Teach, what's the good word?"

Henry Dees hesitated. He glanced at Ray and then back at me. He'd always broken my heart, truth be told. A man like him. Maybe he put me too much in mind of who I would have been without Ray. That night, I felt lucky. I thought I had everything just the way I wanted it. Betcha by golly, wow. A new porch, a garage, a mess of Kentucky Wonders, and summer in all its glory. "Go on," I told Henry Dees. "Don't be bashful. Tell Ray what you need."

Mr. Dees

I HADN'T INTENDED to do it, promise Raymond R. that money, but that night, he took me out to his truck, and he poked around in his toolbox for a screwdriver just right for tightening my glasses. I can barely say the feeling it gave me to watch him hold my glasses in his fingers and reach in with the tip of that screwdriver. It was delicate work, and he took care.

Looked after. I guess that's what I felt. Seen to. And who among us hasn't wanted that?

When he was done, he slipped the glasses onto my face, and I leaned toward his hand to help him. "How's that?" he said, and I told him it was good.

I was thinking what a puzzle we were, the two of us. He was so chatty and I was so used to being alone. "People," my father always said. "Go figure."

There were all sorts of secret lives in our town. They came out sooner or later on deathbeds, in letters, police reports, whispered confessions. Think of it, and it was true: incest, dope, suicide, adultery, arson, theft, murder. The lunatic and the maimed. So many feeble souls.

The stories came out, and when they did, we had ways to explain the dying: too duty-bound, too fast, too careless, too drunk, too desperate. We died in the war in Vietnam. We took the S-curve west of town with too much speed and smashed into the bridge abutment or left the road and crashed into a tree. We went joyriding, didn't take care at the crest of Sugar Hill and ended up smashing into a gravel truck just then turning onto the highway. We left cigarettes burning and died in house fires, ignored weather reports and got hit by lightning, went swimming at the quarries and got in too deep. We got up on kitchen chairs, tied ropes around beams in our basements, looped nooses around our necks, and then kicked the chairs away.

All these things happened in our small town.

The Dog 'n' Suds across from the hospital had an old wreck of a car—its hood crumpled, its windshield cracked—arranged so it looked like someone had driven it into the side of the building. It was one of the first things anyone saw when they came into town from the west—that optical illusion of a horrible accident and a sign reminding us to take care: *This is not a fairy tale! It's the truth! It's a tragedy!*

We found ways to forget the warning, to think of the crumpled car as a cartoon. We imagined that as long as we lived cautious lives we were safe.

That evening, after he had fixed my glasses, Raymond R. opened his glove compartment and took out an envelope. The flap was tucked in, and he undid it and held the envelope open so I could see what was inside: the fluff of Katie's hair that I kept in the drawer of my night table. Sometime, and this knowledge sent a chill up the back of my neck, Raymond R. had been in my house.

I didn't say a word. What could I say?

"I don't know whose hair this is." He closed the envelope's flap. "But I know it isn't yours. For a price, I'll forget all about it. I won't tell a soul."

Something gave way inside me, not because Raymond R. was threatening me with blackmail, but because here, at last, was someone who knew about me.

It had become too much to hold the secret to myself. My love for Katie was something I couldn't keep quiet forever, and surely I'd been waiting for this chance a good while. I would have paid Raymond R. what he asked just to have him listen. So I told him the whole story. I told him the truth.

Gilley

ONE EVENING that summer—it was the day Katie got her new bicycle—a man came to our house. He was a man who worked for my father. I didn't know his name. I didn't know why he had come. We were on the patio, where my father was cooking steaks on the grill. My mother and Katie were inside.

The man was no one I could describe, the sort you see and then can't call to mind. Dark hair parted on the side and combed over the way so many men then did. I recall that he was neatly dressed, a blue sport shirt tucked into his tan slacks.

He stepped up onto our patio, and he said to my father, "Junior, I ought to have something for those days I worked last week. You can't just let a man go and not pay him for days he worked. I've been with you a good number of years. I thought you'd do me better than this. You'll make things right, won't you, Junior? You know I've got my little girl sick right now. I need that money."

"This is my home." My father was holding a barbecue fork. He waved it in front of him as if swatting gnats. "For Pete's sake, I'm here with my family."

"Junior, you've got to listen to me. You and I, we go back a ways. My daddy and your daddy were friends. I'm trying to be as decent as I can, but damn it, you've got to listen."

"I don't have to listen to a thing you have to say. I don't keep drunk men on my payroll."

"You know I'm not a drunk, Junior. You know it's just I've had a tough time with my girl being sick and all. If you want to let me go, I can accept that. But still, I did the work those days, and I ought to be paid."

"I'm sorry about your girl," my father said. "I truly am, and I'm sorry things have to end like this between you and me. But I can't pay you for time when you were laid up on a pallet sleeping it off."

The man rubbed his hand over his face. "It's true what you say." He pushed back his shoulders and lifted his chin, owning up to whatever he had to face. "I won't deny it. You've always been good to me in the past, but I guess you don't believe I deserve a second chance."

I could see that my father was thinking it over. "Do you need help with your girl's doctor bills?"

"I do, Junior."

"You come in tomorrow," my father said. "We'll talk about it then."

"I'll do that, Junior. I surely will. And I'll be sober. You can count on that from here on."

My father put his hand on the man's shoulder. "There's nothing more important than family," he told him. "You have to remember that. No matter how rough things get, you've got to do what you can to take care of your wife and kids."

You have to understand, because I didn't then, that even as far back as high school days, my father was deliberately and carefully choosing the life that he would one day have. It would be a life of comfort and distinction. He had learned as much from his own father, who had passed the family business to him—had let him "see the future," my grandfather always joked, and left my father, if he "kept a good head on his shoulders" and made all the right moves, "set for life." So much of the world was made of glass, my grandfather said. Windows, doors, dishes, mirrors. That didn't begin to account for it all. A man who made glass would always have as much business as he wanted.

But my father's dreams of the future went far beyond the money he would earn, all on the strength of glass. Not long ago, I found a list of ambitions he had made when he was just a boy. A sheet of stationery slipped from between the pages of his senior-year *Hilltopper*. On it, in the precise and elegant handwriting that men used to have, he had noted that he intended to marry Patsy Molloy, that they would have two children, a boy and a girl. The girl, they would name Katie; the boy would be Gilbert, but they would call him Gilley.

"Gilley," he said to me that evening after the man had thanked him and gone. "Go get your mother and Katie." He speared a steak and held it up on the fork. He winked at me. "Get ready for some good eating, Gilley. Now that's a fine hunk of meat."

A house in the Heights, he had written on his list. *A new car—a Lincoln—every two years. Vacations in the summer: Yellowstone, the Grand Canyon, Hollywood, New York City, Canada.* I've often imagined him daydreaming as he made his list. Maybe he was sitting in class—physics, let's say—and instead of listening to the teacher talk about matter and energy, he was moving on through the future, creating Katie and me and the life we would all one day have as a family.

I believe he needed this dreaming because, despite his family's wealth, he imagined that he had farther to reach than most men.

"Short men have big dreams," he told me once when we were talking about what I would do after I graduated. Like me, he was barely
five-foot-seven. "We're bulldogs, you and me. When we get our jaws
around something, we don't let go."

When I went into the kitchen to tell my mother and Katie that
the steaks were ready, Katie was crying. She was sitting on the
kitchen counter, and my mother was standing in front of her, using
nail-polish remover to take the red polish off Katie's toes.

"It's Gotta Go?" I asked.

Katie rubbed her eyes with the back of her hand. She sniffed
back a few last tears. Then she nodded her head and told me, "The
nail polish or the new bike."

Just to play the devil, I said, "You should have given up the
bike." Although there was no logic to my claim, it was enough to
make her doubt her choice and start her crying again.

My father came into the kitchen and said, "What's all the howl-
ing about?"

"It's nothing," my mother said. "Are we ready to eat?"

Katie wouldn't stop crying.

"Someone tell me what's going on," my father said.

"It's Gilley." Katie pointed her finger at me. "He's mean."

"Shut up, dimwit," I told her, and the heat in my voice surprised me.

"Oh, he's just being a big brother," my father said. "That's what
big brothers do. They try to get your goat."

"My goat?" Katie said, still sniffling. "I don't have a goat."

"Sure you do," said my father. He stooped down and put his face
next to hers. "Just listen." He made the gruff baaing noise of a goat,
and then he chanted a rhyme. "There's an old billy goat. Where's

that old billy goat?" He traced his finger down Katie's chin. "Right here, my dear. Right here, in Katie's throat."

Katie giggled then, and just like that my father had made her forget that just a few moments earlier she'd been upset. We all went out to our patio to eat, and my father said with a big smile, "Well, here we are," and I could tell at that moment he was, like the rest of us, in love with this life we had.

Later that night, when I was in bed, I heard my mother talking to my father. Her voice, low and even, drifted up from downstairs, and the last thing I heard her say before I fell asleep was this: "Junior, how well do you know Henry Dees?"

It was a question that I would forget by morning, and only remember later. I've never been able to put it out of my mind, any more than I can forget my father's senior quote from his *Hilltopper*: "The measure of a man's real character is what he would do if he knew he would never be found out."

Clare

Ray told me later. It was after the sun had gone down, and we'd come in from outside. He was at the kitchen sink washing his hands, and to this day, whenever I smell that soap—that Lava soap, strong and clean—I think of that night and the way he told the story so la-di-da as if it was nothing at all, just a little piece of chitchat he'd carried home in his pocket.

"He's one of them," he said. "That Henry Dees. He's a kid fruit. He's got short eyes."

I didn't know what he meant. I was at the counter dumping the Kentucky Wonders into a drainer so I could rinse them, and I said, "Short eyes? Sounds serious. I thought he just needed his glasses straightened up."

Ray turned off the tap and shook water from his hands. "He's a puppy lover, Clare. An uncle. A chicken hawk. Do I have to say it plain?" He dried his hands on the dish towel. "He gets his jollies from being with those kids. He's a pervert."

"Henry Dees? I can't believe that."

"It's hard to know someone," Ray said. Then he said the rest of it, told me that Henry Dees snuck around in the dark and kept his eyes on those kids, one in particular, a little girl who lived in the Heights, a little girl named Katie Mackey. One night, he took a snatch of hair from her brush.

"Ray, did he go into that girl's house?"

"I believe he's capable of doing that, Clare. I really do."

"He told you all this?"

"Darlin', do you think I'd make it up?"

I didn't even wonder then how Ray knew all those names for what he claimed Henry Dees was, and when I finally got around to asking, he said, Well, you know, it's just things you hear. It's just talk.

Mr. Dees

WHAT I TOLD Raymond R. was this: I didn't think of Katie
Mackey, or any of my other pupils, with lust. I loved them the way I
would have loved my own children, had circumstances allowed me a
family. I loved them because I had no one else to love. My parents
were both dead. I'd never understood the art of courtship. I wasn't
like the purple martin who could sing his croak song and attract a
mate. The only affection I knew came from children. They found
me to their liking. I prefer to think there was a kindness to me that
they trusted, that made them overlook the fact that I let my hair
grow too long, wore crooked glasses, sewed patches on my clothes.
My students at the high school took note of such things, and sometimes I overheard a cruel comment or saw a piece of graffiti written
on a desk, but the children like Katie were at an age when they could
still see beyond a person's oddities to the real person inside, and
there, I believed that I was good-hearted and above reproach. I gave
thanks for those children. They were all there was between me and
the rage I felt because I was, at heart, a lonely man.

But then they started to come to me in my dreams, Katie most of all. One night, I dreamed we were on her porch swing and she took my hand. Sweet child. What father hasn't dreamed like this and woke feeling the joy of his love for his daughter? But when I woke I felt ashamed because, of course, I had no right to this dream.

I told Raymond R. all this because it had become too much for me—too big, too frightening—and he was the one who had patched the cracks in my porch steps. Work the point in deep, he'd told me. Tamp in that mud. Fill that crack all the way up so the damp won't get in and set in the cold and cause that concrete to heave open. He'd patched those cracks and now I could barely tell that they had ever been there.

Sometimes all you can do is tell the truth. That's what I was thinking when he showed me that fluff of hair in that envelope. I couldn't have explained this then, but now I suspect that I had started to sense that he carried his own secrets, that he was expert in covering them over, that we were bound together by the dark lives we tried to hide.

"You came into my house," I said to him that evening. "I thought you were my friend."

"I fixed your glasses, didn't I?" He folded the envelope and put it in my shirt pocket. "You loan me some money—like I said, a thousand, two if you've got it. Don't worry. I won't tell anyone your secrets about that little girl. Teach, you give me that money, and I'll be your friend all the way to the sweet by-and-by."

The Heights

IT WENT WITHOUT saying in the Heights that Junior and Patsy Mackey were blessed. One look at their house, that Queen Anne with its gingerbread trim and its dramatic roof gables and its bay windows and that marvelous wraparound porch, said it all. Everyone anticipated the Holiday Parade of Homes that took place each Christmas so they could have a peek inside and, if they were lucky, perhaps a word or two with the Mackeys themselves.

In the meantime, unless someone was lucky enough to be a close family friend, glimpses would have to suffice. Anyone driving past could slow just enough to get a glimpse of the house and the wreath on the front door, which changed according to the seasons. Sometimes a car would turn onto Shasta Drive and then down the alley that ran behind the Mackeys' house all for another look at the patio, its pavers cut from blue limestone shipped in from Virginia's Shenandoah Valley, at least so word had it at Burget's Sand and Gravel. Along the edge of the patio a fishpond caught the water trickling down over a wall of that blue limestone. The lawn was always freshly mowed and edged, and Patsy Mackey's rosebushes were glorious in the summer. No one could raise roses like Patsy, and why shouldn't that be so? Just take a look at her children. Handsome and full of vigor. Everything about the Mackeys—their children, their roses, their patio, their house, the luminaries that lit their driveway during the Holiday Parade of Homes—announced that they were golden.

Sometimes people stopped their cars and took snapshots. It was that kind of home. They were that kind of family. Nearly nine years had gone by since President Kennedy had been assassinated, long enough for the shock to fade, but not so long to make people forget what it had been like to have a family like the Kennedys, who captivated a country with their charm, their wealth, their good looks. In Tower Hill, that was the Mackeys.

In the days after Katie disappeared, Pete Wilson, who took care of film developing at Fite Photography, said he couldn't begin to count the number of rolls that came in with shots of the Mackeys' house and yard. "It was like we'd all gone away," he said. "The whole damned town of us, and all that was left was that house."

What no one knew was that in the weeks leading up to Katie's disappearance, Junior Mackey, at moments when there was nothing to keep him on the sunny side—no canasta parties, or basketball games at the high school, or home-staged talent shows featuring Patsy and Katie—found his heart seized and aching. He was the sort of man who, by nature, brooded over his mistakes; often the smallest, most commonplace things set him to sulking: catching his reflection in a window as he passed, hearing an owl calling in the night, or the creak of bedsprings as Katie or Gilley or Patsy turned over in their beds.

He crossed over then—left the life he thought was his and

found himself, poleaxed and weak-kneed, stumbling about in a place where he saw himself, his true self, and he couldn't, as much as he wanted to, look away.

It was then that he thought of the moment—all those years ago—when he and Patsy, both of them only eighteen, stood in the alleyway behind the doctor's office in Indianapolis on a night when snow was dusting their heads, and she turned to him and said, "Gil," said it like a plea, and he squeezed her hand and told her, "You can do this. Jeez, Patsy. It's the best thing."

That was the moment he now wished he could change. He wished he had said, "All right. Yes, we'll go home. Yeah, sure. We'll go home and we'll get hitched and we'll have this baby." If only he'd said that. If only he hadn't given a hang about what his father would say. His father, who had told him, "You're going places, Junior. You don't want to get tied down with a wife and a kid."

Junior knocked on the door, three deliberate knocks as the doctor had requested. When the door opened, a smell of disinfectant and rubbing alcohol and fuel oil from a heating stove washed out into the alley. Junior put his hand on the small of Patsy's back—he could barely bring himself to touch her there now—and pressed until she stepped from the alley and up the back stairway to the doctor's office, where he asked Junior for the money.

"Stupid boy," his father said when Junior told him that Patsy was in trouble. "You think with your head, not from down here." He grabbed Junior's crotch and squeezed. "Stupid boy," he said again. "I'll only bail you out of a jam like this once. If it happens again, you'll have to own up to it." Money, he told Junior, could buy whatever they needed, but above all else it could buy them convenience. What he didn't say was that it could also buy secrets, enough secrets to last Junior and Patsy a lifetime. Secrets that reared up late at night, or sometimes, without warning, in the middle of the day. A gargle of Listerine, a swab of alcohol, a sniff of kerosene from a heater. All these things were enough to make Junior close his eyes and swallow hard because he had caused the child—their first child—to be taken away.

He brought himself back from his misery by concentrating on what was around him—the blue limestone pavers, Patsy's roses, the new bicycle he had bought for Katie, anything to keep him anchored in the here and now—and when he returned he loved his family more fiercely, determined not to surrender to regret.

It was Katie whom he cherished most of all—Katie, his darling girl. Soon Gilley would be making his own way through the world—already he had a head of his own. He didn't want to sweat at the glassworks in the summers; he had no interest in that. Well, what could Junior do? He was disappointed. Sure. But boys were different than girls. A boy got his chest all puffed up, his head stuck on stubborn, and went off to prove he was his own man. But a girl? It was just like the old song said: her heart belonged to Daddy.

Nights, that summer, he lay with Katie on a blanket in the backyard, and he named the constellations. He pointed to the sky, and she followed the handle of the Little Dipper to the brilliant star at its end—the North Star, he said, Polaris, the star of the northern hemisphere toward which the earth's axis pointed. He told her how someone, no matter how lost, could always find his way by looking for that star. Then he moved on to Orion, the hunter, and named the stars that marked his shoulders and feet. Katie loved the chant of their names: Betelgeuse, Bellatrix, Rigel, Saiph. He spoke them in a whisper as if they were too precious to say. In the silence that followed, she reached for his hand, and he let her take it. He closed his eyes and thought of that night all those years ago when he and Patsy had driven back from Indianapolis, and she had cried, and he had told her, "Don't worry. We're going home." And now here they were: Junior and Patsy and Gilley and Katie. Life had gone on. It always did. That's what you learned as you got older. Time. It kept moving. You couldn't stop it. You couldn't go back to the moments you wished you could change. They were gone. They left you in a snap. You knocked three times on a back-alley door. You put your hand on the small of a girl's back, a girl you loved, and together, you stepped inside.

What was that joke? A snail comes into a bar. The bartender takes one look at him and gives him a swift kick out the door. A year later, the snail comes back into the bar. "Okay, wise guy," he says to the bartender. "What was that all about?"

Katie rolled around on the floor in a fit of giggles the afternoon that her father told her that joke. It was the evening before the last day of school. Summer vacation—three glorious months—stretched out ahead of her. She was giddy with the thought of all those days. She and Renée Cherry would have tea parties in Renée's playhouse; they'd invite their Barbie dolls. They'd make Ken and Barbie kiss and then giggle about it. Katie would do Barbie's voice. "Oh, you smoothy," she'd say, which is what her mother said sometimes when her father kissed her. And there would be sleep-outs in the pup tent in Katie's backyard, and long afternoons on the front porch swing reading or playing another heartbreaking game of It's Gotta Go. In a few weeks, the stores downtown would have their Moonlight Madness sales. They'd close off the streets around the square, and there'd be carnival rides and cotton candy and saltwater taffy and lemon shake-ups. This year there was supposed to be a live elephant. An elephant that you could ride. Holy moly. All of this and trips to Shakamak State Park to fish in the lake and the curlicue slide at the city park and whatever else she and Renée Cherry wanted to do. That was the joy of summer. It was yours. You owned it. If you wanted to laugh yourself silly over a corny snail joke, you could. If you wanted to roll around on the floor until your hair was a mess and you were dizzy, hey, who was there to stop you?

Katie heard her mother's high heels clacking on the hardwood floor. From where she was lying, she could see her mother's feet, still in her dress-up shoes, the ones she had worn for an after-school meeting with Katie's teacher. The shoes were black and shiny. They had pointed toes. One foot was tapping the floor.

"Oh, Katie." Her mother sighed. "Oh, dear."

A gust of wind caught the front door, and it slammed shut. The curtains at the windows, which had been merrily lifting with the wind, sagged and flattened against the screens. Katie remembered the time right before Christmas vacation when her mother told her that she had to go into the hospital to have her tonsils out. It could happen like that. You could think you were sailing along, and then something could throw everything, as her father said, "all jabberwockers."

This time it was math. She'd just barely squeaked by. "By the skin of your teeth," her mother said. "The skin." Katie rubbed her tongue over her teeth, which were hard and not like skin at all. "Miss Silver says you're going to need help if you're going to keep up next year."

Katie sat up. "Help?" she said.

"That's right," said her mother. "A tutor. A summer tutor."

Katie fell back on the floor, her arms stretched out to her sides. "I'll die," she said. "A tutor? In summer? I'll just die."

Patsy Mackey would think back to that moment often that summer, and in the years that would follow. She would remember how she and Junior, getting ready for bed that evening, agreed that Henry Dees was the one who could help them. Henry Dees, who lived in Gooseneck. A bit of an odd duck, that Henry Dees, but he got results. Patsy knew more than one mother who swore that her children would have never gotten through fractions, long division, or algebra without Mr. Dees.

"I'll go down to Gooseneck tomorrow morning," Junior said. He sat on the edge of the bed, watching Patsy at her vanity table. She was braiding her hair, which she still wore long, and even though he had watched her do this every night for nearly twenty years, it still fascinated him. She put her hands behind her head as if she were fastening a necklace, and her fingers separated her hair into three sections and then began to weave those sections together. He loved to watch this graceful crisscross, Patsy's fingers gathering and twining, because when he did, he felt that the world held still, that the storm he sometimes felt brewing inside him died down. The hatred he felt for himself over what he had done that night in Indianapolis went away. He could forgive himself, forgive his father. He could sit on that bed and watch Patsy braid her hair, and he could think that he was, all things considered, a lucky man. "I'll talk to Henry Dees," he said. "Don't worry. We'll get Katie back on track."

As they lay down in the dark and waited for sleep, Junior didn't know that Patsy thought of the lost child, who would be a young man or woman now. She wondered what joys that child might have had, what miseries. Oh, that was all part of being alive, wasn't it?

The what-ifs? She remembered how scared she had been that night in Indianapolis. It was snowing, and she was wearing her new car coat, the camel's hair her mother and father had given her for Christmas. She kept worrying that the snow would ruin the coat, and that was the part that made her feel silly now to recall it. How young she had been. What a fool. Worried about a coat on a night like that. Somewhere down the alley, a radio was playing. The song was Perry Como's "When You Were Sweet Sixteen." Sometimes, even now, a line or two of that song popped into her head, and she felt a tenderness for the girl she had been, the one who had believed Gil when he told her they had no choice. They couldn't get married. Jeez, they were still in school. And how would he go to college with a wife and a baby to support?

She had gone ahead and made a life with him. She had lived so long that sometimes the night in Indianapolis seemed as if it had happened to someone else, not her. Then there were moments like tonight when the two of them lying together in silence became too much for her, and she knew with a heartbreaking sureness that it had been no one's fault but hers. She should have been stronger. She shouldn't have gone along with Junior's plan—his father's plan. But—and this was the part that caught her breath, made her feel like she was suffocating—she had been afraid to have the baby. Secretly, she had been glad for someone to tell her what to do. She wanted to ask Gil on these nights, when she knew that they were both having trouble falling asleep, whether he ever thought of that night, whether he ever wished that they had turned around and come home and never knocked on that doctor's door, but she knew she couldn't ask him that, couldn't whisper a word about that night, and this was the saddest part of all. They could never admit that they shared the same regret, the same heartache. They could only talk of the here and now: Gilley's golf game, a new variety of tea rose, and now Katie's problems with math, which they would have to solve. What was it their high school calculus teacher had told them, something from a famous mathematician, something about what to do when you couldn't solve a problem? Oh, yes. *If you can't solve a problem, then there's an easier problem you can't solve. Find it.*

THE NEXT morning, the music was so loud at Mr. Dees's house that Junior had to pound and pound on the door. The song playing was one he had heard Gilley play on his stereo—"Candy Man"—and for a moment he wondered whether he had made a mistake and gone to the wrong address.

He shielded his eyes with his hand and peered in through the diamond of glass in the front door. What he saw amused him. Such a sight. Henry Dees with a spatula held like a microphone as he sang along. "Oh, the Candy Man can." Who would have thought that he fancied himself a singer, that mornings he strutted around his kitchen, his head tossed back, his fingers snapping, his arm flung out, as if he were onstage at an Executive Inn dinner show, a spotlight following him as he reached toward the audience? "Yes, the Candy Man can."

Junior couldn't bring himself to knock again, to disturb Mr. Dees and let him know that he had found him out. But he couldn't back away. Watching Mr. Dees, unguarded and exposed in this private moment, made him happy, glad to know that all manner of folks could manufacture joy—even a bachelor schoolteacher who, as far as Junior knew, had never even had a chance at love. He could sing into that spatula. He could turn up the volume and not care who heard. He could sing, sing, sing on this bright morning in June.

Then the music stopped, and Mr. Dees went to the stove and used his spatula to turn a pancake. Bacon was frying in a pan. He speared the slices with a fork and stacked them on a saucer. He was all business now. He was making time. He buttered toast, poured coffee, slid the pancake onto a plate, and spooned out batter for another. Soon there was a stack and syrup on the table, and he was ready to dig in. He paused and snapped his fingers twice. He tapped his foot. That song. That "Candy Man." Junior knew it was still in his head, that little bit of dum-di-dum, and he was glad to know it, satisfied with the news that Henry Dees was a man who could make room for the cockle-fruity-do, a little bit of a silly song to give him a chuckle. It gave the earnest part of him, that by-the-numbers dignity, all the more weight.

Junior tapped on the glass and watched as Mr. Dees looked up from his breakfast. He squinted toward the door. He touched his napkin to his lips and then folded it into a neat rectangle before pushing his chair away from the table. It had been nearly twenty years since Junior had spoken to him. The last time—he could recall it clearly—had been in school, the night of graduation. In the hallway before the line for the processional formed, Junior bent to tie his shoelace and it snapped. Henry Dees had a spare one in his pocket, and he gave it to Junior. "Why do you have an extra one?" Junior asked him, and Henry told him he liked to think ahead. Who knew what might happen? He wanted to be ready. Junior had always remembered that, how Henry Dees had given him that shoelace, had been right there when he needed him.

Now he had come to ask for his help. "It's my girl," he said when Mr. Dees opened the door. "You remember me, Henry. I'm Junior Mackey. It's my girl, Katie. She's having trouble with her arithmetic."

Mr. Dees asked him to come in. He poured him a cup of coffee, offered him pancakes and bacon. The house smelled of the coffee and food. A breeze lifted the curtain at the kitchen window. Outside, birds were singing. Those were his purple martins, Mr. Dees said. For a while, he and Junior sat at the table and said nothing. They sipped coffee, two men taking their time on a summer morning.

Then Mr. Dees said yes, of course he knew him. Gilbert Mackey. He'd married Patsy Molloy. They lived in the Heights. He'd had their son, Gilley, in his calculus class. A smart boy, a polite boy. Very nice. And he'd seen their daughter around town. A little brown-haired girl. What was her name? Katie? Yes, Katie. So it was Katie who had hit a snag with her math? Of course he could help her. He hadn't found a child yet that he couldn't teach.

He wasn't boasting. Junior had no doubt of that. Mr. Dees was merely stating a fact in that quiet way he had, bowing his head as if it embarrassed him to have to say it. Such a claim was far from a boast. It was the simple truth stated with the same shy and quiet dignity Junior remembered from that night at graduation when Henry Dees loaned him that shoelace. Everything would be all right with Katie. He felt sure of that. Henry Dees was someone they could count on.

"Don't worry about your Katie," he said. "I'll take care of her."

HE CAME the first time on an afternoon when Katie and Renée Cherry were outside, sitting cross-legged on the grass. Mr. Dees wore a poplin suit—powder blue, the color of the sky in early June before the heat came and the clotted air. He paused on the sidewalk and listened to the girls. He memorized the lilt and chirp of their voices. As bright as pennies. They were talking about books they had read. The Henry Huggins books were *magnifique*, Renée Cherry said. She had copper-colored hair. Glorious hair that fell to her shoulders, that wreathed her narrow face. It was her mother's hair. Margot Cherry, née Legrand, who was Mr. Dees's old classmate. Margot Legrand, who had spoken French and smoked cigarettes and tried once, unsuccessfully, to kill herself by slashing her wrists with her father's razor. Even she had managed a family. A husband and this beautiful daughter sitting in the shade on this glorious summer day. "*Magnifique*," Renée said again, and Mr. Dees grinned, convinced that she had heard her mother use that word and now was trying to make it her own.

The air smelled of the cedar shrubs and the attar of Patsy Mackey's roses. Mr. Dees was content to linger and eavesdrop. He let himself imagine, just for a moment, that this was his home, these girls on the grass his daughters, and soon he would call to them and they would come running, each of them reaching for one of his hands.

Yes, said Katie. The Henry Huggins books were funny, but, really, wasn't the Little House series so much better? Laura and her sisters, Mary and Baby Carrie, and Ma and Pa Ingalls. "*On the Banks of Plum Creek*," Katie said, "when the grasshoppers eat the wheat crop, or *The Long Winter* when the snow's so deep and the trains can't get through with food or coal? Didn't those books break your heart?" Mr. Dees could see that her cheeks were flushed and damp with tears.

"Oh, I know," Renée said. "Absolutely heartbreaking. *Très triste*."

They went on debating the merits and disappointments of each book, but Mr. Dees wasn't listening now. He was watching Katie.

She was sobbing. Her shoulders shook. Her breath came in hiccups. Her hair fell over her face and she pushed it back with her hands. He wanted to run to her, gather her up in his arms, and tell her not to worry; nothing could be as bad as all that. He understood now that the girls were playing a game that required them to eliminate one of the books, pretend it never existed, and how could they make that choice when they loved each so dearly? A child's game. That was all, and yet at the moment nothing could have seemed as dire to Renée and Katie, especially Katie, who blubbered and bawled and said, between her hiccups, "Laura . . . and Mary . . . and Baby Carrie . . . and Laura's friend Almanzo . . . Oh, Renée."

Mr. Dees felt an ache in his throat, and he wasn't ashamed, not a whit, to know that his own tears were about to come. Katie's anguish touched him. He removed the handkerchief, freshly ironed that morning, from his breast pocket and blotted his eyes. How could anyone behold the miseries of children and not take them in, not feel them as his own? He couldn't bear to hear Katie cry. Not for another second could he stand it.

So he called out. "Hello, hello," he said, waving his arm as he came up the driveway. "Which one of you girls is lucky?"

"Lucky?" said Katie.

"Why, sure," he told her. "I thought you were the one."

He began the first lesson by explaining how to divide a whole number into fractions. They sat on the patio at the table with the big green umbrella opened above it. From time to time, Mr. Dees caught a glimpse of Patsy Mackey at the kitchen window, pretending not to be watching. She had brought them a pitcher of lemonade. "Katie, this is Mister Dees," she had said. "He's a very nice man who's going to help you with your arithmetic."

He told Katie that any whole number could be divided, even one. It could be divided in half; it could be split into thirds, fourths, sixths, eighths, and on down the line. He showed her on his tablet how to write one-half by putting a one over a two: $\frac{1}{2}$. The bottom number, the 2, was the denominator. It showed how many equal portions made up the whole number. The top number, the 1, was the numerator. It showed how many of the equal portions they were taking away.

"So if we have the fraction one-fourth," he said, "it means we've split the whole number into four equal parts and we're going to take one of those parts away. Do you understand?"

She had her arms crossed on the table, her chin on her hands. She nodded, and she looked so glum Mr. Dees almost called their lesson to an end. He imagined that she'd rather still be with Renée, that she'd rather be doing anything than learning about fractions.

But he had a job to do, so he went ahead and explained how to add $\frac{1}{4}$ and $\frac{3}{4}$ to return to the whole number, 1. "You add the numerators. One plus three. See?"

"I know how to add," Katie said with a dramatic sigh.

"Of course you do," he told her, determined to stay patient and cheery. "But I want to make sure that you really understand."

"I said I did, didn't I?"

"All right. Show me." He wanted to win her over. He wanted to convince her that learning mathematics could be fun. "Let's say you have four of something, four . . . oh, I don't know . . . four children. Let's say their names are Laura and Mary and Carrie and Almanzo."

She raised her head. "From the Little House books?"

"That's right. And let's say one of them wanders away from the others, gets lost in the woods perhaps."

"Lost?" Her eyes opened wide. She was interested now. Mr. Dees congratulated himself on having the good sense to turn the math problem into a story. Katie, he could tell, was a girl who understood narrative, mystery. A girl with curiosity. Someone who wanted to know what happened next. "Which one?" she asked. "Which one of them got lost?"

"Oh, I don't know," Mr. Dees said. "It could be any one of them, any one at all. You just have to pick one."

Right away, he recalled the game Katie and Renée had been playing and the anguish it had caused them. He knew he had made a mistake. Katie's eyes narrowed with concern. "Pick one?" she said. Her chin started to quiver. "I have to pick one?"

Mr. Dees tried to erase his error. "Tell you what. I'll pick one."

But that only made matters worse. "Who?" Katie was even more worried now. "Who has to be the one who gets lost?"

Mr. Dees could see that any answer he gave would be the wrong one because Katie couldn't bear to think of any of the four children lost in the woods. "Maybe we should forget the children," he said. "We could do the problem with something else. Dogs or cats or zebras."

Katie's voice shook. "A dog? Lost? Like Lassie? Lost?"

Then the tears were coming, and she jumped up from her chair and ran into the house, leaving Mr. Dees alone, cursing himself for how foolish he had been. He hadn't meant to hurt her at all, but that's what he had done. He had convinced himself that he knew what it was like to want the best for someone like Katie, but now he had done this stupid thing, and it made him realize how clumsy he was when it came to dealing with people.

He didn't know what to do, whether to wait on the patio, or

knock on the door so he could apologize, or just slink away, a lost dog starved and alone. He put the cap on his fountain pen and clipped it to his shirt pocket. He closed his writing tablet.

The door behind him opened, and he heard Junior Mackey say his name. "Henry," he said. "Jesus, Mary, and Joseph. What did you say to my girl?"

"Didn't she tell you?"

"Christ, she could barely talk. Henry, she came running in bawling her head off."

Mr. Dees was angry, disgusted with himself for bringing up the Little House children. How had he even managed to recall their names? Why hadn't he seen that the very mention of them would upset Katie? He was also irritated with her for being so sensitive. But wasn't that what he loved most about her? The stories of those children had broken her heart, she had told Renée, and he had ached for a child like Katie who could take in the miseries of people, could feel them as if they were her own.

"We were doing our work," he said, and then, though he was furious, he told Junior Mackey in a calm voice what he had said to Katie and why it had disturbed her so. "I was wrong," he said. "I miscalculated."

"Good God," said Junior Mackey. "Don't you know a thing about kids?"

Mr. Dees was standing up now. He buttoned his coat, smoothed his tie, tugged at his shirt cuffs. He stepped toward Junior Mackey, his gaze level. He took off his glasses, folded the temples, and slipped them into his breast pocket. Later, he would think how silly that was; it was what he had seen high school boys do before a fistfight. Did he really think that he and Junior Mackey would come to blows?

"I was wrong," he said. "Sometimes people make mistakes. If you'd rather I didn't teach your daughter, then say so, and I'll go home and not come back. Otherwise, you'll have to trust me."

He never raised his voice. He never stomped a foot or shook a fist. He didn't have to. He narrowed his eyes and said what was on his mind, and because no one, particularly Junior Mackey, was accustomed to hearing him talk with such force, his words, quiet as they were, had weight.

Gilley stepped out onto the patio, golf club in hand. He saw his father and Mr. Dees, and something about the way they were standing told him he should turn around and go back into the house. He saw his father take a step back from Mr. Dees. He rubbed a hand over his head.

"A misunderstanding," he said. "That's all. Come back tomorrow and we'll give this another try."

Gilley stood there and watched Mr. Dees walk across the yard to the street. His back was straight, his shoulders squared, and he wasn't in a hurry. He took his time, and Junior stood there, watching him go.

"Something wrong?" Gilley said.

Junior brushed past him on his way into the house. "You don't know anything," he said. "That man's got backbone. You're a kid."

Gilley was accustomed to his father's moods—the way he could fall quiet, go inside himself—but this was something different. This was hostility. This was a remark meant to belittle, and Gilley didn't know what to do with it. All he knew was that something had shifted between them. Ever so slightly, something had turned. He would feel it all through that evening, the slap of those words: *You're a kid.* Even at the supper table, when his father, back in good spirits, would tell the joke about the horse who walked into the bar and the bartender who said, "So, tell me. Why the long face?" Gilley, laughing, would feel something catch inside him, and he would wonder what it was about him that his father had found to scorn.

Then one afternoon, a few days later, when he was in the display window at Penney's, slipping a sleeveless summer blouse onto a mannequin, he suddenly sensed that someone was watching him. When he turned toward the sidewalk, there was his father. Their eyes met, and his father immediately looked away, turned on his heel, and walked on up the street, his arms swinging with purpose, as if he couldn't move fast enough from the sight of his son dressing that mannequin, his fingers nimbly buttoning the blouse, smoothing out the collar.

Gilley felt the distance spreading between them, and though he couldn't name its source, he knew that somehow he had disappointed his father.

They never spoke directly about that afternoon, but that evening, when Gilley got home, his father asked him whether he'd been working hard, and he told him yes.

"Let me tell you what real work is," his father said, and Gilley knew then that their trouble had come about because he had refused to work at Mackey Glass. "Of course, you're probably not interested in hearing it. You're probably too pretty for that."

Gilley lay awake a long time that night, hearing those words again—*too pretty*—and the way his father sneered when he said them and then stalked off to his office and closed the door. Immediately, in his heart of hearts, Gilley knew that it was so. Not that he was on the other side of the street when it came to the baby-oh-baby between boys and girls—not that—but because he was more finicky than a seventeen-year-old boy should be, overly concerned with trifles; the slightest details gave him concern, and he would work and rework them until everything was just the way he wanted it. He was, as he often heard Katie say about Renée Cherry, a fusspot, or, as his father had suggested, a pretty boy.

He thought of all the nights he spent in the backyard working on his chip shots, going through the mechanics of his swing, bringing the club back, pausing to see how his weight was distributed, repeating a single motion until he was satisfied that his body had memorized it. He practiced the same obsession with his wardrobe, taking time to press creases into the legs of his blue jeans, choosing colored socks to match the shirts that he wore. These summer days, when he dressed for work, he stood in front of the mirror, knotting and reknotting his tie until it pleased him.

There was, he realized now, something womanly about him. That's what his father had seen that afternoon when he watched him buttoning that sleeveless blouse. He had tugged at its hem, smoothed its collar, then stepped back and done it all again to make sure that the blouse hung just so on the mannequin. It was that meticulous attention to detail that served him well on his job. No one did a window like him, his boss had told him, and when it came to folding shirts, well, he was a natural.

But there was a flip side to his fastidiousness. He saw that now. It was a nose-in-the-air way of moving through the world. In every smoothed wrinkle, every perfected motion, there was an air of moral judgment, though he didn't intend it. There were people, he implied, who lived sloppy lives, and then there were people like him.

His father, who made his living from glass—relied on a mix of sand and soda ash and limestone melted in furnaces where the heat could get as high as 3,600 degrees—had seen as much that after-noon at Penney's. He had seen that his son was a prig, and he won-dered—surely he did, Gilley thought—how a boy like that would ever be of any use to him.

So that was how Gilley found himself, a few days later, saying to Mr. Dees, "All right. I guess. Sure."

Mr. Dees had come into Penney's late in the afternoon—the dead time in summer, the time when Gilley folded the shirts moth-ers had picked through earlier, unfurling them, holding them up to their sons' chests, then leaving them discarded in wads. He folded the shirts and then the trousers, stacking them according to size. He used a feather duster to clean the display shoes. The store man-ager had stepped over to the Coach House for coffee the way he always did that time of day, and the girl at the cash register was filing her nails while she sang along with the radio. WTHO had started its Top Fifty Countdown, and the woman who worked in Ladies' Apparel called over to the girl. "Turn it up, sweets. Let's live a little."

The question Mr. Dees asked took Gilley by surprise. He wanted to know whether it would be all right—"whether it would be permissible," he said—to take home a few lightweight jackets, maybe three or four, so he could see which one might suit him.

"Mine has a rip." He turned his shoulder so Gilley could see the iron-on patch. "See? I've tried to mend it, but now I'm thinking I need new. It's embarrassing, yes? To wear torn clothes."

It was a cool day. Gilley could see the branches rising and falling on the trees across the street on the courthouse lawn. All morning, women had come in with scarves on their heads and they smelled of the cool air, and some of them—the country women—of coal smoke. They had lit fires, they told him. That's how cold it was. "Feels like March," more than one of them said.

Mr. Dees's request was, to say the least, unusual. "You could try them on here." Gilley pointed to the tri-panel mirror outside the fitting room. "I'll be glad to help you."

"Oh, no," Mr. Dees said. "I couldn't do that."

"It's the way people usually do it."

"I don't like to look at myself in the mirror." Mr. Dees bowed his head. "And three of them? I couldn't bear to see so many of me and from so many angles. Like I was sneaking up on myself. At home, I have someone who will help me. Someone I trust." He raised his head and looked Gilley straight in the eye. "Please."

Gilley took in Mr. Dees's meek look, and he thought of the way his father had called him pretty and then left him to wish the word gone.

"You must be a size forty," Gilley said. "A forty long. Just look at your arms."

Ordinarily, he would have refused such an unreasonable request. Imagine. Someone wanting to take home jackets. But today, when he was mulling over the ways men could choose to live their lives, it felt proper and right, a good fit—geez, what would his father think now?—for him to say yes.

At the rack of poplin jackets, he picked out a green one and a yellow one and a red-and-blue plaid.

"I can pay for them." Mr. Dees reached into the pocket of his trousers and took out a roll of bills. "All three of them. Then tomorrow, when I bring back the two I've decided against, you can give me a refund."

Gilley shook his head. He was practically dizzy with what he was about to do. "Keep the money," he said. "I know you'll be back."

He asked Mr. Dees to follow him to the rear of the store, and there the two of them slipped through the stockroom—past the cardboard boxes full of shirts and blouses and trousers and skirts, past the racks of hangers, past the shelves where the layaway items waited to be claimed—to the alley door. When Gilley pushed it open light came flooding in, along with the cool air and the sound of a mower running on the courthouse lawn and the smell of the freshly cut grass. Gilley loved that smell. He loved the chill in the air, the wind rising, and how sharp the day had become.

"Thank you." Mr. Dees hugged the jackets to his chest. "Thank you very much for understanding."

"Come back tomorrow," Gilley told him. "Same time. I'll be waiting. Knock on the door and I'll let you in."

It happened that way. Gilley let him take the jackets, without a dime put down as security, and the next day, when the store manager was once again at the Coach House, the knock came. Gilley opened the alley door and there was Mr. Dees.

"I've chosen the plaid," he said. "Usually I choose blue, but my friend convinced me. The plaid. What do you think?"

Gilley was relieved. He had the two jackets back, and already Mr. Dees was reaching into his trousers pocket to pay for the one he had chosen. What a wad of bills he took out. He snapped off a twenty with a flick of his wrist.

"I think it suits you," he told Mr. Dees.

Mr. Dees pressed the twenty into Gilley's hand, squeezing. "I've never worn plaid before." A tremor of a smile came to Mr. Dees's lips. "Who would have thought?" he said. "Plaid." He refused the few dollars change owed him from his twenty, telling Gilley to please keep it for himself. "A good-looking boy like you," he said. "A popular boy. I'm sure you can find something to spend it on."

"You won't tell, will you?" Gilley said. "What I did? If my boss found out . . ."

"I won't tell. You can trust me." Mr. Dees put his finger to his lips. "Our secret." Then he turned and disappeared down the alley.

Nothing had changed on planet Earth. Gilley knew that. In fact, that evening he would sit down with his father while he was watching Walter Cronkite give the news on television, and he would think, What did it matter, what he had done for Mr. Dees? What difference had it made to the whole, big world spinning on beneath them? What had it mattered to the 236 people dead from flooding in Rapid City, South Dakota; or the 118 who had lost their lives in Hurricane Agnes; and when he thought of the 62,000 people starving to death because of the drought in West Africa, not to mention the casualties in Vietnam . . . how important was the fact that he had played fast and loose with J. C. Penney merchandise and come away clean? What difference at all did small favors between people make?

Still, he couldn't stop the crazy, giddy-assed feeling coming over him even as he sat in the glow of blue light coming from the console television and heard Walter Cronkite naming the world's mayhem and disaster. He knew he was grinning like an idiot.

"What's so hilarious?" his father asked, and he told him, nothing. Not a thing. Just something funny that had happened at work.

THE CARNIVAL came to town: a merry-go-round, a Tilt-A-Whirl, a Ferris wheel. The police blocked off the streets around the courthouse square—High, Thirteenth, Taylor, Fourteenth—and the carnival set up shop. The downtown merchants carried tables and racks of sale items out onto the sidewalks and kept their stores open until ten o'clock: Minnie's Discount, Volk's Clothiers, Helene's Dress Shop, Bogan's Shoe Store, Sherman's Five and Dime, J. C. Penney, where Gilley stood in the twilight, listening to the calliope music coming from the merry-go-round, watching the painted horses slide up and down on their silver poles.

People on the Tilt-A-Whirl were screaming as the cars spun them around. A boy and a girl at the top of the Ferris wheel kissed while their gondola swayed. Their silhouettes were dim against the darkening sky. Barkers called out: "Take a chance. A little luck, a little skill. Everyone's a winner." Katie and Renée Cherry came running up to Gilley, their mouths sticky with blue cotton candy. The air smelled of it—that burned sugar smell—and there was popcorn and corn dogs and saltwater taffy.

"Gilley, Gilley, Gilley," Katie said, all out of breath. "Oh, Gilley. Look what we won."

It was a rubber snake. Katie shook it at him.

"Doesn't it look real?" Renée asked.

"Oh, it really does," said Gilley.

"We picked up a duck," Katie told him. He knew the game, a stream of plastic ducks floating on water, idiotic looks on their painted faces, just bobbing along, la-di-da. Some of them had lucky numbers painted on their undersides. Pick up a winner; take home a prize. "We picked up a duck," Katie said, "and we won."

She shook the snake in Renée's face, and both of them screamed and went running back into the crowd.

A man stepped up on the sidewalk, a stocky man with a sunburned face. He turned and watched Katie and Renée as they ran past him. Then he turned to Gilley. He pointed his finger at him.

"Bub," he said, "I want to shake your hand." He was wearing a white painter's cap, and black-framed eyeglasses with flecks of gray on the lenses. Something had splattered up and hardened. He grabbed Gilley's hand and squeezed it. "You're all right," he said. "You're an ace."

Then, before Gilley could ask him who he was or what he wanted, he let loose of his hand and moved on down the sidewalk, tipping his cap to a woman in front of Bogan's, digging into his pocket for a dime that he gave to a little girl. He patted her head. Gilley watched him until he came to the Coach House, where a woman was waiting: a scrawny woman with short hair gone to gray, a cook's apron still tied around her neck. She was sipping something from a wax cup, and when she saw the man, she lifted her face from the cup and she smiled. It was a beautiful smile, a smile full of joy and thanksgiving, and Gilley was grateful that he had seen it.

He heard his name, and he knew it was his mother calling him in her loud, brassy voice. She was across the street waving her arm. "Gilley," she said. "Look at your sister."

Katie was riding the elephant. She sat up high on a velvet-covered gondola with gold tassels swinging from it. A man in knee-high boots and riding pants blousing around his legs and a pith helmet on his head led the elephant around the straw-littered ring. He put a hooked pole beneath the elephant's trunk and used it to turn him.

Gilley followed the circle the elephant made, and as he did, he saw his father watching from the crowd. At one point, when the gondola shifted and slipped just a tad to the side, Junior Mackey made the slightest move forward, and his arms started to lift. Later, Gilley would remember that—how his father had been ready to catch Katie. But there was no need. She was fine. People were watching because how often in this itty-bitty town did you see a girl, her glorious brown hair draping her shoulders, riding atop an elephant? Mercy.

When the elephant turned again, Gilley saw the man and woman in front of the Coach House. Mr. Dees was with them. He was wearing his plaid jacket even though the night was warm. Gilley knew the weather was about to turn. Soon there would be hot, dry days, the air still and sultry. The man with the sunburned face took off his painter's cap and waved it in the air. He raised his other arm and pointed at Katie. "Woo-hoo," Gilley heard him shout. "Look at that cowgirl."

Then he put his cap back on. He laid one arm over the woman's slight shoulders and the other around Mr. Dees's, and the three of them walked on up the street.

"Gilley, I'm riding an elephant," Katie said.

She looked splendid. She was sitting up very straight and her chin was lifted. "Exotic," he would tell her later when she would sneak into his bedroom, still talking about the elephant. "Oh, yes, you looked exotic," he would say. "Like a princess. An Indian princess."

"I wasn't afraid," she would say. "Not a bit."

He would tell her that he had seen that. And it was true. He knew, as he watched her, that she wasn't afraid. Later, he would have to remind himself of that fact. She hadn't been afraid. Not her. Not then. Not on that night, on the courthouse square, in the center of this small town, where so many people, enchanted with the sight, were watching her.

Raymond R.

And i still can't see anything that involves me in any way in this thing other than the fact that I was a neighbor to Henry Dees.

Mr. Dees

It was a Friday, June 30, when Raymond R. came to my house around noon. I was sitting out under the catalpa tree, just sitting there on an old metal yard chair, drinking a glass of iced tea. From time to time, a martin swooped down from the sky and perched atop one of the houses. Raymond R. squatted down on his heels just the way he had that first time when he showed me how to patch the concrete steps. He pulled snatches of grass out of the ground and tossed them into the air. When he finally spoke his voice was flat and used up.

"They canned me today," he said. "That hospital up in Jasper. The foreman gave me the sack."

He reached into his shirt pocket and took out a tin of Sucrets throat lozenges, but when he opened it I could tell that it wasn't Sucrets that he had inside. They were pills, some of them purple and some of them yellow. He fished around with his finger until he had the one he wanted, a yellow one. And all the while he was telling me how he'd always tried to get ahead, how he got tired of all the rich bastards, those ones like Junior Mackey. Just look at him sitting high and mighty. "I build houses for people like him," Raymond R. said. "I build their factories and their schools, and what do I get out of it? Not enough to amount to a pinch of shit. That's for sure."

Story of his life, he said, and then he snapped the Sucrets tin shut.

The first time he tried to get a leg up, he told me, was when WWII was on. He was eighteen, and boys in his hometown in Minnesota were going off in bundles to fight in the Pacific and North Africa. He saw them downtown on Mitchell Street, jazzing with their best girls before they shipped out. He saw them at the Snow White Sandwich Shop, playing records on the countertop jukeboxes, snuggling up to Glenn Miller's "String of Pearls," or Bing Crosby's "You Belong to My Heart," or Vaughn Monroe's "There I Go." The girls wore plastic flowers in their hair; the boys had on neckties and smelled of Bay Rum Aftershave. They went out into the night, got into cars, and drove up Mitchell Street, turned west on Chestnut, angling along the north shore of Silver Lake, heading to the Rocks Cabins.

Raymond R. followed them in his father's Buick 90. He saw the girls with their heads laid over on the boys' shoulders. He fought the urge to keep following them, to sneak up to a cabin and get a peek at what was going on.

The Army wouldn't have him, nor would the Navy or the Marines. He even tried the Coast Guard, and they told him the same thing. Go home, they said. You didn't pass the physical. It's your leg. Sorry, bub, but you understand.

A broken leg when he was a kid, he told me. It never healed right.

He watched the boys home on leave after boot camp. They

paraded down Mitchell Street in their uniforms. Man, they were sharp. All spit and polish. Everything crisp and neat. They strutted around and let everyone give them the glad hand. Men dragged them into bars and bought them drinks. Girls gave them their scarves, their lockets, their bracelets, their stockings—anything for good luck. Then the boys went away, and the girls wrote them letters, and each week in the evening newspaper there was "News of Our Boys in Service." If you were a soldier, you were by God somebody.

So he stole an Army Air Corps uniform from a surplus store and wore it up and down Mitchell Street until he could work up the nerve to saunter into the ballroom at the Northwood Hotel and ask a girl to dance. She wore a red felt hat with a sloped brim and lace netting that fell over her eyes. The band was playing "Moonglow," the clarinets all sleepy and whispery, the muted horns raspy and slow. The girl had small hands, and he liked the way his palm covered hers. She laid her head on his shoulder; the netting of her hat tickled his neck. They danced under soft blue lights until a policeman tapped him on the shoulder and asked him to please step outside.

That was the first time he'd been arrested, he told me, and he wasn't sorry. That girl. That dance. The gardenia scent of her cologne. Those small hands. It had all been worth it. Every day he spent in jail.

He stood up. He took the glass of iced tea from my hand. He popped the yellow pill in his mouth and drank it down with the rest of my tea. "I've beat men before." He let the glass drop to the ground. "It's no skin off my nose. Teach, I'm in a pinch. I figure you can help me get a leg up on those pricks like Junior Mackey. How about it? What'd you say?"

Clare

Iт was midafternoon when Ray came into the dining room at Brookstone Manor. I was on my break, just sitting at one of the tables, drinking coffee. A couple of the girlie-girls who worked in the kitchen were sitting across the room, sipping Cokes through straws. They were talking with loud voices. "God," one of them said, and she drew it out—*Gawd*—like now she'd heard it all.

Ray sat down next to me. He kissed me on the neck. "I'm sorry, old girl." He whispered it in my ear. "They gave me the heave-ho. 'Grab up your tools and don't come back.' That's what the boss man said. That son of a bitch."

I whispered back. I didn't want the girlie-girls to hear. "Ray, was it those cement blocks? The ones you took? Was that why they let you go?"

By this time, he'd finished the porch and then hauled home more blocks and built that garage out behind the house. He'd put on a tin roof and hustled up some doors from the salvage yard. One evening, he backed his truck into the garage, closed the doors, and fastened them with a chain and a heavy Yale padlock. He pulled on the lock, and the chain rattled. Now he could shut up his truck at night, he told me, and not have to worry about someone breaking into it on the street and stealing his tools. "There it is," he said. "Everything safe and sound."

No, he told me, it wasn't those blocks. He got the heatstroke again. He was on the scaffold wall when he felt it coming, that spin in his head, and soon he saw the black spots swirling in his eyes, and his knees gave way. He heard a voice—one of the other men—and it seemed to be coming at him from a long way off. It was like he was in a tunnel and the openings were closing and the light was going out. "It's Ray," the voice said. "Jesus, he's gone again."

When he came to, he was in the shade with the men crouched around him, and he said, "Well, hello there, boys. Long time, no see."

They gave him a cold drink. They took off their shirts and fanned his face. They went back to their work and left him there in the shade.

It wasn't but a little while when the foreman come to tell him he was through. That's how it happened. That's how he ended up, middle of the summer and no job.

I tried to think about what it meant. Where would we get the money to let us stay through winter? Florida was no good for Ray. All that sun and sticky air. And we were already in debt, only I didn't know that then. I thought Ray had been putting money back— leastways that's what he'd been telling me. I didn't know about the dope then. Didn't know about the yellow jackets and the pep pills and the LSD. Didn't know he was putting out twenty dollars a day for all that junk. Some nights he came home sleepy or chatty, and I thought it was the beer. Call me stupid, and you'd be right.

Or, really—and I think it was this—I just wanted to hold fast with love. I'm not afraid to say it, not even now. There was a time when I loved Raymond Wright. Nothing that happened can change that fact. I'm not even sure I'd trade it if I could. Don't ask me. Just know there are days when you thank your lucky stars, when the world doesn't seem quite so old and used up. I lay in bed those mornings and listened to the martins singing. Sing, sing, sing—just like Mama said, all over God's Heaven. Now, these last summers—*my* last summers—when I hear them, I think back to those mornings, Ray in the bed beside me, and my heart balls up so tight I can't tell what's love and what's misery. It's all the same, always will be. That's what I'd tell those girlie-girls now if I could somehow travel back to that afternoon at Brookstone Manor—that lazy afternoon when one of them said, "God," not like a prayer but like there wasn't a thing left to surprise her. I'd tell her there's always something around the corner, no matter how old you get, no matter how much you're sure you've got a handle on things. Sooner or later you live long enough—I hope that girlie-girl got the chance—and the love and the heartache get all mixed up, and that's what you've got.

Once upon a time, there was me and Ray and Henry Dees and a little girl named Katie and her mama and daddy and brother. That's the way it was, always will be. Nothing we can do to make it different. It's a story now, and stories have endings even when you don't know—fools like me—that you're already in the middle of one, and you're already making choices. "Let's go for a ride tonight," I said to Ray, trying to cheer him up. Choices that will bring you to places you never thought you'd be, places in your heart you'll mourn and love the rest of your life. I'd tell that to the Mackeys if I thought it'd do any good. But then I really don't have to. I'm sure they know it. At least in that one way, they're like me.

Gilley

I WENT TO Renée Cherry's mother because that night of Moonlight Madness I had a dream. I dreamed that Katie and I were riding
an elephant—not just any elephant, but Dumbo from the Disney
movie. So we really weren't riding. We were flying. Dumbo was flapping his ears, and we were rising past the courthouse clock tower.
We were soaring over the carnival, over our mother and father waving good-bye to us. "Good-bye," Mother called. "Good-bye."

My father threw his arms up above his head, reaching, but we
were gone. We were flying over the square, over my father's glassworks, and Gooseneck. Then we were so high, there were only
clouds—all that white nothing—and Katie said, "It's cold up here." I
put my arms around her, and then out of nowhere, the way things
happen in dreams, there was Mr. Dees. He wasn't flying. He was just
walking along—walking through the clouds. He was wearing that
plaid jacket.

"How can you do that?" I asked him.

"You're riding an elephant," he said. "Explain that."

"It just happened."

"Here's the secret." The vapor of the clouds was swirling around him. "I'm invisible. No weight."

"But I can see you." I stretched out my hand to touch him. "You're right here."

But he wasn't. My fingers closed around his jacket sleeve, and there was no arm in it. I flailed about with my other hand and caught the jacket by its collar. It was like I was grabbing it off a hanger. It collapsed in my hands. I was holding the jacket, and I realized then that Mr. Dees, wherever he had gone, had meant it for Katie, who was so cold. Only she was no longer there with me. I hadn't even felt her slip from my arms. "Katie," I called out, but there was no answer. Only the sound of wind, and this is the ridiculous part—the nutty stuff of dreams that leaves me stupid, no way to explain it—Dumbo said to me, "Holy moly." He sounded like Katie, but of course he wasn't, and it was like she was there and not there all at the same time, and when I woke, I was shivering.

"My sister," I said to Margot Cherry a few days later. "When she was born, I didn't know what to make of her. She was the most amazing thing. I wouldn't even hold her. I couldn't. I was afraid."

I hadn't meant to say any of this. I hadn't intended to confess that there were times when I didn't know how to love Katie enough. She was our sweetheart, come when I was eight years old. "She's our little girl," my mother told me when she and my father came home from the hospital. Katie's face was my face in my baby pictures displayed on our fireplace mantel, hung from our walls, set on my mother's dresser. "She's your sister," my mother said, and the word amazed me, as it did even that day in Margot Cherry's living room. Sometimes, to this day, I hear myself say it—*my sister*—and I feel this trembling inside me.

That dream was still in my head, that crazy dream about Katie and me on Dumbo the elephant and Mr. Dees walking in the clouds. When I opened my mouth, the dream was on my tongue, as was the feeling that I'd had ever since—the sensation that sometimes life was so wonderful it was scary, not to be trusted. Maybe that was what I learned the first time I held out my finger to Katie when she was a baby—"Go on," my father said, "for Pete's sake, Gilley, she's your sister"—and she closed her hand around it, and she looked at me with those green eyes, and she smiled. Maybe I learned then that I'd never be able to love her as much as she deserved.

Now I'm a parent myself. Each night before I go to bed, I step into my son's room and then my daughter's, where moonlight comes through the windows and falls over their faces. I stand in the shadows and watch them sleep, register each rise and fall of breath in my own chest, and each time I do, I think about that summer. How many times did my father, climbing the stairs at night, do the same? How many times did he look in on Katie and think himself a lucky man?

"Is it too late?" I asked Margot Cherry that afternoon. It's been more than thirty years and still I can remember how my voice shook. "How do we know when we've loved someone all that we can?"

We were sitting in her living room on a green sofa. A painting of a red barn hung from the wall across from us. I thought what a perfectly ordinary house this was. Throw rugs littered the floor, put down in front of chairs and doors. The rugs were green with yellow daisies on them. A vase shaped like an ear of corn sat on the coffee table, a bouquet of lilies gathered in it. The room smelled of lemon-scented furniture polish. Margot Cherry had a red bandanna tied around her hair. She held her dust rag in her hands.

She told me about the light that was coming. She said I would be chosen.

"Love," she said. "It finds you. Be ready."

Clare

So we went for that ride. We rode through the long evening light on that Friday when Ray lost his job. He had his binoculars, the ones he used to scan the horizon for the tall arms of cranes and the frames of steel girders when he went out looking for construction sites he'd read about in his union bulletin. The tilled fields flashed by, flat and brown, stretching back to woodlots. The corn was nearly knee-high, and the bean plants were getting a hold and growing up from the clay dirt. Orange tiger lilies swayed in the fence rows. Quail gave their cheery, two-note call: *bob-white*. The air smelled sweet from clover hay, cut in the pastures and curing in windrows. We met a car now and then, but for the most part we didn't see anyone, maybe a farmer climbing off his tractor in his barn lot or a woman scattering feed to her guinea hens. They gave us a wave, and we waved back, and I liked the way that made me feel, like we were regular folks on this summer evening when we didn't know how anything would work out for us. We were just driving.

We drove out Route 59, all the way to Georgetown, and crossed the White River. We turned onto a gravel road to a place called

Honeywell, a heap of run-down houses, bird dogs and beagle hounds staked and chained in scrabbly yards, rows of mailboxes nailed to posts along the road, a lot of them with their lids hanging open.

He wanted to take a look, Ray said.

"For what?" I asked him.

"That power plant, the one they're building outside Brick Chapel."

He drove to where the houses stopped and the road dipped into the woods. After a while, he pulled the truck over to the side and got out. He stepped up on the running board. I opened the door out into the tall turkey foot grass and did the same, standing on the running board, so I could get a level look at him on the other side of the cab. He had his elbows resting there, his binoculars up to his eyes. Woods spread out to the east, trees rising up, a mess of green.

"Ray, you can't see anything from here."

All I could see were glimpses of old shale roads winding back through the trees. The light was fading, dusk coming on.

"Do you know what that foreman said to me?" Ray was still looking through his binoculars, and his voice was low. I knew that he was embarrassed to tell me what he was about to say. I thought then that he'd come out here, to this Honeywell—this place of lost chances, this place of people hardly getting by—to tell me a shameful thing, to speak words he could only stand to hear in the deep woods when dusk was falling. When the only people who might bear witness were folks who knew what it was to be down on their luck, to have people treat you like dirt. "He said I was a no-account man. I tried to tell him he was wrong. Dead wrong. It was just the sun, I told him. That's when he said it: 'Asswipe, you're done. And if you keep giving me guff, I'll run this trowel right though your guts. Now get out of here. Go on. You ain't nothing but your daddy's wet dream.' That's what he said. Like I was nothing."

Something was moving in the grass. I looked down into the turkey foot, and there was a quail. Why it didn't lift up, I don't know.

"There's mean people," I said. "It's no secret."

"No call for it," said Ray. He lowered the binoculars and banged his fist down onto the cab. With a flurry of its wings, the quail rose from the grass and flew off into the woods. That pop of wings— it's a sound I can't hear today without a chill passing over me. "It's no way to talk to a man," Ray said. "Mean makes mean, and who's to blame?"

On the way back home, we came up behind a pickup truck loaded down with hay bales. The bumper barely cleared the ground. The truck was taking it slow, and Ray, even though we were starting down a hill, pulled out to pass. Just then, a set of headlights crested the hill in front of us, dipped down, and sped our way.

I pushed my hand against the dashboard.

"Relax," Ray said. "We've got time."

The headlights were so close they lit up the inside of our cab. It was one of those souped-up cars with racing stripes down the hood and the back end jacked up. We were so close, I could see the boy inside. He had his T-shirt sleeves rolled up. His girl, a blondie with long, straight hair, was sitting up close to him. She had her hands over her eyes.

Ray jerked the steering wheel and whipped the truck back into the right lane as the car went speeding past, its horn blaring and then dying away.

"I guess they'll have something to talk about, won't they?" Ray said. "Tough guy and his queenie." He stepped on the gas, threw his right arm across the seat, and pulled me to him. "Hon," he said, "I bet they'll see me in their dreams."

July 5

In GOOSENECK, Clare unplugged her iron. Ray was in the bathroom, shaving, and he was whistling that song, that "Candy Man." She folded his trousers over a wooden hanger, taking care that the seams were straight. Saturday, they had bought the khaki twills uptown at the J. C. Penney. She had just enough to spare from her paycheck. Got to have some new pants, Ray said, if he was going to look for work after the Fourth of July holiday. The clerk, a polite boy, told them the khakis were on sale. "I remember you," the boy said to Ray. "You were on the square during Moonlight Madness. You shook my hand." Ray said no, sorry, I'm afraid you're thinking of someone else. The boy was handsome, so well mannered, and Clare wondered what her own children would have been like—hers and Bill's—if they'd ever had any.

She carried the trousers into the bedroom and hung the hanger on the knob of the closet door. Outside the sky was just beginning to brighten in the east. She raised the window blind and looked out over the backyard at the clothesline poles, the garage Ray had built, and the old oil drum where they burned their trash. She smelled the dew on the grass and listened to Henry Dees's martins warbling. This was her favorite part of the day, just before dawn, when the air was cool and the birds were singing, and it was easy to believe, if she chose, that the day wouldn't turn hot and muggy. She wouldn't have to spend all those hours in the kitchen or the laundry at Brookstone Manor. She and Ray could just lollygag.

Saturday, after they came home from Penney's, they sat out on their porch to catch the little bit of air that was stirring.

"Name your heaven," Ray said.

It was a game that he liked to play. Ray and Clare Own Paradise, he called it. Together, they came up with as many names for prosperity as they could. Names called outside the bright forever, Clare thought, recalling that old hymn that promised a "summer land of song."

"Easy Street," she said, even though it made her feel guilty to play the game. There was always someone worse off. Across the street, for instance, the curtains were drawn on Lottie and Leo Marks's house. They'd gone off to Indianapolis to be with Lottie's sister when the news came that their nephew had died in Vietnam. Clare saw it every day in the paper or on the news: mothers losing their sons, car bombs going off in Northern Ireland, airplanes being hijacked, that man running for president—that George Wallace— shot and left a cripple. In the light of all the world's misery, who was anyone to wish for an ounce more than what they had? Why tempt fate, Clare thought, by wanting too much? Still, she played along with Ray because she liked the way his voice went all soft and whispery, and it was love, she thought. It was just love. This wanting more.

"Shangri-La," he said.

"Never-Never Land," she told him.

Then, for a long time, they didn't say anything, and that was good, Clare thought. That was just them together, no thought of time moving on, no worry because Ray had lost his job. It was Saturday. It was summer. They had a new porch, a new garage. Why fret? Maybe this was all there was. Maybe this was paradise. All this. Right here, right now.

Now Ray came into the bedroom, his face shining with aftershave. "Old girl." He put his arms around her waist and hugged her. "Things are looking up. This is my day."

He drove her to Brookstone Manor in his pickup and said he'd be back for her come evening when she got off at eight. He was all spiffed up in those twill trousers, a grass-green sport shirt, and the brown pull-on boots he saved for good. He had polished them and buffed them with the horsehair brush he always used. He thought he'd drive down to Brick Chapel to check out that power plant. He gave her a wave when he pulled away from the curb. He slowed down for a moment. His brake lights came on, and she thought he had forgotten to tell her something. She thought he was going to turn around and come back. But then he stuck his arm out the window and waved at her again. She waved back. He tooted his horn, and then he was gone.

HE DIDN'T come back at eight. One of the girlie-girls asked if Clare wanted her to run her home. "No, don't trouble yourself," Clare told her. "Ray said he'd be here. I'll just wait."

The girl's name was Pat. She had a boyfriend fighting in the war. She wore his high school ring on a chain around her neck.

Sometimes she picked up the ring and tapped it against her teeth. She was the sort of girl Clare had never trusted in high school even though she had wanted to. She had harbored more than one secret crush, had spent hours daydreaming about being friends with such girls, those pretty girls with the bright smiles and the merry voices. She knew she would never be one of them. She was too plain, too tall and skinny, her chest caved in, her shoulders slumped. She was too timid, too ordinary. She knew how to crochet and cook, but no one really cared about that, and they didn't care that she had a good heart, not unless they were girls like her, the spooks, the ones the other girls, the popular ones, acted like they never saw.

"I could wait with you," Pat said. "Really, Clare. I don't mind."

"You've got things to do," Clare said. "You don't need to be wasting time with an old dame like me. He'll be here in a jiff."

But he wasn't. She walked uptown and stood on the curb in front of the Coach House, thinking maybe she'd see his truck coming up High Street. It was nearly eight-thirty. She wandered up and down the block a ways, glancing at the new ladies' dresses on the mannequins in the front window of Helene's Dress Shop—goodness, how short the hems were—turning back to the street from time to time. She would see headlights coming and she would think, There, that's his truck, but it never was. She remembered once, when she was a girl—probably no more than six or seven—coming out of a matinee picture show on a winter afternoon and looking for her mother, who had said she would be there waiting for her. But she wasn't. Clare stood in the cold, snow coming down, not knowing what to do. "Just stand still," her mother told her when she finally arrived. "If you think you're lost, don't move. I'll find you."

Clare knew she should have stayed at Brookstone Manor;

maybe Ray was there waiting for her. She almost turned around and went back. She almost started walking the rest of the way home. Finally, she couldn't bring herself to do either. The longer she stood there, the more worried she became. She was afraid to move, afraid that if she walked away from that corner, Ray would pull up in his truck and she wouldn't be there to get into the cab beside him, to hear his familiar voice, "Oh, hon, did you think I'd forgotten my best girl?" To slide over next to him and let him drape his arm over her shoulders and to ride along, the breeze coming in through the open windows, as they went home. He would be jabbering about everything he'd done that day—oh, how she loved to hear him talk—and she would close her eyes and revel in what she had missed those long months after Bill died, the sound of someone talking to her, the sense that she was part of someone's life.

Finally, it was a quarter of nine, and cars of teenagers were cruising up and down High Street. A few men who were staying at the Litz Hotel came out onto the sidewalk and started passing a pint bottle back and forth. Across the square, in front of the J. C. Penney store, a man and a boy loaded a bicycle into the trunk of their car. Clare hated for people to see her there, like she was lost and didn't know where to turn. She gave up on Ray and started walking to Gooseneck.

When she got home, the house was dark, and Ray was nowhere to be found. She heated up a can of vegetable soup and tidied up the kitchen when she was finished eating. She dragged a kitchen chair out onto the new porch and sat there awhile, again imagining that each approaching set of headlights belonged to Ray's truck. She got sleepy in the dark, and the mosquitoes came out, so finally she went back inside, put on her nightgown, and went to bed.

~~~

IT WAS THE smell that woke her, well past midnight—the smell of something burning—and when she opened her eyes, she saw the glow on the bedroom walls. She rolled over toward the window and saw the reflection of the flames, watery on the glass.

Ray was in the backyard at the burn barrel, poking at the fire with a stick. He was in his T-shirt and jockey shorts, and his pull-on boots were still on his feet. Bits of ash fluttered at the tips of the fire's flames.

Clare put on a robe and walked barefoot across the damp grass. She came up behind Ray and touched him on his arm. He didn't look at her. He kept staring into the fire. She could see his new trousers, his green sport shirt, charring and curling in the burn barrel. She wanted to tell him that she had waited and waited for him. She wanted to ask him whether he had found a job. Where had he been all this time? But she didn't say a word. It was such a strange sight—her husband in his underthings, burning his clothes—she had no idea what to say.

"I went fishing," he finally told her. "I went down to Patoka Lake. Me and another fella, we cleaned up a mess of perch, and I got fish guts all over my clothes. Well, hon, I just ruined them, that's what I did. My shirt and my new pants. No good for nothing but to burn."

He stirred the fire, and the flames crackled and sparks flew up into the air.

"I could've washed those clothes," she said.

All the houses up and down the street were dark, and the night was still. The only sound was the crackling of the fire.

"No," said Ray. "Nothing you could've done would've ever got them clean. Now go on back to bed. I'm going to pull my truck into the garage and then I'll be in."

SHE HAD JUST settled back into bed when a knock came on the front door. It was a loud knock, three impatient raps. She thought it must be Ray, but why would he be knocking? She came out into the living room, this time without her robe. Her long cotton gown swept over the floor. She opened the front door, and standing on the porch was a policeman. He was tall, and his shoulders slumped a bit as if he were ducking under a low ceiling. "Ma'am," he said. A soft-spoken young man in a light-blue shirt, a silver badge pinned to the pocket. He had thick sideburns. "Ma'am," he said again. "I'm sorry to bother you, ma'am, but it's your husband." He lifted his right hand and scratched at a sideburn. "You are married to Raymond Wright, aren't you, ma'am?"

"I'm Mrs. Wright." Clare could make out the shapes of men coming up the driveway. Three city police cars were parked along the street, but their lights weren't on. She could hear boots kicking up gravel and leather creaking, and she knew the men were police-men, and that it was their gun holsters she was hearing. "I'm Clare," she said, and then she felt foolish for having said it, as if she were a little girl. But that's how she felt, like a girl bumbling through some-thing she didn't understand. She told herself to listen hard, to do what this nice young man was telling her.

It was her husband, he said again. That's who he was looking for. Had she seen him?

Once when she was just a girl—this was when the Depression

was on—she let a tramp into the house and gave him a plate of food. He ran off with the only thing of value that her family owned, her grandmother's gold earrings, the ones with jade insets. "If Hitler was dying of thirst," her father said when he found out, "she'd carry him to the well." She couldn't help herself. She knew too much about misery. When she saw someone else hurting, she couldn't help but fall in love with that hurt. If she couldn't be pretty or smart, she decided, at least she could be generous and kind. And she could make a nice home. She knew how to cook and sew and how to keep the house spic and span.

"He's out to the garage," she told the policeman. It came to her then what this was all about. Later, she would feel foolish for having such a simple thought, but at the time it made sense to her because she didn't want to think that what was happening might be anything else. "Those cement blocks," she said. "I told Ray not to steal them. I said, 'Ray, what if someone finds out?'"

The policeman bowed his head. When he looked back up at her, there was such a pain on his face, she wanted to touch him and tell him it was all right. Whatever he had to say, it was fine.

"Ma'am, you seem like a nice lady." His voice was so low she had to lean close to hear it. "I don't know how you hooked up with Raymond Wright, but ma'am." He rubbed his hand over his mouth as if he were trying to pull out the words. "Ma'am," he said again, "the truth is, those cement blocks, they're the least of your troubles now."

THE POLICEMEN brought Ray out of the garage. They had handcuffs on his wrists. His head was hanging down, and he wouldn't look at Clare, who stood in the backyard, her hands trying to rub the chill out of her bare arms. The flames from the burn barrel cast an eerie glow over the faces of the policemen and Ray in his jockey shorts and T-shirt.

"What's burning in that barrel?" the policeman with the side-burns asked Clare.

"Ray?" she said to him.

"It's just clothes," he said. "Just dirty clothes. I went fishing."

"Ray, what's this all about?"

"It's a mistake," he told her. "Whatever they say I done, they're wrong, Clare. They're dead wrong."

Soon there would be questions, plenty of questions. But there was a first one, and the soft-spoken policeman put it to Ray now. "Ray? Ray, listen to me. What have you done with the girl?"

MR. DEES saw the police cars go by his house. They didn't have their red lights on or their sirens, but he knew that's what they were, and he knew where they had been and who they had come for. He knew because at eleven o'clock, he finally worked up the courage to call the courthouse and tell the dispatcher who answered that he understood they were looking for a Ford truck, green with black circles painted on the doors. How did he know? It didn't matter. No, it wasn't important who he was. He just had the information they needed. He'd seen that truck uptown around five-thirty—and that girl, the one they were looking for?—he'd seen her up on the running board of that truck, talking to the man who was driving it. "That truck," he said. "You come down to Gooseneck. You'll find it. That odd-looking truck. It belongs to a man named Raymond Wright."

Now he was up, pacing the floors, tired of tossing and turning in his bed, going back over everything that had happened that night.

Earlier, around ten o'clock, when the policeman with the fat fingers had come to his house, he had only told as much of the truth as he could bear to hear coming from his mouth. Yes, he had been with Katie Mackey that afternoon. Three-thirty until five. An hour and a half working on story problems. Then he lied: No, he said, he hadn't seen her since.

The truth of the matter was, that afternoon, when he was with Katie, he found himself, without knowing that he was about to do this, leaning down and kissing her. They were sitting beside each other on the Mackeys' porch swing, swaying back and forth in the shade, a lone bird singing somewhere in one of the oak trees. The scent from Patsy Mackey's petunias was fragrant, and Mr. Dees would never be able to smell petunias from that day on without remembering how Katie had solved a story problem using the Parker 51 he had bought for her—"Fifteen banana Popsicles. Holy moly, Mister Dees"—and when she lifted her face to look at him, the light came into her eyes and she was more beautiful than he could stand, and he did what he had wanted to do all that summer since their lessons began—what he had done only in his dreams: he kissed her. He kissed her on the cheek, and it was only a fleeting moment— that quick kiss. Later, he would be tempted to believe that it hadn't really happened. Only, he knew that it had. He had kissed Katie Mackey on her front porch, in plain view of anyone who might have happened to have been watching.

Katie didn't even seem to notice. She was a girl who was used to being loved. He could tell that she thought there was nothing out of the ordinary about the fact that he had kissed her. But he was horrified over what he had done. He called the lesson to an end.

"Wasn't I right?" Katie said. "Fifteen banana Popsicles? Isn't that the answer?"

Yes, he told her. "Yes. Oh yes, Katie. You're absolutely right."

He heard the front door open, and there was Patsy Mackey stepping out onto the porch. In an instant he stood up from the swing, saying in a rush, good-bye, good-bye, it was time for him to go. What a good girl Katie was. What a smart girl. "She's really coming right along," he said to Patsy.

"Wait. Don't go just yet," Patsy said. "I need to make out your check. Katie, let me borrow your pen. It was so kind of you to give her that pen, Mister Dees. You've done wonders for her, really you have."

Yes, yes, the check, he said, of course. He folded it once and put it in his shirt pocket. Then he was hurrying down the steps, eager to be alone, still stunned by what he had done, and only a few seconds before Patsy had come out on the porch. What if she had been watching from inside the house?

When he left the Mackeys' he didn't go straight home, as he had told the fat-fingered policeman. He made it as far as the downtown square before the heat became too much for him, and he had to sit awhile on the courthouse lawn. He slipped off his poplin suit jacket and thought what a fool he was for wearing it, trying to look like an upright man. He had kissed Katie Mackey. God forgive him. He took the handkerchief from the breast pocket of his jacket, the dark-blue linen handkerchief he had folded carefully so three points made a line of pickets. He shook out the handkerchief and used it to blot the sweat from his forehead. He sat on one of the loafers' benches in the shade and loosened his necktie. It was nearly five-thirty.

He watched the traffic go by, taking note as he always did of the makes and models of cars: Ford Fairlane, Chevy Impala, Buick

Sebring. Later, at home, he would note them in his journal. He would uncap his Parker 51 and jot down the names of the cars and the snatches of song lyrics he heard coming from their radios. He would record the day's high temperature, ninety-three, any fact that would keep him from thinking of Katie Mackey and what he had done. All those people passing by him, and none of them knew what had happened. None of them had any idea. He tipped back his head and closed his eyes. Then he felt a stir of air, and a shadow fell across his face. When he opened his eyes, he saw Raymond R. looking down on him.

"Teach, you look tapped out." Raymond R. leaned over and took Mr. Dees's face between his rough hands. He patted his cheeks. "Jesus in a basket," he said. "You look like you're ready to give up the ghost."

"It's the heat," Mr. Dees said.

"Jesus, yes. I know what you mean. Come on. Let's go home."

Mr. Dees let Raymond R. take his arm and pull him to his feet. He followed him down the slope of the courthouse lawn. Later, he would think how easy it had been to do this, to put one foot in front of the other and follow Raymond R. to his truck. He was going home. He would lock the doors, pull down the window shades so no one could look in. He would sit inside his house and tremble with the thought of what he had done that afternoon.

By the time they got to Raymond R.'s truck, Mr. Dees was weeping. He was making no sound, but the tears were running down his face.

"Here, now." Raymond R. opened the truck door, took Mr. Dees by the shoulders, and eased him in. "You just sit there. We don't have to go nowhere. Not just yet. You tell me when you're ready."

It wasn't bad there in the shade. A breeze moved through the truck. Raymond R. got behind the steering wheel and he didn't say a word. Mr. Dees appreciated that, the way he just waited, and he remembered the night that Raymond R. had repaired the martin house. They were in Mr. Dees's garage, and Raymond R. hammered in the finishing nails with such gentle taps, careful not to split the wood. Finally, he laid down his hammer and he told Mr. Dees that any time he needed him he should just call. If he had something that needed getting done, Raymond R. Wright was his man.

Now, in the truck, he was merely waiting, letting Mr. Dees dry his face with his handkerchief, saying nothing that might embarrass him, respecting whatever it was that had shaken him to the point that he could cry in broad daylight on the courthouse square, where anyone passing by would see him.

It touched Mr. Dees, this courtesy, and before he could help himself he had started to speak. He said it all in a whisper, and what he said was this: there were times, he told Raymond R., when he felt like a little boy, the boy he had been all those years ago when numbers had started to make sense to him. He could add one to another and come up with an answer; he could subtract them, multiply, and divide. He could write out an equation and then see the proper moves that would isolate the unknown and solve it. Numbers he understood; they had a science to them, an integrity—they were what they were. But people—ah, people—they were a different story.

He told Raymond R. about the hours he had spent, even as a child, trying to understand where he went wrong when it came to making friends. It wasn't that his classmates didn't like him. He had opportunities to join their games, though he was never athletic, and their clubs—he tried Cub Scouts, the Methodist Youth Fellowship, the Junior Jaycees. But he was shy. Once in junior high, during an MYF hayride, a girl said to him, "Why don't you ever smile? If you'd just smile, you wouldn't be so weird." He practiced at home, looking at himself in the mirror, but always there was something unnatural about his smile, a forced and hesitant stretching of his lips that made him look like a ventriloquist's dummy. Better to ixnay the smile, he decided, no matter what the girl had said. Her name was Bonnie, and because she had made that suggestion to him about smiling more, he got the idea that she liked him. She sat in front of him in their seventh-grade English class, and when she slouched in her chair, her long blond hair often fell over his desk. One day he started wrapping her hair around his pencil. It fascinated him, that hair. It was the color of wheat, and it gleamed in the sunlight slanting through the tall windows. He loved the feel of it on his hands and the way he could wind it around that pencil. Then the teacher noticed what he was doing and she said, "Pity sake, Henry. Leave her hair alone." Bonnie tried to turn around, but his hands, that pencil, they were in her hair, and when she moved her head, he got all tangled up, and the teacher had to come and patiently work him free, and all the while Bonnie was saying, "Ew, ew. Henry Dees, you're a creep."

That was it, he told Raymond R. That's how it was done. From that day on, to his classmates, he was that kind of boy. "I thought she liked me," he said. "I guess I figured she'd understand that I liked her, too."

"You don't have to say anything else," Raymond R. said, and then he told Mr. Dees the story of having to eat his lunch each day in the dimly lit hallway outside the school cafeteria. He told him about the steam pipe and how it leaked water on his head and how the kids, the ones who ate the hot lunches in the cafeteria, pointed their fingers at him when they came out into the hallway.

"People," Mr. Dees said. It shook him to think of all the misery wrought in the world. He found himself telling Raymond R. that he had kissed Katie Mackey. "I shouldn't have done that. It's not right. A man like me."

"Maybe you're a different kind of man than you figure." Raymond R.'s voice was soft, kind. It held no note of judgment. "Maybe it's like that."

Mr. Dees knew, as much as he hated to admit it, that Raymond R. was right. He'd been going through his life thinking he knew who he was, when all along he was dumb to his own mysterious heart. It was a frightening truth to run up against. Here he was, a man in the middle of his life, lost, desperate now for the chance to atone for kissing Katie and to move on to a better way of seeing himself. He wanted to erase that afternoon from his mind, from his heart. He wanted to go to sleep and not have Katie come into his dreams. He wanted to sleep a dead sleep and not wake, tormented with shame and guilt. He wanted to sleep through the night and let the martins wake him, their dawnsong a joy bubbling up inside him.

"Sometimes." He couldn't stop himself. He'd had no idea that he felt this until he heard himself giving it words. "Sometimes," he said again, "I think if she weren't here. Katie. If she didn't exist, I'd be all right."

He sat there, stunned. What a thing for him to say. He wished he could snatch the words from the air and stuff them back into his mouth.

"How much would that be worth to you?" Raymond R. asked. Mr. Dees was about to tell him that no, it wasn't like that at all, but before he could speak, Raymond R. said, "Jesus in a basket." He pointed toward Fourteenth Street, where Katie was coming down the sidewalk on her new bicycle. Mr. Dees recognized the black T-shirt and the orange shorts that she had worn that afternoon. She was barefoot. She stood up on her pedals, and he could feel the hard rubber digging into his own arches. Then her foot slipped, and she almost took a tumble. She got off her bicycle in front of the J. C. Penney store. She leaned the bike on its kickstand and squatted down beside it. The chain had come off its sprocket. "Lordy, Lordy," Raymond R. said. "Speak of the devil. Yonder's your little girl."

July 6

Just after dawn, the skies opened up, and rain fell. It came in silver sheets, falling straight down. It fell over the cornfields and the wheat fields and the soybean plants in their straight green rows. It fell over the woodlands, soaking down through the canopies of the hickories and the oaks and the sweet gums. It drummed the tin roofs of barns and grain bins. It flattened pastures of timothy and the turkey foot grass on the prairies. It pocked the White River and the lake at Shakamak. It muddied the shale roads and left them slick and black.

The searchers moved through the rain—slowly, deliberately—the way the police had told them. They were just ordinary folks, people who the day before had been wishing for this rain, who had planned, when it finally came, to be enjoying it from inside their homes, their businesses, or else cozied up in their cars, glad for the shelter, thankful that all they had to do was sit there. Nothing required of them but their slow, easy breathing as they imagined going out to their gardens later to check their rain gauges. They'd gab about the rain with their neighbors. "It was a toad strangler," they'd say, and they'd linger in the cool air and hope that it might be the start of blackberry winter, that cold snap that always seemed to come when the blackberries were in bloom.

But now they were out in the storm, sweeping in lines across fields and meadows, disappearing into woods, down quarry roads. They were looking in ditches, barns, abandoned cars, anything that was in their path, eyes open for any clue that might lead them to Katie Mackey.

In Gooseneck, Mr. Dees watched the rain streak his windows. Down the street, Clare was watching it, too. She was standing at the back door, keeping her eyes on the policemen who were going in and out of the garage. Earlier, they had moved the burn barrel in there to get it out of the rain. They had been there all night. This was after they had taken Ray away in a police car. They didn't even let him put on clothes. Now the police officers went in and out of the garage, and some of them left in cars and then came back. Sheriff's officers and state patrolmen arrived, and men in suits with gleaming white shirts. Clare stayed in the house, letting the feeling sink in that nothing was hers any longer—not the house or the garage or the person she was to herself. Nothing in her life. It was all slipping free from her, attaching itself to whatever had happened that night of July 5 while she waited for Ray to pick her up. Whatever had happened then was larger, more potent than she could ever be. She knew that. She knew how Ray must have felt every time the sun overwhelmed him, everything going dark, shrinking in the glare of that bright light.

The soft-spoken policeman, who identified himself as Chief Evers, showed her a search warrant. She listened very carefully to what he was telling her: a little girl, eyewitnesses, a green Ford truck with black circles on the doors.

She kept quiet. She couldn't think of a thing to say that would make any difference. What could she tell Chief Evers? That Ray had always been good to her? He'd built that porch, that garage. He'd kissed her hand at the Top Hat Inn one night. They'd driven down to Louisville and gotten married, and she'd never regretted it. He called her *darlin'*. He kept her company through the winter, and then spring came, and he lay beside her in the mornings while they listened to the martins singing. What would any of that matter to Chief Evers, who was convinced, he told her, that he had the right man?

Just after dawn, he came into the house and said he needed to ask her some questions. Where had Ray been that night, he wanted to know. What time did he get home? What had he been up to?

She told him that he had gone to look for work. "He dropped me off at Brookstone Manor," she said, "and I didn't see him until he came home. It was late. After midnight. I was asleep."

They were in the kitchen. She was sitting at the dinette. Chief Evers was standing beside her, jotting things down in a notebook. "Clare," he said. For the first time, he called her by name, and it startled her. "Clare," he said again, "I want you to help me. You'll do that, won't you? I want you to tell me the truth. Do you know a girl named Katie Mackey?"

"I've heard tell of the name." She was worrying a thread coming unraveled from the hem of her housecoat. "Katie Mackey. Yes."

"From Ray? Have you heard him talk about her? Did he have his eyes on her?"

It was that one word, *eyes*. That was what did it. She was speaking before she even knew what she meant to say. "It's Henry Dees," she said. "He's got short eyes."

"Short eyes?"

"He's an uncle." She was talking fast now. "A puppy lover, a chicken hawk, short eyes. Henry Dees. He likes little girls. He had his eyes on Katie Mackey. You go talk to him."

MR. DEES was ready when the police came. In the night, he had found the petal that he had torn from one of Patsy Mackey's roses on the evening when she and Junior took the kids to the Dairy Queen. What a small thing. A petal from a pink rose faded now to white. Who would think a thing about it if they found that petal, pressed and dried between the pages of Mr. Dees's Bible? But now everything was suspect. Carefully, he slid the petal onto his palm and carried it out the back door. He crushed it to powder with his thumb and forefinger and then dusted it from his hands, letting the wind, which had come up in the early morning hours, carry it away from him.

The hair—that fluff of brown hair taken from Katie's brush—it was dawn before Mr. Dees could bring himself to let it go. He took it from its envelope and once more, for the last time, he rubbed it on his cheek, knowing it was a pitiful thing to do. His life had come to that. He let the hair tickle his face, thinking, Katie, my Katie. He started to slip the fluff of hair back into the envelope, but it fell from his fingers, and then a gust of wind caught it and sent it skittering through the air.

A purple martin swooped down from above and snatched the hair up in its beak. The martin curved up and disappeared into one of the houses atop the tall poles. What a thing to have happen. Mr. Dees told himself he would have to get a ladder. He'd have to climb up to that martin house and try to get that fluff of hair. He took a step toward the garage, but then he heard a man's voice calling for him.

"Mister Dees," the man was saying from the front of the house. "Henry Dees."

It was the police chief—Evers, Tom Evers. Once upon a time, he had been a student in Mr. Dees's calculus class. A soft-spoken boy with a sharp mind. The center on the basketball team. Mr. Dees remembered his square jaw and thick neck, the sad look in his eyes that told Mr. Dees he had accepted the fact that he was sturdy and dependable. He had resigned himself to always being someone people could count on. When Mr. Dees looked at him in class all those years ago, he saw the boy he wished he had been.

"Hello, Tom," he said.

"You're up early, Mister Dees."

"I couldn't sleep."

"Yes, sir," Tom Evers said. Thunder was rumbling in the west and the first drops of rain were hitting the windows. "Mister Dees, I suppose you've heard about Katie Mackey."

By this time, few people in town didn't know that Katie had disappeared. They'd either heard it the night before or as they rose and turned on their radios. Katie Mackey, nine years old, four feet three inches tall. Seventy-two pounds. Green eyes. Brown hair. Last seen wearing orange shorts and a black T-shirt. The police claimed they had the man who had kidnapped her—Raymond R. Wright, a construction worker from Gooseneck—but he wasn't saying anything that would help them find her.

Only a few months before, in March, the biggest news in town had been the high school basketball team winning the state championship. There was a parade down High Street. It was Sunday, and the team and cheerleaders rode on fire trucks. Sirens blew. The cheerleaders waved green-and-white pom-poms. The players, many of them in their green letterman's jackets, held the championship trophy aloft. Fans lined the parade route and later crowded into the high school gymnasium, where the coach and several of the players spoke to their adoring fans.

The next day, Monday, the *Evening Register* reported that Mrs. Madeline Brokaw had picked the year's first ripe tomato. She found a volunteer plant in her backyard in early December, dug it up, put it in a flowerpot, carried it into her house, and set it near a south window, where it would get sun. It grew to be five feet tall, and on March 10, she picked the first tomato. It was a Golden Boy, she reported. A yellow tomato, sleek and bright, large enough to cover her palm.

That was the news folks talked about: the basketball team, the first ripe tomato, hamburgers five for a dollar at the Dog 'n' Suds, the grand opening of the Super Foodliner, the Carnival of Spring Fashion show at the high school.

But now, on this Thursday morning in July, all anyone could think about was Katie Mackey. Downtown, all the stores were closed. Everyone who was able was out in the rain with the search parties, sweeping through the fields and the woods. They could tell, though no one had the heart to say it, that the storm was one of those cloudbursts that came after a string of humid days, came as a torment really. Soon the clouds would break, and the sun would come out and heat up all that rain. The ground would steam, and the temperature would inch back up into the nineties. The gnats would come out, and the horseflies. The searchers would slog through the mud, hold the sting of sweat in their eyes. Soon there would be search dogs, and airplanes with infrared sensors, and Margot Cherry, who claimed she could see in her head what everyone had missed with their eyes.

But first there were these people out in the downpour, these gray figures, shoulders hunched against the rain, and what no one spoke was the secrets they carried in their hearts, the weight of all their sins. That day and all the days after, every bit of wrong they'd ever done was knotted in their chests. What they thought, but never said, was this: It should have been any of us but her. If God had any interest in punishing the wicked, it should have been us. They had gone about their business the evening before, not taking note of that girl, that man, that bicycle, that truck. Only now were they starting to come forward, to say what they remembered, hoping that they weren't speaking too late.

AT THE Mackey house, the grandfather clock in the foyer was ticking, its pendulum swinging back and forth. Patsy, who had been awake all night, opened the cabinet and threw the lever that stopped the works. It was two minutes after seven.

"I couldn't stand it," she said in a quiet voice, hoarse and weary. "That noise."

All night, Gilley had listened to her crying, praying, bargaining with God. If only he would bring Katie home to them, she would never again let her out of her sight. And she would tell Junior exactly how she felt about that night in Indianapolis, and she would admit her sin—right now she'd confess it, and please, dear God, wouldn't he forgive her and see to it that Katie was safe? At one point, she got down on her knees at the back door where Katie's sandals were still on the mat, and she pressed her hands together and held them at her chest, and her lips moved so quickly with her prayer that Gilley couldn't tell what she was saying in her fast, desperate mumble of words. He didn't know what she was saying, and he didn't know what she meant about that night in Indianapolis or what she had to confess. He had his own guilt. At the supper table, he had told his father that Katie hadn't taken back her library books that day, and that had started the chain of events that had brought them, finally, to this moment, two minutes after seven on a Thursday morning in July, when the rain was falling and they had no idea where Katie was.

He tried to comfort his mother. He rubbed his hand in slow circles over her back, telling himself to remember this, to memorize the way it felt to touch her with tenderness, to store it away so he would know it all through the years, no matter what happened from this point on. This touching, this love: he wanted it to be theirs forever.

"They'll find her," he said. "They have to find her."

At first, after they had discovered Katie's bicycle in front of the J. C. Penney, Gilley had told his father that maybe she had left it there and walked home. "The chain's off," he said. "She couldn't get it back on."

"She would have pushed it," Junior Mackey said. "Don't be stupid."

By this time, the library was closed. As they walked around the courthouse square, Gilley imagined that at any moment they would see Katie gazing in a store window, enchanted with something that had caught her eye, or at the Rexall Drug on the penny scale that would tell her weight and fortune. "Gilley, Gilley, Gilley," she would say the way she always did whenever she wanted to show him something. "Look."

At the Rexall, there was no one but the pharmacist and the high school girl who worked the cosmetics counter. Neither of them had seen Katie.

"Well, she's somewhere," Junior said, and the pharmacist, a round-faced man who wore a red bow tie, said he was sure she'd turn up soon. "Kids," he said, and then he shook his head.

But she didn't turn up. She wasn't at Renée Cherry's house or the city park or the Dairy Queen. Later, after they had given up and called the police, Gilley stayed with his mother, as his father ordered, while Junior rode through the Heights in a police car, revisiting with Chief Evers all the places where Katie might have gone.

All night, police cars cruised up and down the streets in the Heights and downtown around the square and out Tenth Street past the glassworks. They knocked on people's doors. Have you seen this little girl? they asked, showing them Katie's school picture, the one Patsy had given them from her photo album. In the picture, the ends of Katie's hair curled over her shoulders and onto the front of her jumper. Her blouse was covered with a pattern of roses and daisies. Her hair was pinned back at the temples with two gold barrettes, as it had been that evening when she had ridden away to the library. The next afternoon, the picture would be on the *Evening Register*'s front page. Her round face and big eyes. A pretty nine-year-old girl, grinning to beat the band.

It was 7:05—Gilley checked his watch—when the front door opened, and his father, water dripping from him, stepped inside. He didn't bother to wipe his feet. He walked straight to Patsy and took her in his arms. He had his eyes closed, and Gilley could tell he was squeezing his mother so tightly that it was uncomfortable for her. She put her hands against his chest and tried to push herself free.

"Is it Katie?" she said. "Gil, is it some news about Katie?"

Gilley felt as if the house were shrinking, the walls closing in on them. He waited for his father to answer, and when he did, what he said was this: "Patsy, they've got a man. The police. They picked him up in Gooseneck." Junior was speaking calmly, as if he were explaining how glass was made, or the way to read a green before making a putt. He had spoken to Gilley in those same hushed tones more than once on a golf course, encouraging him to keep his cool, and now he was doing the same with Patsy. "They think he knows something. This man. They're talking to him now."

Patsy broke away from Junior. "Did he take her? For God's sake, Gil, is that it?"

"They're trying to find out."

"I want to go there. To the courthouse." She was already striding toward the door, which Junior had left open. Gilley watched the rain blowing up onto the porch, where one of Katie's pencils, all silver-and-gold glitter with a troll doll on the eraser end, was getting wet. He wanted to go out and bring it in and comb out the troll's hair and put it somewhere to dry, but his mother was already in the doorway. "I'm going to talk to that man. I'm going to ask him what he's done with my little girl."

"Patsy," Junior said. "I'll take care of things. You stay here and leave this to me."

"No." She turned on her heel and pointed her finger at him. The word came out with a force that had been gathering through the long night. "You won't tell me what to do. Not this time. Not like in Indianapolis."

Gilley saw his father's shoulders stiffen. "For God's sake, Patsy," he said.

"I mean it," she told him. "I'm going to talk to that man."

Junior followed her out into the rain. Gilley stepped out on the porch and watched them get in the truck and then drive away. He bent down and picked up the pencil. Then, out of the corner of his eye, he saw something on the porch swing. It was a snapshot of Katie, the one that he had taken earlier that summer with his Polaroid camera. She had been sitting on the stone bench between the two Japanese maple trees in their backyard, and the sun had been slanting just so through the low branches so that the light fell over her, and her hair shimmered. She was sitting on the bench with her back against one of the trees. Her bare feet were on the bench and her knees were drawn up to her chest. She had on a pair of pink-framed sunglasses, and later when she saw the snapshot, she said she looked just like a movie star. She loved that picture, she said. Loved it, loved it, loved it, darling Gilley, because it made her look a little bit like Marcia Brady—well, almost—and everyone knew how pretty and popular she was.

All summer, the picture had been tucked into the corner of Katie's dresser mirror, but now here it was on the porch swing. Gilley picked it up, and when he did, he noticed that on the back, in a handwriting he didn't recognize, someone had written with what he could tell was the rich indigo ink of a fountain pen: *Katie, Age 9.*

BY THE TIME Junior and Patsy got to the courthouse, the rain had stopped. The sun broke through the clouds. When Junior got out of the truck to follow Patsy up the courthouse steps, he had to shade his eyes with his hand.

"Patsy," he said. "Patsy, wait."

She marched ahead of him, her arms swinging. In the truck, she had said, "I won't have another child taken from me. I won't."

Finally, he caught up with her on the steps. He grabbed her arm and swung her around, more roughly than he had intended, and that force broke her. She leaned into him as if her spine had turned to dust. He took the dead weight of her in his arms and he held her while she wept. He held her, and he said very quietly, "We'll do whatever we have to, Patsy. I swear that to you, whatever it takes to bring Katie home. Believe me, whatever it takes, I'll do it."

She clutched the front of his shirt. She balled the material up into her hands. "That man," she said. "I want to look that man in the eyes. I want to ask him what he knows."

Raymond R.

*P*ROVE IT.

Mr. Dees

I STOOD IN my kitchen with Tom Evers, and I told him as much as I could stand to say. Yes, it was true that I'd told Raymond R. about the way Katie had struck my fancy. Such a darling little girl. Who couldn't help but love her?

"But Tom," I said, "you know me. Do you really think I'm the sort of man Clare Wright claims I am?"

"Right now I'm just asking questions," Tom said. "I'm just trying to find out what's gone on." He was facing me, but I could tell his eyes were glancing around my kitchen, taking everything in, and for an instant, I wondered if I'd forgotten anything. That rose petal, that fluff of hair. Then I remembered the snapshot, the one of Katie sitting on that stone bench. I'd looked for it earlier and hadn't been able to find it. I had no idea where it had gone. "Mister Dees," he said, "I need to know where you were last night."

"I told the officer who came here. Tom, I was home last night. I was right here preparing lessons."

"Is there anyone who can vouch for that? Anyone see you out in the yard maybe? Anyone call you on the telephone or see you in the house?"

It pained me to have to answer that question. "Tom," I said, "I don't have many friends. I pretty much keep to myself." He studied me for a good while. "Is there call for me to prove something?" I finally asked him.

"I can't say that there is. No, I can't say that. I'm just trying to eliminate whatever I can. You understand? Some people say you were a friend to this Raymond Wright."

"He's done some repair work at my house. Not long ago, he gave me a ride home from the Moonlight Madness Carnival. Neighborly things like that. I wouldn't say exactly that we're friends."

"I'm just trying to whittle things down, trying to learn what happened to Katie Mackey."

"I understand that, Tom. Like I said, Katie is a splendid little girl."

"If you know of anything that might help me, I trust you'll let me know."

"Believe me, Tom. If I had something to tell you, I would."

I didn't tell him about the nights I hid myself away and watched the Mackeys in their backyard. I didn't tell him about taking the petal from Patsy's rose or the fluff of hair from Katie's brush—thank goodness Clare hadn't said anything to Tom about that—and I didn't tell him about the time that summer when I went into Katie's room.

It was only that one time. Trust me; this is true. It was a Sunday morning, and I knew the Mackeys would be at church. It was easy to get into the house. Most folks in our small town only used their locks when they went away on vacation. I opened the back door and stepped inside.

It was quiet there: the refrigerator humming, the grandfather clock in the foyer ticking—so quiet that I could hear the chains and gears in the clock as the weights rose and fell.

I stood at the foot of the stairs. I had waited in this foyer more than once that summer, eager for Katie to come down for her lesson, but this morning I was free to go wherever I chose. I could imagine that this was my home and soon it would be filled with the sounds of my family: Patsy's sharp, bright laugh; Gilley's rock-and-roll music playing on his stereo; and Katie—oh, my dear, dear Katie—she would come hopping down the stairs, singing some silly rhyme:

Eenie, Meenie, Disaleenie
Ooh, aah, Gotchaleenie
Hotchy Totchy
Liberace
I love you!

I laid my hand on the stairway railing, put one foot on the carpeted runner, and then it was easy—one foot after the other, climbing the stairs to Katie's bedroom.

The house smelled of roses—vases and vases of roses—but in Katie's room the scents were more varied, and to me, who had never lived with a child, more exotic. There was a necklace of candy beads and a chain woven from Fruit Stripe gum wrappers, bottles of Avon Sweet Honesty cologne and Maybelline Rose Lustre nail polish, modeling clay and rub-on tattoos, crayons and Magic Markers, construction paper and paste, stuffed bears and snakes and dogs.

I memorized each scent. I took my time. I told myself I would never do this again, never be in this room. That certainty made me bold, and I opened her dresser drawers. One held neat stacks of shorts and tank tops and T-shirts; in another were balls of socks and tights. A third drawer was for her camisoles and underpants, and I know you expect that I lingered there—pervert that you've surely decided I am—that I pressed my face into cotton and rayon, perhaps even wadded up a pair of panties and stuffed them into my pocket. I know you expect the worst of me. I'd be ashamed to have the thoughts that you do now.

The truth is this: I was a man who didn't know what to do with his passion. I was a teacher of mathematics, and numbers taught me that there was always an answer. Noodle around long enough, and I could solve any problem. But this love I felt for Katie, this child I wished were my own—that was a knot I couldn't untangle. I was trapped in it, helpless. I trembled with the thought of how far I had gone. There I was in her room, overwhelmed. Me, a decent man. You have to believe me. I have nothing to offer as proof except the rest of my story.

I closed her dresser drawer, the wooden runners squealing just a bit, and that's when I saw the picture wedged into the corner of the mirror: Katie sitting on a stone bench in her backyard, smiling at the camera, her eyes hidden behind dark glasses. It seemed that she was smiling at me, and I couldn't help myself. I plucked the picture from the mirror and slipped it into my pocket before stepping out into the hall.

A door opened before I could make it to the stairs, and Gilley came out of his room. He was in his boxer shorts and bare-chested, his hair tousled from sleep. I remembered how kind he had been to me when I had asked him whether I could take home the jackets from Penney's and then return the ones I didn't want. How he had trusted me.

"Mister Dees?" he said, his voice full of surprise and wonder, and I knew immediately that I could tell him any lie, and he would believe me.

But you, I won't lie to. Don't worry. You, I'll tell the truth. Every bit of it. No matter if you want it or not.

Gilley

It was the Sunday before Katie disappeared. I woke and heard a drawer open and close and then footsteps in the hall. I thought I'd slept so long that everyone was back from church. Normally, I would have been with them, but instead I'd slept in and finally my parents had given up on rousing me.

When I got out of bed and went out into the hall, I was surprised to see Mr. Dees about to go down the stairs.

"Mister Dees," I said, and he turned to me, a sheepish grin on his face.

He said, "I was just using the bathroom while I waited for Katie. I let myself in. I'm here for her lesson."

"It's Sunday," I told him. "Katie's at church."

"Sunday," he said after a pause. "I thought it was Monday. In the summer, you know, one day's just like the rest. I feel like a ninny. Such a mistake."

At the time I thought it was strange, but not so odd as to be unbelievable. Mr. Dees always acted a little different from most folks, like he was in his own world. A confusion. Nothing more.

"I didn't hear you knock," I said. "I didn't hear the doorbell."

"Oh, sometimes people forget I'm coming. Sometimes they go somewhere and they're late getting back. I usually let myself in and wait."

So there I was, face-to-face with Mr. Dees, and I didn't know what else to say. Later, I would wonder why, if what he told me was true, he hadn't used the guest bathroom downstairs. It would come to me that the sound of the drawer opening and closing had come from Katie's room.

"I'll be going then," he told me. Then he shook his head. "Such a dolt I am. Sunday. Don't tell your parents. Please. They'll think I'm an idiot. They'll think, What can he possibly teach Katie? He doesn't even know what day it is."

He walked down the stairs. He didn't hurry. He even stopped at the mirror by the front door and straightened the knot in his necktie. Then he let himself out, and our house was quiet, that lazy, Sunday quiet I'd always loved.

Clare

THERE CAME a time that day—yes, I'm talking about that Thursday, the sixth—when the police finally stopped asking me questions (mercy, so many questions my head was spinning) and it was just me, alone in the house, the way it was after Bill died, when I didn't rightly know how my life, without him, would pick up and go on.

Keep looking up, Mama used to tell me. There's nothing on the ground but your feet.

The police took away a pair of Ray's overshoes. They took a pair of knives he used to cut bait. I told them that's what they were, but they took them anyway. They took the burn barrel. A tow truck came and hauled away the pickup.

Could I see him? I wanted to know.

"No, ma'am," Chief Evers said. "Not just now."

It was so quiet in the house after everyone had gone—only the Regulator clock ticking and the refrigerator humming when it came on. The policemen and the detectives had left their smells: the leather of their gun holsters, their aftershave lotions, their hair tonics, the cigarettes they smoked. Everything seemed strange to me.

I moved through the house the way I did after Bill died, afraid to sit down, unable to sleep, staring at the furniture, the rugs, the pictures and doodads hanging on the walls—things I'd seen every day of my life for years, only now it seemed that they belonged to someone else. That was how I felt the day they took Ray away in handcuffs— like I was in someone else's house, like I was living some other woman's life.

I kept imagining that soon I would hear the back door open and then Ray calling to me like this was just any night, "Darlin', name your paradise."

Did I think he'd kidnapped Katie Mackey like they said— snatched her off a street corner uptown when it was still light?

Don't ask me such a thing. Do you really think I could lay down every night with a man I thought might do like that?

If that's what you think, then you won't want to hear the rest. You won't have room in your heart for the story of how that evening, after the police left me alone, I opened the bedroom closet, stepped inside, and closed the door. There in the dark, I breathed in air that was still familiar to me, still a comfort, not dirtied up with the smells the policemen left. I picked out what I knew: the powdery smell of my Secret deodorant cream on my uniform dresses, Ray's Hai Karate cologne on his good shirts, the smells of sweat and mortar and clay bricks on his twill work suits. I ran my hands over that twill, petting the shirts and pants, and at one point I put my arms around a shirt and I hugged it to me, just like I was a young girl mooning over a boy, only inside I knew I was old and at the end of something. The shirt was all air. It caved in when I tried to hold it, and I cried because I missed Ray so much, and maybe, just maybe, I sensed somewhere deep inside me that he wasn't ever coming home.

That's the part you won't abide if you've already made up your mind—if you've decided that there are people in the world whose lives don't matter because they're ragtag, full of wrong turns and dead ends and stupid choices, if you've decided I'm one of those.

You'll want to hear instead about later that night when I was sitting in the dark house—just sitting, not knowing what to do with the strange turn my life had taken—and suddenly there was a knock on the front door. I hoped in my heart of hearts that it was Ray, that the police had finally seen that they had made a mistake and now he had come home to me, but deep down I knew it wasn't true. That knock was a mousy tapping, not the sort of knock he would have made, and anyway, why would he knock on his own door? Then I heard a voice—"Clare? Clare, are you awake?"—and I knew it was Henry Dees.

I went to the door and laid my hand on the knob. It was cool in my palm, even though the night was sultry and still.

"Clare," he said, and it gave me a spooky feeling, like he could tell I was standing there on the other side. "It's about Ray," he said. "Clare, let me in."

I didn't want to open the door. If I opened it and saw Henry Dees, I'd know the police had questioned him and then let him go. I'd know what that meant about Ray.

"I know all about you and that little girl," I said. "That girl they're looking for."

"You don't know everything. Clare, it's not your fault."

Yes, you'll want to know about how I opened the door and let Henry Dees come into my house. You'll want me to tell you that we sat in the front room—me in the rocking chair by the window, him across from me on the couch—and I never turned on a light.

I listened to his voice—calm and gentle—and I never said a word until he was done.

He said he knew I'd turned the police onto him. He said he didn't blame me for that. He knew what it seemed like, especially if Ray had told me the stories he suspected that he did. Did he spy on Katie Mackey? Yes. It was a fact he couldn't deny. Did it mean that he was guilty of something? Just loving her, he said. Like she was his own.

We sat there in the dark a good while, and I could hear him swallow from time to time, as if he was trying to choke something down. When he finally spoke again, it was like there were twigs stuck in his throat, bits of dried leaves, dead grass, straw, a bird's nest made from misery.

"Clare," he said, and it was like everything had gone away—all the noise—and it was just us, me and Henry Dees, saying things no one else could hear. "Clare, after Bill died, I used to think about you down here in this house. I used to walk by after dark and see a light on back in the bedroom—oh, it was so faint, just a little speck of light—and I'd know you were getting ready to go to sleep because it was better to do that than to face all those minutes alone. You and I know that, don't we, Clare? That loneliness. I've known it all my life."

"Bill had a mermaid tattooed on his arm," I said, because I didn't know how to tell Henry Dees what I really wanted to, that yes, he was right. When someone you love disappears, it's like the light goes dim, and you're in the shadows. You try to do what people tell you: put one foot in front of the other; keep looking up; give yourself over to the seconds and minutes and hours. But always there's that glimmer of light—that way of living you once knew—sort of faded and smoky like the crescent moon on a winter's night when the air is full of ice and clouds, but still there, hanging just over your head. You think it's not far. You think at any moment you can reach out and grab it. Bill used to sing "Fly Me to the Moon," and he'd really jazz up that part about playing among the stars. "Do you remember that mermaid?" I asked Henry Dees. "Bill could make it dance the hootchy-kootchy." Then, although I hadn't planned to say anything like it at all, I said, "I'm sorry Bill and me never had kids. A boy. That's what I wish. A son so I could see Bill in his face. So I could have that much the rest of my life."

Henry Dees let that be. Lord love him. He didn't say a word. He didn't tell me I was silly to be as old as I was and to wish such a thing, didn't throw a pity party and say, "Oh, I know what you mean." He didn't have to. I knew that already, and what's more, I knew that I had told him, without saying as much, that I understood how lonely all these years had been for him. That I knew how a girl like Katie Mackey could carry a light to him, that I believed him when he said he never would have hurt her.

That's when I felt the truth rise up in my throat, a knot of grief so hard and tangled I swore it would choke me. This is the part you've been waiting for, the ones of you who think I only got what I deserved. This moment when it all hit me. I tried to take a breath, felt the ache in my throat and chest, thick and rough like the cement blocks Ray had stacked and mortared to make that garage, the place where he hid his truck that night I found him setting fire to his clothes in the burn barrel. The sob that tore loose from me was a miserable sound I've never been able to forget, like everything inside me was scraped away and I was nothing more than a white uniform dress or a cook's apron hanging from the clothesline, flapping in the wind.

Henry Dees got up from the couch. I felt him move toward me in the dark. I heard the soles of his shoes scuffing over the floorboards. He laid his hand on my head. He stroked my hair. "Clare," he said in a voice, patient and kind, the way I imagine people talk all the time in Heaven.

Raymond R.

AND I HAD nothing to hide then, and I don't have anything to hide now.

July 7

It was raining again on Friday. Gilley woke to the pop and crack of thunder, the rattle of the rain beating against his bedroom window. It was barely daylight, but he could hear his parents moving about downstairs. He suspected that they had been awake for hours, had perhaps never gone to bed. He heard the tap-tap of cupboard doors closing, the rattle of teacups. Coffee was brewing. The radio was playing the State Farm Insurance jingle about being a good neighbor. It might have been any summer morning: the fresh coffee, the radio, the rain. Only Gilley knew it could never be that kind of morning—ordinary and carefree—never again. Katie was gone, and no one could find her. What was worse, though he could barely allow himself to think it as the days went on, he feared that no one ever would.

He sat up in bed, and through the rain-streaked window he watched the tree branches jerk and thrash in the wind.

Junior and Patsy were sitting at the breakfast table, talking about Henry Dees.

"I remember something that happened awhile back," Patsy said.

"He told me Katie was a pretty girl. It gave me an odd feeling. The way he said it. That was the day you brought Katie the new bike."

It was all too much for Patsy, remembering the way Katie had ridden the bike in lazy circles on the drive and how her squealing laugh had sounded. How many times since Wednesday evening, when they first knew that she was gone, had Patsy imagined that she heard that laugh, that this had all been a terrible dream and now Katie was home?

She took her hands away from her eyes and reached them out to Junior. "That night in Indianapolis," she said. "We were so young. Both of us. We were just kids."

"Patsy." He held her hands and felt the strength of her fingers curling over his. He knew that she was trying to say that no matter how much she regretted that night and what she believed he had forced her to do, she had finally spoken her piece about it, and now the important thing was that the two of them were together, bracing themselves for whatever lay ahead. "Patsy," he said again, "I can't pretend to know what makes some folks do what they do, but I'll tell you this about Henry Dees: I trust him. Besides, Tom Evers told me someone called that night and said he'd seen Katie talking to that man, that Wright, downtown where we found her bicycle. I think Tom's got the right man."

Gilley came down the stairs and moved into the dining room. There, through the archway that led to the kitchen, he saw his parents at the breakfast table. They were holding hands, and they had tipped their heads forward until they were touching. In that way, they sat quietly, and Gilley imagined that they were gathering strength from each other, trying to shut out the noise of the rain and the storm raging outside.

Just for this little while, they were alone together—no police officers milling through the house, no news reporters knocking on the
front door, no neighbors breezing in with casseroles and good
wishes. Gilley took it all in, the stillness of this scene: his parents
holding hands, their heads tipped forward, nuzzling. They might
have been young and just then falling in love. He felt he had no
right to disturb them with what he was about to say.

Junior heard footsteps. He pulled his head up and saw Gilley
coming into the kitchen, a look of misery on his face.

Patsy recognized it as her own. She could feel it in the slackness
of her jaw, the tightness around her eyes, the knitting of her brow.

"Gilley," she said. She got up from the table and went to him
and hugged him, knowing that she was greedy for his substance, for
the feel of his solid body in her arms. "Dear Gilley. You're shivering." She held him more tightly. "I can feel the goose bumps on
your arms."

Junior looked out through the window and saw that the rain
was still coming down hard. He thought of all the searchers gathering now for another day of combing fields and woods. Some of the
people were strangers to him. Some had come from other towns.
There were Boy Scout troops and church fellowships, farmers and
store owners, horseback riding clubs and lodge groups. Civil Air Patrol planes, Army helicopters, a team of search dogs flown in all the
way from Portland, Oregon. Everyone looking for Katie. Soon he
and Gilley would join them. He would tell the boy to get dressed, to
grab rain gear, to shake a leg.

Then Gilley showed them the snapshot of Katie, the one he had
found on the porch swing. He told them that on Sunday, when
everyone but him had been at church, he had found Mr. Dees in
the upstairs hallway. "He was just there," he said. "He claimed he'd

gotten the days confused, and he'd come to give Katie a lesson. He let himself in. He came upstairs."

Patsy put her hand to her throat. "Gil, I told you. There's something odd about that man. How can you trust him?"

Gilley held out his hand. In it was the snapshot of Katie, the one he had found on the porch swing. "Look on the back," he told his father.

Junior turned the snapshot over and saw the handwriting, neatly spelling out Katie's name, her age. He showed it to Patsy. She looked at the handwriting, the letters made of crisp lines and curls and tails. She'd seen that handwriting on Katie's story problem sheets. She knew that Henry Dees had taken that snapshot from the corner of Katie's dresser mirror, where it had been all summer, and, with his fountain pen, he had written her name and age on the back as if she were his child. She turned the snapshot over and saw Katie posed on the stone bench, the sunlight falling across her face.

"Gil," Patsy said, "I know that handwriting. It belongs to Henry Dees."

JUNIOR DROVE THROUGH the rain, thinking about the way Henry Dees had come into their home, had climbed the stairs to Katie's room. At the time, what did it mean? An absentminded man. Odd duck. But now, of course, it was everything. He had stolen that snapshot, had written Katie's name and age on the back as if he were claiming her. What else might he have done? Junior intended to find out.

The rain was still falling, slanting down with such fury that the trees and houses and the smokestacks at the glassworks wavered behind the curtain of rain as if they were shaking. Junior turned down the Tenth Street spur and drove into Gooseneck.

He didn't even knock. Mr. Dees's front door was unlocked, and Junior threw it open and stomped in, rainwater dripping from him.

Mr. Dees was at the kitchen counter, unwrapping the white butcher's paper from a cut of meat. "I woke up feeling like a beefsteak for breakfast," he said, not even bothering to give Junior a glance, as if he had been expecting him. "Steak and eggs," he said. "Maybe some fried potatoes."

Junior put his hands on him. He took Mr. Dees by the front of his shirt and shoved him back against the counter.

"You know something," he said. "Something you're not saying."

The rainwater was running down his face, smarting his eyes. He squeezed them shut, and when he opened them, he saw that Mr. Dees had picked up a dish towel from the counter and was holding it up to him, inviting him with that simple gesture to take the towel, to dry his face, to tell him calmly what he wanted.

And that's what Junior did. He let loose of Mr. Dees and took the towel and used it to dry the water from his face and arms. Outside, the rain had stopped. Junior could see that through the window above Mr. Dees's sink. The sky was brightening. A single purple martin perched atop his tall house and began to sing. An ordinary thing like that. It overwhelmed Junior, made him think that if things were different, this would simply be another summer day. He sat down at Mr. Dees's table, and for the longest time he couldn't speak.

Mr. Dees didn't move. He didn't make a sound. He let Junior have the martin's song with no noise to disturb it. Junior understood that—the kindness that Henry Dees was paying him—and he felt small in its presence.

Finally, he took the snapshot from his shirt pocket and laid it on the table. He raised his head and looked at Mr. Dees, not knowing what to say.

As it turned out, he didn't have to say anything. Mr. Dees came to the table and sat down beside Junior, and quietly he said yes, he had been in Katie's room, yes, he had taken the snapshot. He spoke about the life he had—years and years alone in this house—and how the children were the only light that got in. His children, he said, as bright as Heaven. And above all the others, Katie. His dear Katie. He loved her more than he could ever find words to say, loved her because she was funny and smart and spirited. But more than all that, she was kind.

"I can't say I know what this is for you," he told Junior, "but it hurts me, this trouble. It knocks the air right out of me. I feel it in my chest—this knot. Every time I close my eyes, I see her— Katie—and I'm sorry that my life is such that I feel this way about your little girl, but that's the truth of it. I'm not ashamed to say it. I took her picture, but that's all. I swear. Now I'd do anything—any- thing at all—to have her back."

He said all this in a way that managed to maintain his dignity. He wasn't asking, Junior knew, for anyone to feel sorry for him. He was only stating the facts as plainly as he could. As much as Junior wanted to match his calm, to stick only to the facts, the idea of Henry Dees in Katie's room, making off with that snapshot, angered him, and he could barely keep himself from putting his hands on him again.

That wouldn't help anything now, he told himself. He needed more information, so he kept his voice even. "Have you told the po- lice everything you know?"

"No, not everything."

"Will you tell it to me now?"

Mr. Dees stood up. "Excuse me, please," he said. "Please, just a moment."

He went down the hallway to his bedroom, and Junior heard a drawer open and then close. When Mr. Dees returned, he was holding his hands behind his back. "I'm not much of a man," he said. "I keep to myself. I know people think I'm odd. I never chose Raymond Wright for a friend. I want you to know that. I was trying to patch concrete on my porch steps one day, and I looked up and there he was."

Mr. Dees reached out his right hand and laid a book on the table. It was *The Long Winter*, and Junior knew it was one of the books that Katie had been taking back to the library. He started to reach for it, his hand trembling, but then he stopped, unable to touch the book, remembering how he had scolded Katie for not returning it that Wednesday the way he had told her. She had gotten on her bicycle and ridden away. Seeing the book now was too much for him. He could barely speak.

"Where did you get this?" he asked Mr. Dees in a whisper.

Mr. Dees was whispering, too. "From his truck." He cleared his throat and spoke more firmly. "From Raymond Wright's truck."

"That night? Wednesday night?"

"He came here late, almost midnight. He needed money, he said. He was in a fix. He had to go down to Florida for a while." Mr. Dees took a breath. Junior could see that he was trying to steady himself. "'I don't have any money to give you,' I said. 'Money?' he said, like he didn't know what I was talking about. Like he was drunk or hopped up on drugs. 'You should go home,' I told him. I led him out to his truck. He couldn't walk straight. When I opened the driver's door for him, this book fell out of the truck, and I picked it up. 'What's this?' I asked him. 'Some kid's book,' he said. 'I never seen it before.' Then he got in his truck and drove on down the street."

Junior let it all sink in: Katie in Raymond Wright's truck. "Why haven't you told all this to the police? Why haven't you given them this book?"

"Who do you think told them where to find that truck, where to find Raymond Wright?"

"That was you who called that night? You're the one who saw Katie talking to Wright on the square?"

Mr. Dees nodded. "I guess it's common knowledge that I pretty much hold to myself, but that doesn't mean I don't know how to help folks. Your Katie? She means the world to me. I couldn't bear to let this book go, this thing of hers. But I'm giving it to you now, and I'm telling you that whatever you need from me, you just have to ask. I'll do whatever I can."

Mr. Dees

I LIED TO Junior Mackey about the way I got Katie's library book—it wasn't that way at all, the way I said Raymond R. came to my house and the book fell out of his truck. Now I've lied to you, and that's what makes me the most ashamed. I asked you to trust me, and then I lied. I wouldn't blame you if you left me now. After all, what can you believe? But if you do—if you close this book and walk away—you'll never know the end of it all. Maybe you're good with that. We all make our choices.

You can, if you like, go to the public library in Tower Hill—perhaps it will be a summer day in July and you'll think, This is what it was like that evening. It was hot and muggy and all drowsy, and there was a little girl on a bicycle. You can go to the library, find the old newspapers, and get the facts.

But the facts don't tell the whole story. They never do. For that, I'm afraid you'll need me. I'm all you've got.

Or maybe you think you already know the end. Maybe you've made up your mind about who's good and who's evil, and if you have—if you're one of those—God help you. Ask anyone who was

living in the middle of it all and they'll tell you: it didn't have anything to do with good and evil; it was all about love.

Maybe someday you'll sit in the public library, listening to the
drone of the oscillating fan, and you'll hear a car going by. You'll
lift your head toward the window where the curtains will be barely
stirring, and everyone you've been reading about—me and Raymond R. and Clare and Junior and Patsy and Gilley and Katie—
will come alive, and you'll feel your heart in your chest, and you'll
travel back thirty years and you'll think, This is what it was; it was
people like me going about their business while there was that girl
and those two men and a queer-looking truck. You'll wonder whether
you could have made a difference. Would you have heard something, seen something, that would have mattered?

Here, let me give you the details again: a little girl with a slipped
bicycle chain and three library books; a dope fiend and his green
truck with the black circles on the doors; and me, a summer tutor, a
thief, a voyeur, a man who could kiss a little girl on a porch swing on
a summer afternoon. So there we are, the three of us. You write the
rest of the story. I'm done with it. Go on. Try.

The Searchers

BY NIGHTFALL Friday we'd come up with nothing. We'd put our-selves out in the rain, and then the blazing sun, and we'd come back into town covered with mosquito bites, our arms and faces scratched from blackberry briars.

We went home and stood in showers for a long time, lay down in hot baths and closed our eyes, and when we did, we saw her. All slender arms and legs and a round face and that brown hair. We'd seen her earlier that summer riding an elephant at the Moonlight Madness Carnival. We'd seen her at the public library sitting cross-legged on the floor, reading a book. Sometimes in the afternoon she'd be in the Coach House with a friend, sipping cherry Cokes through paper straws.

It was amazing what we remembered about Katie—small things you wouldn't think would stick in your head. Her hair smelled like strawberries, and the girl at the Rexall said yes indeed, Patsy Mackey would come in every so often and buy a bottle of herbal shampoo. That Friday night, when we came downstairs after our showers or baths—after we scrubbed our heads with Head & Shoulders or Prell—we swore we could smell that strawberry shampoo.

We'd seen her at the city park. One night, a group of kids on the bleachers started singing a song about her and a boy: *Katie and Bobby sitting in a tree, K-I-S-S-I-N-G.* We'd seen her at the Super Foodliner pushing the shopping cart for her mother, and those of us who went to the First Baptist Church still recalled seeing her in the children's chorus on Easter Sunday, her white-gloved hands clapping smartly together as she sang "If You're Happy and You Know It."

How many of us would admit now that sometime that week we drove to the Heights and parked along Shasta Drive and took snapshots of the Mackeys' house? We got those pictures developed at Fite Photography, and we spread them out on our kitchen tables and looked at them again and again, allowing the neatly trimmed yew hedges and the blue grass that Spitler's Lawn Service had mowed and edged and the bright house paint (Sherwin-Williams Latex Satin in a shade called Snow White, the paint man at the Western Auto told us) and the fishpond on the patio, its waterfall trickling down over blue limestone, to convince us that no harm had come to Katie. Soon we would find her.

Then that night, that Friday, a woman from Gooseneck—we didn't know this then, but it was Clare Mains, the widow who had married this Raymond R. Wright—told Tom Evers she had a photograph she thought he should see.

Our telephones kept ringing that night, the word spreading. It was hard to know what was rumor and what was fact. The story was that this woman from Gooseneck had taken her own pictures of the Mackeys' house after Katie disappeared. She had carried them to Tom Evers, telling him if he looked through this magnifying glass—she brought her own down to the courthouse for his handy use—he would see through an upstairs window a figure that could only be Katie herself, her back to the camera, her hair fanned across her shoulders.

Tom said later that he only meant to humor Clare by taking a look through the magnifying glass ("She was eat up with what was happening," he told us years later when he finally started to talk about that summer. "You should have seen her. She'd been blind-sided, poleaxed. I felt sorry for her. Still do"), but to his surprise, when he did, he saw what she meant: there seemed to be a figure behind the lace curtains of that window that looked enough like Katie that he had no choice but to drive over to the Mackeys'—it was nearly ten-thirty by this time—to speak to them about it. "I was just doing my job," he told us later. "My God. We were desperate."

At the house, Junior Mackey opened the door, a gun in his hand. It was a Colt Python, a .357 Magnum with a two-and-a-half-inch barrel. "I knew that gun right away," Tom will tell you now. "It was no cap pistol. I'll say that. It could have let in some air."

Junior hadn't shaved, and his hair, normally well-groomed, was mussed. A television was on somewhere in the house. The volume was very low, but occasionally the sound of an audience laughing swelled, and Tom knew that Junior had Johnny Carson on, the way he would on any ordinary Friday night. "That television just about did me in," Tom said. "That laughing, and a couple of times I heard Ed McMahon punching up Johnny's jokes with that thing he did, that *Hi-yooooo.* 'Junior,' I said, 'I need to look through the house again.'"

By this time, Tom and his officers had been in and out of that house more than once: first to take the Mackeys' story that Wednesday evening when Junior called the police to say that Katie hadn't come home, and then again later that night—and on Thursday—on the off chance that they might find something that would turn out to be a clue. "It was SOP," Tom told us. "Standard operating procedure. A kid turns up missing, the first thing you do is check the home. I stand by that. Even if the kid was Katie Mackey and most everyone in Tower Hill thought Junior and Patsy hung the moon. I was just doing things by the book."

The book told Tom that a grief-stricken father, who was more than just a little pissed off—and didn't he have a right to be?—shouldn't be sporting a .357 Magnum.

"You ought to let me have that gun, Junior," Tom said. "You wouldn't want there to be an accident."

Junior let the Colt lie across his palm, and for a moment Tom thought he was going to hand it over. Then he closed his fingers around the grip and said, "I've got a permit. I'm not breaking any law. Tom, if I have to use this, I guarantee you it won't be an accident. I want you to let me see that son of a bitch, that Raymond Wright. If you can't make him talk, I will."

"Junior, you know I can't do that. You've got to let me do my job. Like I said, I need to have another look around."

Tom couldn't bring himself to tell Junior about Clare and that photograph because once he was in that house, the notion that Katie was there and her kidnapping a hoax—a cover-up for something more hideous (here, we could only speculate, and we did so with great shame at the fact that we couldn't stop ourselves from imagining it)—seemed ridiculous, the sort of *National Enquirer* tabloid crap we saw while standing in the checkout line at the Super Foodliner. All right, we can say it now: more than one of us bought a copy now and then and took it home and got a kick out of stories about alien abductions, bigfoot sightings, and women having monkey babies. We thought they were good entertainment, the sort of stories we talked about over after-work beers at the Top Hat Inn or after eighteen holes at the country club, never admitting that yes, sometimes in our most private moments, we got sucked in and could believe that almost anything might be true.

We were reading those tabloid stories when we should have been paying attention to what was really happening in the world. When we look back through newspapers from that time, as we're all apt to do on occasion (we frequently see one another hunched over micro-film readers at the public library, looking again at the news articles about Katie's disappearance), we note what we didn't then—the catastrophes of nature that were all over the globe: the thousands and thousands of people dying (100,000 in North Vietnamese floods; 300,000 in a Bangladesh cyclone; 5,000 in an earthquake in Managua; 4,000 in a blizzard that ended a four-year drought in Iran). We hadn't thought that we were part of that world, this planet bursting and convulsing with calamity, until that summer when Katie vanished.

"What is it you think you're going to find out?" Junior asked Tom.

"I'm just covering all the bases," Tom told him.

Junior stepped back and let Tom come through the door. "All right. You have a look." Junior waved his arm about, the Colt heavy in his hand. "Why don't you invite the whole town? Maybe even sell tickets. That's what folks want, isn't it? A good look? I've seen them driving by, taking pictures. Peeping Toms." It was here that Junior broke down. He laid the Colt down on a table by the door. He put his hands over his eyes, and his shoulders shook.

Tom described for us how he put his hand on Junior's back, and when we listened, we imagined ourselves doing the same, forgiving Junior for calling us Peeping Toms, forgiving him for that Colt Python, forgiving him for his rage.

Tom didn't find Katie anywhere in that house, of course. It couldn't be that simple, could it? But Junior and Patsy, who had come downstairs in her robe, let him look. He looked through all the rooms upstairs, searched the closets. He went from room to room downstairs, and by the time he was done, Patsy had gone back upstairs.

Junior was waiting by the door, calm now, and that's when he showed Tom that book, *The Long Winter*, and he told him what Henry Dees was claiming—that Raymond R. Wright had showed up at his house late Wednesday night, and that this book had fallen out of his truck.

"You've got your man," Junior told Tom. "Now, you better get something done."

Tom held out his hand, and Junior gave him the book. "Don't worry," Tom said. "I'll get Raymond Wright to talk. I'm on my way to Georgetown right now."

These days, he comes into the Top Hat Inn toward evening and he orders a highball, and if someone gets him talking about that summer, he'll tell this story of the Friday night he went to the Mackeys' house. Just before he finishes that highball, he'll say, in a small, ghostly voice, "I showed that book to Raymond Wright, and I said, 'All right now.' He still wouldn't tell me squat. 'Prove it,' he kept saying. Then I went to Henry Dees, and I asked him why he hadn't told me about that book and how he got it when I questioned him that first time. He said, 'Tom, I . . . I didn't want to let it go.' I didn't know what to make of the way he felt about Katie, but I could tell he was hurting. His voice was trembling, and I could see the tears in his eyes. 'Tom,' he said, 'I knew you had the man who took her, who took'—and he paused, his lips working to get out the name so hard for him to say—'who took Katie, and I knew what I had to tell you wouldn't make any difference, you already had your evidence, and I just wanted to hold onto that book because it meant something to me. You see, it was hers.'"

Without fail, someone always asks Tom who it was in that snapshot Clare took. Who was sitting at that window?

"It was just the light making a shadow," he says. "That's all. Just too much light."

Then someone will say, "I remember we used to talk about coming down to the courthouse some night and getting that Raymond Wright and making him talk."

"He wasn't there," Tom tells us. He shoves his highball glass back at the bartender and orders another. "He was down in Owen County, locked up in Georgetown. I thought he'd be safe there."

SATURDAY MORNING, the heat was back. The heavy, damp air closed around us when we stepped out of our houses. It was still, and there were dark clouds in the west and the distant rumble of thunder. As much as we wanted to go back inside and pretend this thing wasn't happening, we were still a town, and Katie Mackey was one of ours, so we got in our cars and trucks and we drove down to the courthouse, where each morning the search parties formed, and we hoped that this might be the day we found her.

The rain came. We tromped through it down by Georgetown, stepping over rows of soybeans, mud sucking at our boots. By the time we came to woods, our feet were heavy with the mud. We scraped our boots on stumps and fallen limbs. We shaved away mud with the blades of our pocketknives. Then we went on through the woods, and when we came out of them, we could see the White

River, and beyond it the smokestacks they were building at that power plant near Brick Chapel. We saw boats on the river and men dropping grappling hooks into the water. We stood there a moment, frozen. We were foremen at the glassworks, sales managers for the local beer distributor, insurance agents, Realtors, owners of all manners of business. We *were* this town; we made things run. We were members of the chamber of commerce, the Jaycees, the school board, the city council. We got things done. But now all we could do was look down on that river and the men in the boats, and imagine those grappling hooks and what they might bring up to light and air.

The rain quit, and all afternoon airplanes flew low in the sky. Pipers and Cessnas and Beechcrafts, and there were helicopters, too, and Army planes with infrared sensors. Their noise burrowed into our skulls and stayed with us that night when we tried to sleep.

We kept going over what we knew, what we'd read in the *Evening Register* and overheard from the police officers and sheriff's deputies and court clerks. There was enough evidence to hold Raymond R. Wright, to charge him with aggravated kidnapping, and set his bail at a quarter of a million dollars. We knew that someone—though we didn't know then that it was Henry Dees—had told Tom Evers that he'd seen Katie that evening, that Wednesday, in front of Penney's, talking to Raymond R. Wright. We knew that the state crime lab in Indianapolis had found charred pages from Katie's library books in his burn barrel. We knew that there had been mud on his truck tires, mud mixed with shale. He'd been at the American Legion that Wednesday, the VFW, the Top Hat Inn. Folks came forward and said so. He claimed he was a retired Air Force colonel, that he'd been in WWII, Korea, Vietnam. He was drinking a lot that day; some folks saw him popping pills.

Later, there would be witnesses, come forward to retrace his path.

Monk Stevens, who ran into him that morning at the Top Hat Inn: "It was probably around eleven o'clock. I was at the bar, drinking a Coca-Cola. Mind you, I never have a highball before noon. This fellow, this Raymond Wright, he moved over onto the stool next to me, and he said, 'Friend, I can't help but notice you got some infection in that cut on your hand.' It was true; I'd jabbed myself on a fishhook, and I hadn't seen to it. 'Peroxide,' this fellow said. 'Douse it with some peroxide; that'll do the trick.' He told me he was always getting his hands nicked up with cuts and that's how he doctored them to keep the infection out. He laid his hands on the bar. 'Lookit,' he said. 'See how that one's healing up? Peroxide.' His hands were clean. I took note of that. His fingernails, too. A polite fellow. And he was right about that peroxide. Fixed me right up."

Clifford Ford, who tended bar at the American Legion: "He come in with Monk Stevens. Must have been one-thirty. 'Hi-dee-ho,' he said. 'I'm Colonel Raymond R. Wright, United States Air Force, retired.' He had a membership card, Post #591 down in Macon, Georgia. So I give him what he asked for, a Budweiser, and one for Monk, though Lord knows by that time he didn't need it. You know Monk and the booze. Story too sad to tell. Anyway, that blowhard, that Raymond R., he got under my skin, squawking about how he'd been base commander up at Scott over in Illinois and before that at Robins in Georgia. Said he had two sets of twin boys—'Now that's something, ain't it?' he said. 'That's the kind of starch I've got where it counts.' Claimed those four boys were all in the Air Force, dropping napalm over in Vietnam. 'How old are they?' I asked him. That got him all flustrated. 'Hell,' he said. 'Old enough to serve their country just like their old man.' Finally, I'd had enough of his gab, so around about three o'clock I cut him off. He put his arm around Monk. 'You've got to serve us,' he said. 'I'm Colonel Wright and this boy was a command sergeant major under me.' I just laughed. What a peckerhead. I was in the Air Force myself and I knew. No such rank as a command sergeant major."

Tubby Carl, who played pool with him at the VFW: "He was alone. Yeah, I knowed him. Married Bill Mains's widow, Clare. Knowed him and didn't like him. I run the table on him, and he said he'd buy me a drink. 'Let's drink to all you bastards who never gave me and Clare a chance,' he said. 'Then we'll drink to the asshole who put me out of work.' And that's what I done. Just exactly that. Liquor's liquor, and I'm no fool. If you're buying the drink, I don't give a good tinker's fart what you think of me. Bring it on."

Betty Mallow, who was driving up Fourteenth Street to the Super Foodliner: "I saw him cross the street, headed toward the courthouse. That man. The one you're asking about. He waited for the 'Walk' sign before he crossed. He went over to his truck and he put some money in the parking meter, and I thought it was funny because by that time—it was after five—the parking was free."

Emma Short, who was sitting on a bench outside the Little Farm Market on Tenth Street: "The truck came from the south. I know it was after seven because I was listening to the Cardinals game on my transistor radio. It was the top of the first. Bob Gibson on the mound against the Phillies. This truck came into town from the south. I couldn't see if there was a little girl. But I can tell you this. The man driving that truck was Raymond R. Wright. I picked him out of a police lineup. He looked over at me when he went past. He even tooted his horn. Now it gives me chills to think about it. He looked right at me. Him."

So we knew all that, but the one thing we didn't know was how to find Katie. And Raymond R. Wright still wasn't saying a word. We even knew that Tom Evers had gotten so desperate for answers that he had gone to Margot Cherry, the woman up in the Heights who claimed to have ESP.

"*J*," she told him. "Look for the letter *J*, and you'll find her."

J, we kept thinking as we lay in our beds. *J*. But we didn't have any more of a clue than Tom Evers what it might mean.

Mr. Dees

So that much you know, but you don't know this. You don't know that on Sunday morning, close to one o'clock, Junior came to my house and said, in a low, even voice, "I want you to bring him to me. Raymond Wright." He was carrying an attaché case. He laid it on my kitchen table and opened it. The bills were in bundles, neatly stacked. "I want you to bail him out." He closed the attaché case, and he looked me square in the eyes. "I want you to do what I say."

He told me he'd hashed it out with Patsy. He'd told her that Tom Evers was so out of leads, so down-to-go-for-broke, that he'd gone to Margot Cherry. "A woman who claims she has that ESP," Junior told me. "It's clear Tom doesn't know where to turn, and time's just slipping away, and I've got to do what I can for Katie. I said to Patsy, 'Now, I can't stand by and let this go on. I'll get that Raymond Wright. I'll make him talk.'" He was at the end of something. I could see that. "Henry," he said, "I can't do this alone." Someone would recognize him, he told me—the police, Raymond R.—and everything would go haywire. They'd know what he was up to—a tormented father out for revenge. That's why he needed me. He said

I had a way about me—collected, dignified. When I said something, people couldn't help but take it as true. "You've made it plain what you think of Katie. You've said you'll do whatever you can to help me. Well, now I'm asking."

I was to drive to the jail in Georgetown—that's where they had Raymond R., Junior said, that was what Tom Evers had let slip. I was to say I'd come to post bail. If anyone asked, I'd say I was family—Raymond R.'s brother from Minnesota. I'd open that attaché case full of cash, and what else would the police be able to do but bring Raymond R. out of his cell and turn him loose?

"He'll trust you," Junior said. "He won't know I'll be waiting. Believe me, I've thought this all out."

Junior would wait in my car, crouched down in the backseat, while I fetched Raymond R. from the jail. "You'll park in the shadows. If Wright sees me, he'll spook." Junior said he would wait until I'd driven away from the jail. Then he'd rise up. Then he'd be calling the shots.

He reached around behind him and pulled a gun out of the waistband of his trousers. "This is a Colt Python," he said. "A .357 Magnum. I'm going to put it right up to Raymond R.'s skull. You don't worry about that. You just keep driving. We'll come back to town. We'll stop at my glassworks. Then we'll get down to business."

It was a muggy night, starless. Cloud cover hung over the moon. It was the kind of night that always made me wish for the cool days of October, bright days full of sun and sharp air and crows calling from the trees.

I had to sit down. I bowed my head, thinking how I'd given away my quiet life. I noticed that one of my shoes was untied, and I bent over to see to it. I fumbled with the laces—my fingers were trembling so—and finally I gave up and sat back in my chair.

"A gun," I said. "Good mercy."

Junior knelt on the linoleum floor, and he took my laces and tied them. How many times, I wondered, had he done the same for Katie? I recalled the rhyme from my own childhood, the one my mother had used when she was teaching me how to tie my shoes: *Build a tepee. Come inside. Close it tight so we can hide.*

"I can't do it, Junior," I finally said. As much as I wanted to agree to what he was asking, I knew I'd never be able to make myself say yes. I had to admit, with a certainty that pointed out the difference between him and me, that I'd never go to the same lengths as he would for the sake of Katie. "I just can't," I said again. "You wouldn't want me to, Junior. Right now you're sure that you do, but think of everything that could go wrong. Someday you'll thank me for saying no. You should go home now. You need to be with Patsy and Gilley, not out in the dead of night with this gun."

He got back on his feet and gave me a hard look. "You just keep your mouth shut," he said. "If you won't help me, at least you keep it quiet what I told you I mean to do."

"Will you go home?" I asked. "Promise me that, Junior."

But he wouldn't answer, and all I could do was watch him walk out my door. He had that money, and he knew any number of men who would do what he needed. I'm certain there were even men for hire who would do that sort of thing, show up in the dead of night and claim that Raymond R.'s family had sent them to post bond.

That's what someone did, someone who never came forward to claim the deed. Of course, there was speculation. In the days that followed, whenever Junior shook hands with someone in the Rexall, or clapped someone on the back at the country club, or leaned in close to whisper to someone at church, people thought, There, he's the one. I heard rumors—I even heard names—but I was never able to say for certain who it was who brought Raymond R. to Junior that night, nor could Tom Evers. Some even said that Tom was in on it, and though I can't say he wasn't, it would pain me to know that about him.

It happened like so many things did in our small town—on the q.t. It happened and then it got hushed up, and for years and years after, people were left to gossip about what really went on. Sometimes I wonder if that man is still alive and how he lives with what he brought to happen. All I can say for sure is it wasn't me, even though later I was there at the glassworks when Junior finally had Raymond R. That much, I'll hold as true.

Gilley

I KNEW WHAT my father meant to do. That night, Saturday, when we were still no closer to finding Katie, he called me into his office, and he closed the door behind us, and he told me to sit down.

"I want you to listen to me." He leaned against his desk. "Gilley, I don't want you to say a word." He told me Tom Evers didn't know which way to turn. That much was clear. "Taking advice from Margot Cherry," my father said. "That's his investigation? Jesus." I could tell that he had made up his mind about something. "Here's the story, Gilley." He walked around behind his desk and opened a drawer. He took out the handgun he kept there, his Colt Python. "I'm going to make that son of a bitch Wright talk."

How my father got the money so quickly, I've never known. I was too young to know it then, and in the years that have passed neither he nor I have mentioned it. All I know is that at some time and in some way outside my knowing, he had come up with twenty-five thousand dollars in cash, 10 percent of Raymond R. Wright's bond.

My father showed me the attaché case and the bundles of bills.

"When you have money," he said, "you can get what you want." He was going to use Mr. Dees to get Raymond R. out of jail, and he was going to take him to the glassworks, and he was by God going to get somewhere. He had things in motion. After three days of nothing, he had a plan. "You need to know this, Gilley. You're not a boy anymore. None of us are anything like what we were. I'm going to do this, and you need to know it because this is about family. This is about standing up and doing what you have to do. Do you understand?"

"I want to go with you," I said.

"Negative." He reached around and stuck the Colt into his waistband. "I'm not sure you could handle it."

When we came out of my father's office, my mother was pacing about in the foyer. She had on a light summer robe over her night-gown. The sash was undone, and one end was dragging the floor. She held the robe closed, her arms crossed over her chest. She turned to face my father, and I could tell that she was waiting for some sign that what he had already discussed with her was indeed going to happen. He was going after Raymond R. Wright.

My father went to her, and he picked up the stray end of her sash and threaded it through its loop. He tied the sash and then leaned over and kissed her on the forehead. She looked at him a moment, and I saw that her eyes were glistening. Then she crossed the foyer to where I stood at the foot of the stairs. She raised her right hand, and very gently she laid it against my cheek. I knew she was telling me, without having to say a word, that whatever might happen this night, she would still love me, and it was all I could do to stand there without breaking down, overwhelmed by the faith women could hold in men.

What else could we do but try this one last thing to find Katie? We always believed that sooner or later she'd come back to us. My mother kept her faith by reading her *Daily Devotions*. Each night, I said my prayers, asking God to keep my sister safe.

My father, though, believed in the power of money, and the sway of a Colt Python .357 Magnum. "It's just persuasion," he said.

I loved him for his optimism. I recalled a joke he'd told earlier that summer about an airplane that flew itself, no pilots, no crew, all computer gizmos and whatnot. On its first flight, as it taxied down the runway, the passengers heard a tape-recorded voice: *Ladies and gentlemen, just sit back and relax. Nothing can go wrong . . . nothing can go wrong . . . nothing can go wrong . . . nothing can go wrong . . .*

Clare

THE CAR WAS in the drive, poked in back there by Henry Dees's garage. There was a light on in the back of the house, and I could see a man moving past the windows. I didn't know who he was.

The night before, I'd come because I couldn't bear to be alone. Henry let me sit in his house. He turned on nearly every light—somehow, he knew I needed that—and I was thankful to sit on his couch and sip the tea that he brewed.

There were paintings on his walls: a horse, a windmill, a ragtag girl with sad eyes. He did them with paint-by-number sets, he said, just something to help him pass the time. He talked about the purple martins and how, come August, they would start to gather in flocks, getting ready for their long flight south. They'd cackle and twitter. Oh, what a racket they'd make, he said, like they were carping about having to leave their cozy summer home. For weeks, they'd say this long good-bye, and then one day they'd be gone.

He talked like that for a while, and then he stopped. We sipped our tea, and finally I said what I'd come to: "I saw him today. Ray. That police chief—that Tom Evers—he drove me down to George-town. He said, 'Maybe he'll tell you something.' I took some clothes for Ray. That night they come for him they took him away in his underthings. I thought he'd need something."

"Georgetown?" Henry Dees said.

"That's where they've got him," I said. "To keep him safe."

Georgetown is a little town like ours. All the county seats in this part of Indiana are pretty much the same: a courthouse, a jail in the basement, stores, cafés, maybe a bus stop, all around the square. Take me out of Tower Hill and put me in Georgetown—or Jasper or Brazil or Martinsville for that matter—and I'd pretty much have the lay of the land.

But that Friday, when I stepped out of Tom Evers's police car and shielded my eyes against the sun, I felt like I was in a place I didn't know. Every which way I turned, the sun blinded me. Its glare was on the cement sidewalks, the chrome bumpers of cars, the windshields, the courthouse windows, the steps that led down to the outside door of the jail.

I was afraid. I don't mind saying so. Think of it: the man you love taken away in the night, arrested, and for something so horrible you can't stand to imagine it. I would have done anything to put it out of my mind. But I had to think on it, so I took a picture of the Mackeys' house on account I wanted something to look at, something to make me understand that this was real. I was so desperate to believe it was all a dream—so stupid with hope—I swore I could see Katie in that picture. That's probably part of the story that you've heard, another reason for you to say, *What a fool.*

There were facts. I'd seen Ray burning his clothes. Pages out of her library books were in our burn barrel. By the time I saw him in the Georgetown jail, I knew that what everyone was saying was true. Ray had done off with Katie Mackey.

So what could I say when I was finally with him but "Ray, can you tell me where you took her? Can you at least do that?"

He looked sick, his face all caved in and his eyes sunk way back in his head. "I've had the sweats," he said. We were sitting in a little room on two straight-back chairs. Our knees were touching. Tom Evers was outside the door. I could hear him talking to someone. "Clare, I've been in trouble with dope." Ray held out his hand, and his fingers were trembling. "I've had the shakes, but Clare, I'm getting myself clean. I haven't been able to hold anything in my stomach, but I'm getting better. I'm almost at the end of this thing. You'll see. I'll be right as rain when they finally see they're wrong and they let me out of here."

"They're not wrong, Ray." I could barely say it. The words stuck in my throat. "Ray, that little girl."

He put his hands up under his arms and tried to keep them from shaking. "So that's the way it is?" he said. "You're ready to hang me?"

"No one's going to hang you," I said. "They just want to know what you did with the girl."

That's when he smiled at me. It was a crazy grin, like any second he'd start bawling. "I told you, Clare. I'm going to get myself right. Darlin', maybe it's a good thing I'm here. Now I can get off the dope and come home a whole man. Oh, won't that be something? Name your paradise, hon."

I couldn't do it. I didn't say a word. In a shaky voice, he started to sing that old hymn, the one I sometimes sang around the house. I didn't know that he'd been listening, had taken it into his heart.

But the night will soon be o'er;
In the bright, the bright forever,
We shall wake, to weep no more.

I almost reached out and touched him then, but I didn't. I knew if I sat there another minute, I'd never be able to get beyond everything that was going to happen from that day on. My life would disappear inside of his. So I got up. I didn't even say good-bye. I left him sitting there. From the hall, I could hear him calling my name; that's the voice I still hear calling, *Clare, Clare.*

When I was finished with my story, Henry said, "He didn't tell you anything?"

"No," I told him. "Nothing."

We sat there awhile longer. A cuckoo clock on the wall struck midnight, and the little redheaded bird came out his door and made his noise.

Then Henry said, "Clare, you can stay here if you want. If it's too hard right now to be in your house. I could make a bed up for you on the couch."

I can tell you it was tempting. All those lights were so merry, and the teacup was warm in my hands. I could imagine then what I would one day have—a life of hiding. I won't even tell you now where I am, only to say I'm not in that place anymore, not in Gooseneck. That place is gone. The glassworks has been torn down, and without it to work at, no one needed those houses. The last time I was there—you didn't even know it, did you, didn't know I'd snuck into town?—I went down that Tenth Street spur and saw the empty lots grown over with honeysuckle and wild blackberry. I had to look close to see any sign that those houses had been there at all: a patch of concrete step at Leo and Lottie Marks's, a few cement blocks left from where Ray had built that porch, a single purple martin house, leaning over on its pole at Henry Dees's.

The purple martins come each spring where I live now, and when I hear their song, I think of Henry and that night when he offered me his couch. I thought for a minute about staying there and waking in the morning to the martins' singing. But what would that have been like? Me, sleeping the night there? What if someone knew it? Wouldn't that make for talk? Me and Henry Dees.

So I told him, "No, thank you. I just come to say my piece. I thank you for listening to it."

"You come anytime," he said. "I mean that."

I told him, "I know you do."

So I was back on this night. Actually, it had got so late, we'd turned into Sunday morning—the ninth day of July. I'd come to tell Henry what I'd seen plain as day in the dream I'd woke up from. It was me and Ray in Honeywell, and the quail was in the grass, and Ray had his binoculars up to his eyes and he was looking out on the hills and the old roads snaking back into the woods. It came to me in the dream that he wasn't spying for those smokestacks at that power plant in Brick Chapel at all. "Ray," I said, "what do you see?" "Junk," he told me. "A dump back there in the woods." He let me look through the binoculars, and when I did, they turned into one of those kaleidoscopes. All I saw were whirling colors—pieces of bright glass. Then everything cleared, and a blinding light came into the kaleidoscope, and it was like all the trees in the woods had fallen and every bit of color had gone away. There was just this light, so bright I swore Heaven must have opened up, and I knew it had to mean something—that place, that Honeywell—so I came to tell it to Henry. I couldn't tell it to the police myself, not after the fool I'd made showing Tom Evers that picture.

But there was that man in Henry's house, and pretty soon he was coming out the back door. I was afraid that he might see me, so I slipped back into the shadows. I turned around and went back home, thinking that what I'd come to say could wait till morning.

July 9

M**r. dees** drove a powder-blue Mercury Comet, bought new in 1965 and used mainly in the winter when it was too cold for him to make the walk to school and whenever he wanted to drive to Bloomington to do some shopping. Otherwise, he preferred to walk.

But on this night, when he needed to be able to cover ground quickly, he backed the Comet out of his garage and started toward the Heights, where he meant to put his mind at ease by seeing that Junior Mackey had left Gooseneck and gone home, as Mr. Dees had recommended, rather than driving to Georgetown with that crazy scheme still in his head.

It was a sweetheart, that Comet. A Super 289 V-8 engine, multidrive Merc-O-Matic transmission, a deluxe sixteen-inch steering wheel, only twenty-one thousand miles on the odometer. It hummed along the Tenth Street spur, and even though it wasn't one of those jazzy Mustangs or GTOs like the kids drove, it was in apple-pie order—Mr. Dees saw to that; he brought it in regularly to have the oil changed and made sure the tires had the proper pressure—and he felt confident driving along the empty street.

Then, as he was passing Mackey Glass, he recalled the details of

Junior's plan, and he had the thought that it wouldn't hurt just to turn in and drive around behind the long buildings to make sure that everything was quiet there.

He pulled back into the yard behind the humped ridges of sand and limestone, and there he came upon a sight that stunned him. He had to step hard on his brakes to keep from rear-ending Junior's truck. The Comet's headlights swept over Junior and Gilley and a third man they had crowded up against the truck's front fender. All three of them swung their heads toward the Comet's lights to see who was finding them. Mr. Dees could see that the third man was Raymond R. and that Junior had the gun, the one he had carried into Mr. Dees's house.

Mr. Dees switched off his headlights and the sight in front of him faded into the darkness. Little by little, as his eyes adjusted to the dark, the image came back to him, the three figures reemerging. Behind them, he could see the shadows of the smokestacks from the glass furnaces. Even though it was after midnight on Sunday and the glassworks were shut down, he could smell the heat from those furnaces in the muggy air.

He heard Junior shouting, intent on his business, unconcerned that Mr. Dees had happened to appear to witness it.

"All right, now," Junior said. "Here's what I want. I want to know what you've done with my daughter."

Raymond R. was trying to get his breath. "I swear, mister. It's like I've done told you. I don't know."

Junior held the Colt to the soft flesh under Raymond R.'s chin. He drew back the hammer. "You better know," he said.

Gilley

I WENT DOWN there. My mother said, "Gilley, don't." But I went. Why did I do it? Because I'd taken to heart what my father said. This was about family, and I had something to prove—that I was man enough to stand beside him and do whatever we had to do to bring Katie back. *Love finds you,* Margot Cherry had told me. *Be ready.*

"Gilley," my father said when he saw me. He had that Colt up under Raymond R.'s chin. "Gilley," he said again, as if he were trying to make sure that what he saw was true. I'd had the nerve to come there, to be with him, to be whoever he needed me to be on this night when we didn't know what would happen next.

July 9

Mr. Dees sat in the Comet, and he closed his eyes. He wished he could put the car into gear and drive away and be finished with this night. But he was afraid to move because Junior had Raymond R. up against that truck, a gun under his chin, the hammer back. That was the last thing Mr. Dees saw before he closed his eyes: Junior pulling back that hammer. The sound lingered in his ears, that ratcheting that reminded him of the martins' alarm call.

"Tell me," Junior kept shouting, and Mr. Dees was afraid to do anything for fear that if he did, that gun would go off and Raymond R. would be dead, and then they would never know what had happened to Katie.

"I mean it, brother," Raymond R. said, his voice quivering. "I don't remember. That night? I was hopped up on booze and dope. I was a different man then. My life wasn't mine. That night you're wanting me to remember? It's gone from me. I took too much junk, twice as much as usual, and now the truth is I don't remember anything that you want me to. Believe me, brother. I've tried. It's all gone. It's like it never happened."

And there they were, in a fix. What do you do, Mr. Dees wondered, when your daughter's been missing nearly four days, and you have a gun to the head of the man you're sure is responsible, and he can't—or won't—tell you what you need to know?

You go back. That's the thought that came to Mr. Dees. It was what he told his students. You break the problem down into its parts; you zero in on a simpler computation and you learn it. You work your way back until you've learned everything you need to know to find the answer you thought was beyond your reach. You work your way back.

So he started. He got out of the Comet and came to where Junior and Gilley had Raymond R. pinned against the truck. "Let me talk to him," he said to Junior. "You're not the one to be doing this. Not now. You're not in your right mind. I don't blame you. Not for a second. It's a horrible thing. Let me talk to him. Let me try."

"Now you want to help?" Junior said. "After you already turned me down? Now you come sticking in your nose. This isn't your affair. Go home."

But Mr. Dees was already talking. "Listen now, Ray," he said. "You know you had Katie that night." Mr. Dees knew that he was risking that Raymond R. would recall that the two of them had seen her on the courthouse square, but he was willing to do that if it would mean information in exchange, information that would lead them to Katie. "Ray, all we want is for you to tell us what you did with her. Where did you take her? You need to tell us, Ray."

"I'll tell you what I know," Raymond R. said. "Brother," he said to Junior. "I know this uncle here, this Teach, he had his eyes on your girl. I'll tell you that much. If you want to know what happened to her, you ought to ask him."

"What's he talking about?" Junior said.

"He's talking out of his head," said Mr. Dees.

"Teach, you know you took that snatch of hair from that little girl's brush."

For a while, no one said a word. Then Junior said, "Like you picked up that snapshot of Katie? Henry, what's going on here?"

Then Mr. Dees had no choice. He had to say the words. He told Junior that on summer evenings he had hidden himself in the darkness and watched the Mackeys on their patio, had seen Gilley in the backyard practicing golf shots, Patsy tending to her roses, and Katie running over the grass, chasing after fireflies. "And you," he said to Junior. "You were lucky. You were all lucky, and you didn't even know it."

He kept talking, and Junior let him. Everything that Mr. Dees had kept hidden came out. One night, when the Mackeys had driven to the Dairy Queen for ice cream, he had come up on their patio and taken a petal from one of Patsy's roses and a fluff of hair from Katie's brush. And yes, later, as he had already admitted to Junior, he had come into their house, had made his way to Katie's room. He had opened her dresser drawers. He had stolen the snapshot, the one Gilley would later find on the porch swing. It was on that swing where the shameful thing had happened, where he kissed Katie, but he couldn't tell Junior that. He could only say that he was a lonely man, that he was afraid of his loneliness. "You had everything I've always wanted," he told Junior. "You had a family—a beautiful, beautiful family—and I couldn't look away from it. I wished your life were mine."

Junior eased the Colt's hammer down and let his arm fall to his side. It was too much for him to listen to Mr. Dees describe how their family had been that summer. He could see the three of them on the patio, their figures dim and shadowy in the gathering dusk. He could hear Katie saying, as she had that Wednesday evening, *The library's open until seven o'clock.* He could hear the noise her bicycle chain made as it rattled against its guard. Her hair flew out behind her as she pedaled away.

It made Junior angry that Henry Dees had seen them when they hadn't known he was watching.

"What kind of man are you?" he said, his voice shaking with rage.

He took a step toward Mr. Dees, and that's when Raymond R. swung his hand down, chopping at Junior's wrist. The Colt fell to the ground. Raymond R. crouched down, his hand reaching out for the gun. Gilley reached for it, too, and he and Raymond R. fell to the ground, wrestling. Mr. Dees couldn't see who had the gun, and for a moment, as the two rolled over and over in the gravel, puffs of dust rising around them, the Colt was held between their chests, each of them trying to get a good grip.

Junior was down on his knees, hovering over Gilley and Raymond R., trying to find his own opportunity to grab the Colt. "Gilley," he called out. "Gilley."

Raymond R. jerked his elbow backward and caught Junior in the head. At the same time, the gun came free, and it skittered over the gravel to lie at Mr. Dees's feet.

He felt weak with everything that was happening so quickly. Junior was shaking his head, trying to get his bearings. Raymond R. had Gilley on his back. He was sitting astride his chest, his hands closing around his throat, choking off his air.

Mr. Dees told himself to move, to kick the gun away, to pick it up, to do something. But then a shadow stretched out over the gravel, and he saw Junior scrabbling on his knees to grab the Colt.

The breath rattled in Gilley's windpipe. Mr. Dees heard it.

Then Junior fired. Raymond R.'s shoulders jerked back, as if someone had suddenly yanked on them. He fell backward onto the gravel. Junior shot him again, and again, and then three more times. Each time, fire flamed at the end of the barrel, and for an instant— Mr. Dees would remember this later—they were all standing there, lit up, unable to escape the brilliant flashes of light.

July 5

Dᴀʀᴋ ᴡᴀs coming on when Don Klinger, manager of the Georgetown Big John Grocery Store, saw Raymond R.'s truck pull into the lot. He parked at the far end by the Salvation Army drop-off box. He got out and walked through the glow from one of the lot's sodium lights, and he took a minute to look at a couch some-one had left. He sat down on it and crossed his legs.

"I couldn't see into that truck," Don says to this day. "Like I told you, it was nearly dark—must have been after nine—but I know it was that Ford pickup, the one with the black circles on the doors, and I know the man who got out of it was that Raymond R. And I'll tell you what else. I could see that truck had wet mud on it. I could sure as shooting see that."

Lois Treadway was working the cash register that night. "He come through my line," she says when someone asks her for the story. "He bought a box of Hostess cupcakes—the orange kind, not the chocolate. That's why I took note of him. 'Not many people like these orange ones,' I said to him, and he said he liked them just fine. When I give him his change, he held out his hand and I saw it was dirty. That's when I noticed. He smelled like wet leaves, like river water, like mud."

Mrs. Mavis Childs was standing at the front door of her house trailer on the south side of Georgetown where Route 59 angles to the east along the White River. "I was looking out for my husband. He was working across the river, building that power plant in Brick Chapel. He was putting in overtime and I was watching for him, hoping pretty soon I'd see his truck coming across the bridge. It was just after eight-thirty. That's when that Raymond R.'s truck went by. I remember thinking what a funny-looking thing it was, that old truck with those black circles on it. I thought, Well, there goes someone down on his luck. I just got a peek as he went by. A little girl? I couldn't tell you. Only that it was that truck, and it went across the river toward Brick Chapel."

Danny Ginder, of Ginder's Farm Service, was on Route 59 north of Georgetown, heading back to town. He'd been out to a farm to fix a tractor tire. "Must have been a little after nine-thirty. Yes, it was dark, but I was sitting up high in that winch truck, and when my headlights caught that Ford pickup, I could see good enough. There was one man in that pickup. One. That's all. And he was driving slow, drifting over the centerline. I had to blow my horn at him to get him back in his lane. I'll swear to it now just like I did then. It was that crazy-looking truck all right, and it was headed north toward Tower Hill."

Tom Evers has long ago retired as chief of police, but even now when he walks into the Top Hat Inn or the Super Foodliner or the Coach House, no one can look at him—even folks who weren't around back then—without thinking of that summer and Katie Mackey.

"We could trace him," Tom says whenever someone convinces him to tell the story. "That Raymond Wright. We had him every move he made except for that time between when Mrs. Childs saw him cross the river and when he showed up at the Big John and then that Ginder boy saw him going back north. About a half an hour or so we couldn't account for, like he just up and disappeared."

July 9

W HEN GILLEY was a young boy, his father showed him how to make glass. Sand and limestone and soda ash went into the furnace, where the fire, its temperature anywhere from 1,500 to 3,200 degrees, melted the mix down until it was like honey. "You wouldn't want to be in that furnace," Junior said. "You'd be vaporized. There wouldn't be anything left but the nails from the soles of your shoes. Now that's no lie."

The night he shot Raymond R., he lowered the Colt and said to Mr. Dees, "I imagine you didn't bargain for this, but now you're in it. Mister, you're all the way in."

Mr. Dees knew it was so. He'd been there as a witness to it all; he'd even involved himself by trying to make Raymond R. talk. Soon it would be clear that Raymond R. had vanished, that someone had come with the bail money that night, and then the man the police knew had kidnapped Katie Mackey was gone. Not a trace of him.

If it got out to Tom Evers that Mr. Dees knew something, he'd want answers, and those answers, if Mr. Dees gave them, would lead to this night and this moment—the one burned into him now for-ever: Junior Mackey and his boy, Gilley, and Mr. Dees, no closer than before to knowing where Katie was, and Raymond R. dead at their feet.

Gilley was sitting up now, rubbing at his throat, gulping breath into his lungs.

"You wanted my life?" Junior was shouting at Mr. Dees. "Well, now you've got it. As close as you're ever going to come, anyway."

He crouched down by Gilley, rubbing his hand in slow circles on his back, telling him to take his time, to breathe, everything was going to be all right. "You did what you had to do," Junior said. "You went for that gun. You remember that. Whatever else you carry away from all this mess, you make sure you remember that you stepped up. You protected your family. That's what we did here tonight, Gilley. We looked out for family, and how can that ever be wrong?"

Soon, Gilley's breath came more easily and Junior helped him to his feet.

Mr. Dees was thinking that if by some chance Tom Evers never knew his part in this—if he went back to his house in Gooseneck and come September he stood at the head of his classroom and the years went on, years and years of other people's children—there would still be Junior Mackey to answer to. Junior Mackey, who came to him now and leaned in close and whispered, "You can't tell this. You know that, don't you?"

"But he was choking Gilley. You had to do something."

"You can't tell it because I got him out of jail. You don't need to know how. No one needs to know that. Tom Evers knows all about this Colt." He held up the gun so Mr. Dees could get a good look at it. "He tried to get it away from me."

"I wish you'd given it to him," Mr. Dees said. "Now look what's happened."

"Listen to me," Junior said. "I got this Wright out of jail and I brought him here under force. That's conspiracy, Henry. Now there he is, dead. Not one bullet in him, the way someone would have shot him in self-defense, but six, the way someone would have shot him for the pleasure of it. Do you understand what I'm saying? Add it up, Henry. What's this going to look like? Whatever they call it— murder, manslaughter—you're in it, too. You were here when it happened. You tried to get him to talk. Is that much clear to you?" Mr. Dees nodded his head to say he understood. "Good. Now I want you to go home. I want you to forget what's happened here. Go on, Henry. Gilley and I are going to take care of things."

Mr. Dees knew he would drive away. He and Junior would seal the secret between them. As full of horror as it was, he would carry it with him the way he did the martins' dawnsong, a memory all fall and winter, until he heard them again come spring. It would be his to recall, this night when Junior traveled so deeply into his love for Katie that he came to something else, something savage and seem-ingly not born of love at all. But there it was: how far a man would go, a man who was powerless to turn away from the most monstrous part of himself—the man he was when he was alone in the dark.

"I suppose you had your reasons for watching us, for taking those things of Katie's," Junior said. "I can't say I understand it. In fact, if you want the truth, it disgusts me. If this was some other night, I'd show you what I think of it. I wouldn't want to be you on some other night, Henry. If we were alone and I had a chance to hurt you, I would. The only thing I regret—I mean it, Henry—is that I still don't know where to find Katie." He leaned in even closer, the way boys sometimes did on graduation night to say quietly so no one else could hear, *Thanks, Mister Dees.* "Henry," he said, and his voice was shaking, "if there's a God, he'll forgive me, don't you think?"

"It'd be nice to think so," Mr. Dees said.

Junior nodded. "Just tell me. You would have done it, too, wouldn't you? Killed him? If she were your little girl and you were sure he was the one who took her, and you were sure . . ." His voice died away, and he couldn't finish. Mr. Dees knew that. How long would it be before Junior would be able to say the words? How long before any of them would be able to say them? So many days had passed now, it was unlikely that Katie was still alive.

"Yes," Mr. Dees said, knowing that he was lying, that the lie was necessary. As soon as he said the word, something opened inside him, and he knew it was his heart filling with a love unlike any he had ever felt: the truest kind, selfless and tolerant and enduring, the love a father had for his child. "Yes," he said again. "I would have done it, too."

July 5

Raymond r. crossed the White River. Fog was starting to settle in the low-lying bottom land. The truck crested a hill, and as it nosed down the other side, he could see in the headlight beams the smoky swirls of fog, and for a moment, his head electric with LSD, he imagined he was flying over the tops of clouds.

Then Katie said, "It's almost dark." He remembered her then, the girl.

"Dark ain't nothing to be afraid of," he said. "You're a big girl, ain't you?"

He could swear she was shrinking. Each time he glanced at her, she seemed farther away from him. Finally, she was so small he thought he could pick her up and stick her in his pocket. Like Tom Thumb, he thought. That was a story he'd always liked. Tom Thumb hidden away in places too small and tight for ordinary folks to go: a mouse's hole, a snail's shell. Tom Thumb swallowed up by a cow and then rescued, only to be eaten by a wolf. Tom Thumb always trying to tell people where he was. *Dear father,* he cried out, *I am here in the wolf's inside.* How dearly Raymond R. had loved the end of that tale: the mother and father blessed again with their wee son, hugging and kissing him, telling him they would never part with him *for all the kingdoms of the world.*

When he was a boy—*Raymond*, everyone called him, never *Ray*—and he had to sit outside the school cafeteria eating his fried-egg sandwich while water from the steam pipe dripped on his head, he wished he could be as small as Tom Thumb, so small no one would see him. Then, as he got older, he started to take note of how boys could swagger through the world. Boys having hamburgs and malteds with their best girls at the Snow White Sandwich Shop, or barbecue red hots and chili at the Club Café. Life was percolating. Couples danced in the ballroom at the Northwood Hotel and later strolled arm in arm down Mitchell Street. One night, when he was coming out of the A&P, he caught the gardenia scent of cologne as a boy and a girl passed by, and the tang of Old Spice aftershave. The girl had red lips and her cheeks were bright with rouge. The boy's face was closely shaved, his hair combed and dressed with tonic. "Hi-dee-ho," he said, and Raymond R. thought that was marvelous. *Hi-dee-ho.* Just like that. Just like that boy owned the world. That's when Raymond R. decided he'd make some noise. He'd make sure everyone, by God, saw him.

So he tried to join the service, and when no one would have him, he stole the Army Air Corps uniform and went to the North-wood Hotel and danced with the girl under the blue lights, and that was what he kept trying to get back to, that top-of-the-world, money-in-your-pocket feeling. Something to last him the rest of his life.

Now the truck was moving through fog, and the thoughts of Tom Thumb and the memories of the dripping steam pipe and the boy who said hi-dee-ho and the girl under the blue lights were gone. Raymond R. lifted his hands from the steering wheel and said, "Wheeee!" He was laughing. "Wheeee!" he said again.

They were gliding through the fog, and for a good while there was only the sound of the truck's tires bumping over the seams in the pavement and the rush of wind coming in through the open windows.

Raymond R. turned off the highway onto a gravel road. He drove another mile north and then found the old shale road that snaked back into heavy woods, the road he had seen through his binoculars the evening he and Clare had driven to Honeywell.

In the woods, all the light went out, and there they were in the dark. The road was narrow and sapling branches whipped up against the fenders and doors, squeaking as they scraped over the paint. The truck tires sank down into the muck of mud and shale. The air smelled of wet, moldering leaves. Trees rose up in the headlight beams, thick trunks laced with wild grapevine. Somewhere in the woods, a screech owl screamed.

"Mister Ray," Katie said.

"Yes, darlin'?" The sweet tone of her voice—hushed and tender—choked him.

"Mister Ray, I'm not to be out after dark. When it gets night, I take my bath, my mother brushes my hair, and I go to bed."

"Are you sleepy?"

"My eyes are."

"So are mine, darlin'. Don't worry. It won't be long."

The road opened up to a clearing off to the right where people had long ago dumped old refrigerators and stoves and washing machines. They tilted and lay over one another. There were piles of glass bottles and tin cans, long ago gone to rust. Broken-handle shovels and rakes and hoes. Old mattresses and bedsprings. Dented-in gas cans and oil drums.

"A heaven's worth of junk," Raymond R. said.

He shut off the truck's engine and the headlights, and it was so black all around him, for an instant, he thought he had closed his eyes and fallen asleep.

Then Katie said, "I'm hungry."

He remembered then where he was. "Shh," he told her. "Now be quiet. I just want to sit awhile."

He thought of Clare, waiting for him to pick her up at Brookstone Manor. She'd be worried. She'd probably give up and walk home. It was the thought of that, her two-mile walk to Gooseneck in the dark, that nearly broke him. He remembered the night he had started home from Mr. Dees's, so tired he could barely tote that ladder, and Clare had come out to help him, had come out in spite of the neighbors who were watching and gossiping no doubt about that old woman and her good-for-nothing man. Together, they carried that ladder home. That was love, he decided. That should have been enough. He should have told her that night. He should have said, "Clare, I'm messed up on junk. Please help me." But he didn't, and now here he was, deep in the woods on a road that year by year was closing over with brush.

His head wouldn't work right. He kept trying to figure out how this was happening. The girl had simply been there on the courthouse square, her bicycle chain slipped from its sprocket, and Henry Dees had said he wanted her gone.

"All right," Raymond R. said now to Katie, but really he had no idea what he was talking about.

He was an idiot, a fool. All the names he could remember people calling him over the years now spun around in his head. He was a *dipshit, screw jack, numb nuts, suck wad, fuckup.*

"Come here, darlin'," he said to Katie. The LSD kept jacking his head like he was a lamp with a short in the wire—bright and burning one minute, then blinking on and off. He had to pick up Clare at Brookstone Manor, he thought. Then he remembered the time for that had already gone. "Just come over here with old Ray."

Katie was trying to find the North Star, the one her father had told her to look for if she was lost, the one that would lead her home. But the trees blacked out the sky. "Mister Ray," she said in a quiet voice. "Do you know where we are?"

"We're just here, darlin'." He took her by the arm and pulled her over onto his lap. He could smell the strawberry scent of her hair. "Just you and me. Right here."

"I'm scared," she said.

"Hush," he told her, rocking her in his arms. "Scared's no good. It's too late for that."

Later, he would find himself tromping through a muddy field, crouching down on his heels, covering his ears, looking up at the sky filled with stars. He would make his way back into the woods, back to that shale road and his truck, and he would drive back to Gooseneck, stopping first for something to eat because he was starved to death.

In the days that followed, Katie's voice would almost come back to him. It would be a sound lingering—the last fading note of a clock chiming, birdsong in the early dawn when he was coming up from the land of dreams—a stirring of air, one impossible to say he heard, one that vanished before he could call it by name.

July 9

Mr. dees couldn't sleep. When he got home from Junior Mackey's glassworks, he tried to lie down and rest, but too much was going on inside his head. He was thinking about Katie. He was thinking that if he had been a better man, he wouldn't have kissed her on the swing—wouldn't have let the love he felt for her get out of hand. He would have stayed to finish her lesson, and then time that Wednesday would have fallen differently. Patsy Mackey would have got supper on the table a tad later. Mr. Dees would have walked straight home instead of stopping to gather himself on the courthouse lawn. Even if Katie had come uptown to take back her library books, he wouldn't have been there to see her, and that little difference in time would have meant that her path and Raymond R.'s more than likely would never have intersected. Maybe he would have gone to Brookstone Manor to see Clare; maybe he would have gone home to Gooseneck. Enough maybes to last a lifetime, but the one thing Mr. Dees knew without a doubt was that he was the one who had brought Katie and Raymond R. together.

Just after dawn, he went out to his garage to fetch his ladder.

He'd been thinking about the fluff of Katie's hair that the martin had snatched up and carried into his roost. He remembered the evening Raymond R. had helped him repair the broken martin house and then reset it on its pole. The Cooper's hawk had passed over, and he thought now that he should have seen that for what it was: an omen of wicked things to come.

When he came out of the garage, he saw Clare coming up the street. The light was gray and there was a haze over Gooseneck, but he could tell that it was Clare, and he could see that she was walking as fast as she could, her arms swinging with purpose. He went out through his yard to meet her.

"I got something the police ought to know," she said. "I want you to tell them. I come last night, but there was a man in your house."

He didn't tell her about Junior. He didn't tell her what had happened at the glassworks. "It was about the girl," he said. "Katie. It was more questions about her."

"Yes, the girl," Clare said. "That's what I come to say. I know where they ought to look."

LIGHT WAS BREAKING when Junior drove into his garage. He and Gilley got out of the car, and together they pulled the garage door down. On the drive home, they hadn't said a word. Now Junior told Gilley to take off his clothes. There was blood on his shirt, blood on Junior's trousers. They had put Raymond R. into the glass furnace; the rest had been heat and chemistry—matter breaking down, something solid becoming liquid and then vapor.

Gilley did what his father told him. He took off his shirt and pants. He folded each of them, a habit he couldn't break from his job at Penney's, and he laid them in the plastic garbage bag his father fetched. He held the bag open while his father undressed and stuffed his shirt and trousers inside.

The two of them stood there in their boxer shorts and T-shirts. "I'll look after you," Junior finally said. "If this comes out, don't worry. I'll tell them you were here, asleep. Your mother will swear to it. You'll be all right. No one has to ever know that you had any part in this."

"What about Mister Dees?" There were bruises on Gilley's throat where Raymond R.'s fingers had dug into his skin, and his voice was hoarse.

"I told you. He's in it, too. He can't afford to say a word."

THE FOG was lifting from the lowlands by the time Mr. Dees started toward Georgetown. Clare had told him about a place called Honeywell and the old shale roads snaking back into the brush and woods. Go across the White River on Route 59, she told him. He wrote down the directions with his fountain pen. Turn down the first gravel road that heads back north. Look for a road that goes off into the woods, one of those shale roads. He wrote down the directions and then capped his pen. His fingers were trembling so badly he couldn't get the pen clipped to his shirt pocket and had to let it slip down into the pocket and lie in its pouch.

"I might be crazy," Clare said, "but I got reasons to think that's where Ray took the girl. You tell the police that. You will, won't you?"

"I'll tell them," he said, but he didn't. After the episode at the glassworks, he didn't want anything to do with the police. He almost told Clare he couldn't go where she was telling him to go; he thought about locking his doors and opening them for no one. Then he thought of Katie, and he knew he would do what Clare was asking of him.

He got in his Comet and drove down Route 59. The highway to Georgetown dropped straight south for fourteen miles and then angled to the west along the curve of the river. It was just after dawn, and the only traffic was a single set of headlights coming from the south, a farm truck, an early bird headed who knew where. Other than that, the only signs of life were the pole lights still burning in barn lots and the occasional lamp in a window at a farmhouse. For the most part, there were the long stretches of prairie, and the white stripe down the center of the highway and the flashing yellow caution light at Alinda, a sleepy little wink-you'll-miss-it town nine miles north of Georgetown. Mr. Dees slowed the Comet, gliding past a Texaco station, and across the street, a grocery store with a neon Kool cigarette sign flickering in the window. Then he pressed down on the accelerator, and the Comet gathered speed. The rush of wind through the open windows carried the sharp smell of cut hay curing in the fields.

Just east of Georgetown, he crossed the river bridge like Clare said he should. Then he turned down the first gravel road, and soon he was in Honeywell. He drove past the run-down houses, following the road as it turned from gravel to shale and then dirt. He pulled off to the side and got out of the car. The heat was coming on. Not a breath of air, the locusts chirring, and the sun full up, and somewhere in the distance a woodpecker drilling at a tree, the *rat-a-tat* carrying a good long ways.

Mr. Dees walked down the road, not knowing where he was headed, not caring that his shoes and the bottoms of his pants legs were getting muddy. The road swung out wide of the woods and opened onto a piece of bottomland where a farmer had planted corn.

It was there, in the soft ground, that Mr. Dees saw the footprints and a ragged patch of black cloth he feared had come from Katie's T-shirt.

INSIDE THE HOUSE, Patsy Mackey heard the garage door come down. She was upstairs in the bathroom, drying herself after stepping out of the shower, the first time she had bathed that week. She'd worn the same pair of golf shorts and sleeveless blouse she'd had on that Wednesday evening when she'd stepped onto the patio and called for Gilley.

Now, to her surprise, she felt no need to hurry. She waited a few seconds, hoping to hear the sound of the door opening to the kitchen and then Gil calling for her as he bounded up the stairs with news—good news—about Katie. Water dripped from the shower-head. Patsy slipped into a robe and moved out into her bedroom. The clock on the night table ticked. When enough time had passed and there was still no sign that Gil had come in from the garage, she picked up a comb from her dresser and ran it through her hair. She watched herself in the mirror, and it was as if she were watching some other woman; it was the way she had felt that night in Indianapolis when she had let Gil lay his hand against the small of her back and nudge her across the doctor's threshold.

Now she took her time getting dressed. She laid out fresh underclothes and went to the closet, thinking she should put on something beside golf shorts and those bright summer blouses she favored, something more somber, something more in keeping with—and here the truth hit her, the thing she had been fearing all night while she waited for Gil to come home, and her legs went weak and tears came to her eyes—something more appropriate for a woman who had lost her child, a mother in mourning.

She was sitting on the bed, threading a needle, when Junior came into the room. She heard his footsteps, but she wouldn't look at him, taking comfort instead in the concentration it required to sight the thread through the needle's eye. She meant to reinforce the hem in a pair of dark-gray slacks she hadn't worn since winter. The hem had come loose one night at the country club and she'd thought, Well, there's something to see to, but she'd put the slacks away in her closet and then spring had come and she'd never gotten around to her mending.

Now she tied off the thread, her fingers nimble and quick. Her robe had fallen away from her leg, and the needle, dangling at the end of the thread, tickled her knee.

"I could sleep," Junior said. "I swear, Patsy. I wish I could sleep for a million years."

She'd been praying that he wouldn't say a word. She wanted there to only be the needle and the thread and the stitches she'd make through the cloth. If he didn't speak—if she only sat there and sewed that hem—she'd at least have that small moment of time, that grace, before she knew for certain how their lives would move on from that point.

But he said what he did about wanting to sleep, and there was such misery in his voice that she couldn't help but look up at him, and that's when she saw that he was in his boxer shorts and T-shirt.

"Your clothes," she said. "What's happened to your clothes?"

He slipped off his wristwatch and laid it on the dresser. "Clothes," he said with a smirk and a shake of his head.

"Junior," she said. "What's happened?" she finally asked. "That man. Did you . . . ?"

"We got him. We got him and he wouldn't tell us anything." He told her how Mr. Dees had refused him. He said the name of the man who had done the job instead. It was a man Patsy knew, the man she'd seen earlier that summer on their patio arguing with Junior. That man who worked at the glassworks. The one who came to ask for his pay. Patsy couldn't even remember what he looked like. He was that kind of man, someone who could bail a man out of jail in the middle of the night and disappear, leaving the ones who had seen him scratching their heads as they tried to describe what he looked like. He wasn't a bad man, just someone like them, Patsy thought. Someone who'd hit some back luck. He had a little girl of his own, a little girl who'd been sick down at St. Jude's in Memphis. He needed money. So he'd been the one. Junior went on to tell her that Gilley had come to the glassworks, that he'd been there when Junior had that Colt under Raymond Wright's chin. "Then Henry Dees showed up. Good Christ, Patsy. It was a mess." He told her about Raymond R. knocking the Colt from his hand and how Gilley tried to grab it, but Raymond R. had it, too, and the two of them wrestled for it. "Then I had it, Patsy, and that son of a bitch was choking Gilley, so I had to do something."

"Did you kill him, Gil? Is that what you're trying to say?"

"He didn't deserve to take another breath. That's the way I look at it, Patsy. Not after what he's done. It's been four days, Patsy. Four days. Good Christ."

She felt that she might faint, and not wanting to slip away, she took the needle and she stuck it into her leg and watched a drop of blood bead up. "What do we do now?"

"What we've been doing, I guess. We wait."

"Only we know now, don't we? That's what you're saying. We know Katie isn't coming back."

For the first time, Junior felt how hard everything was going to be from then on. He could barely speak. "Yes," he said in a choked whisper. "We know."

"What about Gilley? Is Gilley all right?"

"Gilley's fine."

But he wasn't. He was in his room, naked now, wrapped up in his bedclothes, his knees drawn to his chest, shivering, colder than he had ever been.

MR. DEES picked up the patch of black cloth and followed the footprints through the cornfield. Whoever had left them had tromped on the young corn plants. They lay broken over and pressed down into the mud. Mr. Dees stepped carefully over the rows, finally coming out on the other side of the field where the woods took up again.

He followed the prints as best he could, and he found an old road crowded in by brush. It was cooler in the woods—so cool and still in the shade of beech and oak and hickory and sweet gum and ash—and it was nice to be out of the sun. He could hear his footsteps on the roadbed of shale. It was that quiet, only an occasional crow call or a squirrel scrabbling around in the trees.

"So quiet, you'd hardly think it was a place for such a thing," he'd later say to Junior Mackey, and then immediately feel like a fool because by then he would have told the worst of it—how he followed the road deeper into the woods to the old junk pile where people, years ago, had come to dump their used-up refrigerators, couches, kitchen stoves, freezers, tires.

At first, the splintered handle meant nothing to him. He nudged it with the toe of his shoe. It was just another piece of junk someone had got rid of, a wooden handle from a shovel or a hoe. Then he saw a rusted sheet of tin roofing, lying over a mess of dead leaves. The ground was bare outside the cover of the tin, and he could see where the gray dust of the powdery topsoil gave way to clods of darker dirt, the rich loam from years and years of rot. He knew then that the handle belonged to a shovel and that someone, not long ago, had used it to dig in the spot the tin now covered.

He lifted the tin and moved it away. He scraped back the leaves and pressed his hand to the ground, feeling for soft spots where the dirt hadn't filled in. Someone had to do this, he decided. Eventually it had to be someone, and it was better that it was him, who had loved Katie—who was used to being alone with sadness—than someone who would run now from the woods, run to a telephone to call the police, to tell them to hurry, quick.

Soon enough, there would be police cars and sheriff's cars and state patrol cars, and an ambulance. There would be men tromping in and out of those woods, carting away the broken shovel handle, an old galvanized bucket with a brown hair across its bail, a hickory stump stained with blood. But for now there was only him and the quiet and the cool shade and the dirt and his fingers pressing down into the soft spots, digging with his hands, taking his time.

It was Katie's bare leg that he reached first. The skin was the color of ash. Raymond R. had cut her throat; the tips of her fingers were gone.

Her eyes were open—those green eyes—and that was what broke him. He knelt over Katie's body, sobbing, with no one in the world to hear him.

He pulled his shirttails loose from his trousers, and he used them to clean the dirt from Katie's eyes. Then he tried to think what he should do next. If he went to the police, the questions would begin: How did he know about this place? Why hadn't he come to the police instead of going down to Honeywell by himself? Where was he last night? What did he know about where Raymond R. had gone? Had he been with him the night Katie disappeared? He didn't want anything to do with those questions. He didn't even think he could call Tom Evers on the telephone and keep his identity a secret the way he had that night when he called to say that Tom could find the truck he was looking for—in Gooseneck. He wouldn't be able to say the words that he had found Katie and that she was dead.

But he had to do something. The sight of Katie's hurt body was too much for him—that brown hair, those green eyes, the only things that looked to him like Katie at all. He took off his shirt and covered her. He tried to say a prayer. Then he sat there a good while, knowing he couldn't stay there forever, knowing he couldn't just walk away and not say a word about what he had found.

Finally, he decided he would go back to Tower Hill and tell Junior Mackey. They already had secrets between them, and Mr. Dees would ask him to let this be one more.

It came to Mr. Dees then that he couldn't leave his shirt over Katie for someone to find, that he couldn't leave her body out in the open where coyotes might worry it. He knew he would have to slip her back into the makeshift grave, and that was what pained him most of all, having to fill in the dirt and leave her. He put his shirt back on, even though it carried the odor of decay now, and he went back through the cornfield to his car.

When he finally spoke to Junior Mackey, it was on the telephone. He told him how he had taken off his shirt and covered Katie, how he had said as much of the Twenty-third Psalm as he could remember, the parts about green pastures and still waters, about fearing no evil, about goodness and mercy and dwelling in the house of the Lord forever.

"How did you know where to find her?" Junior asked him. His voice was all hollowed out as if he had already accepted that soon this moment would come.

"It was Clare Wright. Raymond's wife. She told me where to look." For a good while, there was only the sound of Junior taking ragged breaths as if he was trying hard not to weep. Finally, Mr. Dees said, "What will you do now?"

"I'll do what any father would do. I'll go get my girl. I won't leave her the way you did."

It hurt Mr. Dees to hear that—made him want to hang up the phone and be alone with that hurt—but he had to keep talking. He had to make something clear to Junior. "Don't do it," he said. "Trust me. Please. Call Tom Evers. Tell him where to go. Please, Junior, for your sake and for Patsy's, let Tom see to what has to be done."

A short time later, when Mr. Dees went into his bedroom to change out of his clothes, he reached his fingers into his shirt pocket to fish out his fountain pen and discovered that the pocket was empty, the pen nowhere to be found.

Mr. Dees

I DIDN'T THINK anything then about where that pen had gone, only that I'd lost it somewhere. You have to understand that I was still shaking with the fact that I had found Katie's body, that I'd left her there in that grave. I could barely think what to do next. I stuffed my shirt into a paper grocery sack, carried it outside to my burn barrel, and set it on fire.

You're probably thinking, That's what Raymond R. did that Wednesday night, the fifth—burned his clothes. A guilty man covering his tracks. You're probably thinking I'm like him.

But wait. We're almost at the end. Stay with me just a while longer. What do you have to lose now? Please, don't go.

July 9

It was midafternoon when the police car turned into Mr. Dees's drive. He watched from the kitchen window as Tom Evers got out of the car. Another policeman was with him, and Mr. Dees recognized him as the one who had first questioned him on the night of the fifth, the fat-fingered policeman who had written with a hacked-up stub of a pencil.

"Mister Dees." Tom Evers was knocking on the back door, and Mr. Dees thought for a moment that if he just kept quiet Tom would go away and not bother him. After a night and day when people required so much of him, he just wanted to do nothing and have everything be all right. "Henry Dees," Tom Evers said, and he said it the way Mr. Dees would have said it had he been scolding a student who had misbehaved. He knew then he had no choice but to open the door and see what Tom Evers wanted.

It was the Comet, Tom said when he and the fat-fingered policeman came into the house. He wanted to have a look at it. Yes, right now.

Mr. Dees let the two men into his garage. The fat-fingered

policeman looked down the sides of the Comet. "It's been in mud, all right," he said, "and not too long ago, I'd say."

Mr. Dees stood in the sunlight, watching as Tom crouched down behind the car and ran his finger over one of the tires. He stepped out into the light and studied the muck on his finger. He raised it to his nose and sniffed at it. He showed it to the fat-fingered policeman, who smelled it, too. "Shale," Tom Evers said.

That's when the fat-fingered policeman said, "Should we show it to him now?"

"Yes," said Tom, "I expect we should."

They led Mr. Dees to the patrol car. Tom Evers reached in through the open window and plucked a small plastic bag from the dashboard. Inside the bag was a fountain pen.

"We know it's yours," Tom said to Mr. Dees. "Burt here." He nodded his head at the fat-fingered policeman. "He remembers that you offered it to him the night of the fifth when he came to question you about Katie Mackey."

"A Parker 51," Burt said.

"We found Katie Mackey's body down near Honeywell, and we found this pen with her in the grave." Mr. Dees was standing with his back up against the patrol car. Tom Evers had his hand on the car and he was leaning in close to him. "Mister Dees, there's footprints in a muddy field down there. A jumbled-up mess of prints. But we've got reason to believe two men made them. Two men going into those woods where we found Katie and two men coming out. On top of that, I've got a suspect someone bailed out of jail and now we don't know where Raymond R. Wright is. You want me to keep going? All right, sir. Junior Mackey came to me shortly before noon, and he said a man had called him and told him where he might find

Katie's body. Mister Dees, I can't say with any degree of certainty that the man who told Junior that wasn't you. Things are starting to add up, and if I was you, I wouldn't like the answers we're starting to imagine, answers about you and Raymond Wright and what you had to do with the kidnapping and murder of Katie Mackey. I think you ought to talk, and this time I think you ought to make sure that you tell us the truth."

Mr. Dees

So I did, and now I'll tell it to you. I told Tom Evers that yes, I was the one who called to tell Junior Mackey that he'd find Katie buried near a junk heap—the letter *J*, Margot Cherry had said—in a wooded area off a shale road near Honeywell. I'd said there were footprints in a cornfield and they led back into the woods. How did I know it? I told Tom Evers I'd been the first one to find Katie, but I'd been afraid to come to him myself and say so.

When he asked me why, I told him I was a shy man. I lived a quiet life. I didn't think it was my story to tell. It belonged to Junior Mackey. He was her father. I gave the news to him.

I said that Clare Wright had been the one to tell me where to look for Katie. "It came to her in a dream," I said, and then I told Tom how one evening that summer she and Raymond R. had driven down to Honeywell and he had used his binoculars, claiming he was trying to see the smokestacks they were building at that power plant across the river in Brick Chapel. "She was too embarrassed to tell you she might have a clue after that mess with the snapshot of the Mackeys' house, the one with Katie supposedly at the window. So she told it to me, and I went down there. People like Clare and me, we've never been anything. Now our lives are too much for us. We don't know how to act."

Then I explained that yes, I'd driven to Honeywell that morning, and I'd seen those footprints in the cornfield and a bit of Katie's black T-shirt. I'd left my own prints in that field. "I won't deny that, Tom." I told him how I'd found the grave underneath a piece of rusted tin—that was the detail that made him start to believe that I might be telling the truth.

"Katie's body," he said. "What do you remember?"

I knew he was looking for the facts that someone would only know if he had been there.

"Her throat was cut," I said, and I could barely get the words out of my mouth. "It was horrible, Tom. You've seen. Her throat was cut, and the tips of her fingers were gone."

He nodded his head. "You've got the facts right, but that doesn't prove you were the one who found her. I hate to say this, Mister Dees, but it could be you know those things because you were there when they were done."

"It's not like that," I said. "Surely you don't think it is."

"For your sake, I hope not, Mister Dees. Now tell me, where were you on Wednesday night between eight-thirty and nine?"

"Is that the time it was done?" I asked. "Is that the time Raymond R. had Katie down that shale road?"

"You need to be able to account for yourself during that time."

"I didn't have anything to do with what happened to Katie. Tom, I can tell you exactly where I was."

July 5

Hε was uptown at the public library. There he put a book, *Henry and Beezus*, into the after-hours returns bin. The book had been checked out on Katie Mackey's library card. It was nearly dark. He put the book in the bin and then he went home, not knowing that only a few minutes before, Tom Evers had gone to the home of the head librarian and asked her to please come with him to the library and open it up so they could see whether Katie had returned her books.

They hadn't been checked back in, the librarian said, and Tom asked her to please look in the after-hours return bin to see if they were there.

The bin was empty. It was 8:33. Tom looked at his watch and jotted down the exact time in his notebook. He ran through the facts: Katie Mackey hadn't come home, her bicycle had been left on the courthouse square, and now he had proof that she hadn't even made it to the library. Something, or someone, had stopped her. That was when he first knew, with a certainty that chilled him, that he had a kidnapping on his hands. A little girl gone.

He asked the librarian to stay there awhile, to do another search for the books just to make sure they hadn't been returned and perhaps shelved incorrectly. He had to run back to the courthouse to talk to the dispatcher, but he promised he'd be back shortly to see whether she'd been able to find them.

When he came back to the library, it was 9:07; again, he jotted down the time. Inside, the librarian was waiting. She slid a book across the counter to him: *Henry and Beezus.*

She'd already checked the records, the librarian said, and yes, that was one of the books that Katie Mackey had borrowed. She couldn't say with any accuracy when it had happened, but somewhere between the time that Tom Evers left to go to the courthouse and when he returned to the library, someone had put that book in the after-hours return bin.

"I checked again," she said. "Just to make sure. You know how it is when you've lost something? You look everywhere you can think to look, and then you start over? I looked in the bin, and there it was, that book."

The odd thing was, she said, Katie had checked out two other books, *The Long Winter* and *On the Banks of Plum Creek.* They were nowhere to be found, and Tom Evers didn't know what to make of the fact that *Henry and Beezus* was in the bin when it had been empty the first time the librarian checked, and he didn't know what it meant that the other books weren't with it. Above all, he didn't know who had put *Henry and Beezus* in the bin or how to go about finding the answer.

July 9

Bᴜᴛ ɴᴏᴡ he had it, or at least a possibility, if Henry Dees was telling him the truth.

"I'm the one," Mr. Dees said. "I put that book in the bin."

"Where did you get it?"

"From Katie."

"So you were with her? You saw her after you left her house that evening?"

"Yes."

"You lied about that, Mister Dees. You said you didn't see her after her lesson. You said you were at home all night. That's what you told Burt when he came to question you. I've got it here in the record."

"Yes, I lied," Mr. Dees said, and he knew he would have to explain why.

It was a hard thing to say to Tom, this man Mr. Dees still thought of as the boy from his class. Tom, who was decent and aboveboard and kind. It was all Mr. Dees could do to confess that he had harbored a love for Katie Mackey, that he was a lonely man who knew he would never have a family of his own, and that in his dreams he fantasized that Katie was his daughter. His voice got small, but he looked right at Tom, met his eyes, and told him all of this.

"So you were fond of her?" Tom said.

"I loved her, Tom, but not like you might be thinking. I loved her so much it scared me. I'd never known I had a right to love someone that much."

"When did you get that book from her? Where were you at the time?"

"Around five-thirty that night. Wednesday. I was walking home from the Heights and I'd stopped to rest on the courthouse lawn. That's when I saw her over in front of Penney's. She was having trouble with her bicycle. The chain had slipped off. She said she had to get her books to the library. I said I'd walk them over there, and then I'd come back and I'd help her. I got to the library and I turned back to see how Katie was doing with that chain. Tom, her bicycle was still there, but she wasn't anywhere to be seen. Well, I didn't know what to do. I thought maybe she'd ducked into one of the stores. I walked around the square looking for her. Then I sat down on a bench to wait awhile. When she never came back, I didn't know whether to take those books back to the library or not. Finally, I decided I'd take them home, and the next day when I went to her house for our lesson, I'd bring them to her. But later, I noticed that they were due that day. Tom, that's when I took those books to the library. I've already told you I couldn't bear to let *The Long Winter* go. But *Henry and Beezus*? That one, I put in the bin."

"Mister Dees, there was another book that Katie had checked out, *On the Banks of Plum Creek*. We've found pages from it in Raymond

Wright's burn barrel. You told Junior Mackey you had *The Long Winter* because Raymond Wright came to your house around midnight and the book fell out of his truck. Now it sounds like you're telling a different story. Mister Dees, something still doesn't add up."

Mr. Dees

I told him to look inside that book. "Tom," I said, "you need to look in *Henry and Beezus*. Look underneath the front flap of the jacket, and you'll see what I'm telling you is true. I couldn't have been with Raymond Wright at the time of Katie's murder because I was the one who brought that book back to the library."

"We've looked at that book," Tom Evers said. "I've got it down at the courthouse as evidence."

"Then you need to look again, Tom. I'll tell you exactly what you'll find underneath that jacket."

July 5

He meant to take the two library books back to the Heights and leave them on the Mackeys' front porch so Katie would find them there once she was home. But as he walked up Fourteenth Street, past the public library, he saw Junior Mackey and Gilley on the courthouse square studying Katie's bicycle. Junior lifted his head and looked all around him, and Mr. Dees slipped behind a pine tree on the library's lawn, afraid that Junior would see him. He watched until Junior and Gilley had lifted Katie's bicycle into the trunk of their car and driven away. He was afraid then to keep walking toward the Heights, afraid to try to leave the books on the Mackeys' front porch. He was carrying too many secrets that might come out if the Mackeys happened to spot him.

So he did the only thing he could think to do: he dropped *Henry and Beezus* into the after-hours return bin. He couldn't bear to let *The Long Winter* go because it had been one of the Little House books that Katie and Renée Cherry were anguishing over that first time he had come to tutor Katie. She had said the Ingalls children's names with such love in her voice, and for that reason alone he couldn't bear to put the book into the bin. He'd keep it just awhile simply because she had touched it, held it in her hands, and he wanted it, like the fluff of hair from her brush and the snapshot he'd stolen from her dresser, wanted it close to him.

He dropped *Henry and Beezus* into the bin, remembering only after the door had closed what he had left beneath the jacket, where he imagined no one would ever see it, and if by some chance anyone ever did, they wouldn't think anything odd about it. Just some kid, they'd say, some kid having a lark.

July 9

Aт the courthouse, Tom Evers opened *Henry and Beezus*. He
peeled back the tape that held the jacket flap in place, and beneath
it, on the hard inside of the cover, he saw written in fountain pen,
Henry + Katie. Whoever had written that had drawn a heart around
it, the way a kid might who had a secret crush.

But it was clear that a kid hadn't written it. The handwriting was
too elegant, too precise. It was the penmanship Tom had seen many
times and remembered well from words of encouragement written
across his calculus exams in high school: *Excellent! Terrific!* He knew
the handwriting he was staring at belonged to Mr. Dees.

Mr. Dees

It embarrassed me to stand there in the courthouse and watch Tom Evers look at such a thing, to see him coming to the picture in his head of me secretly peeling back that cover to write a thing a kid with puppy love would have written. I'd done it that Wednesday evening before deciding I would take the books to the Mackeys' house for Katie to find. It shames me now to say to you that I took pleasure from the thought that when she picked up that book, my secret pledge of love would be there just below where she held her thumb. It was a small thing like that, a thing I can barely stand to say for how foolish it makes me look, but what I hope is you'll understand, despite how I've sometimes deceived you, how far a lonely man like me might go, how much he might risk.

Was it enough? I asked Tom Evers. Enough to prove that I was the one who put that book in the library's return bin during the same time that Raymond R. was driving down Route 59 to Georgetown and then across the river to Honeywell? Didn't it prove that I wasn't with him?

"It doesn't prove anything," Tom said, "only that you wrote what you did inside this book. I can see that. But you might have written that any time, Mister Dees. Katie might have had her book laying out sometime this summer when you came to give her a lesson and you found yourself alone with it and you wrote what you did. Who's to say?"

"All right then," I told him. "Look in the back. Look in that pocket where they keep the card that they stamp when you check out the book." I didn't like to use my teacher's voice, but that's what I did. "You look there, Tom Evers, and then tell me what you know."

That's where I'd hidden the things I didn't deserve, the things I'd meant to return to the Mackeys because I knew I had no right to them.

Gilley

Tom Evers came to our house that Sunday afternoon, and for a while he talked only to my father, the two of them standing on our porch. From the entryway, I could hear them.

"I've got Henry Dees down at the courthouse," Tom said.

"What for?" said my father, and I could tell from his voice that he was suspicious that Mr. Dees would tell what he knew about what he'd done to Raymond R.

"Questions. Things I had to know." I heard the leather of Tom's holster squeak. "Junior, I'm afraid I'm going to need to talk to Patsy."

My father let him into our house, and he sent me upstairs to fetch my mother. She was in the bedroom sitting in the rocking chair she'd had since Katie was a baby. "I used to sit here and rock her," she said. "Do you remember that, Gilley?"

I told her I did, and then I let her sit there a while longer before I told her that Tom Evers was downstairs and he wanted to talk to her.

Tom showed us that book, that *Henry and Beezus*, one of Katie's books. There in our entryway, he showed us what Mr. Dees had written beneath the jacket, and he showed us what was in the manila pocket at the back of the book: a thin, gold bar broken from one of the clips that Katie had been wearing in her hair when she left for the library that Wednesday evening, and a check my mother had made out to Mr. Dees for the tutoring he'd done.

The sight of that broken hair clip nearly turned us all inside out. My mother reached her hand out for it, and I believe that might have been the moment that cost Tom Evers in the end, made him decide not to push my father for answers. We'd been hurt too much by that point; Tom could see it in the way my mother's hand trembled, in the way my father took a sharp breath and said, with a break in his voice, "Good Christ."

"Is it hers?" Tom asked. I could see he was sorry to ask the question. He had to clear his throat. "Is it Katie's?"

My father turned away to the staircase and steadied himself by placing his hand on the newel post. My mother was turning that broken hair clip over and over in her hand, and to her, it must have seemed that no one else was in her house, that Tom Evers hadn't just asked her that question.

Finally, I was the one to answer. "It is," I said. "It's one of my sister's."

Tom nodded. "And she was wearing it—"

I didn't let him finish. "That night," I said. "Yes, she was wearing it on Wednesday night."

There was one more thing Tom Evers needed my mother to do. Could she please confirm that she had indeed written this check out to Henry Dees that Wednesday evening?

She found her voice. "I wrote it," she said. "Right before he left here. I went out onto the porch where Mister Dees and Katie were having their lesson, and I said, 'Your father will be home soon. We'll have lemon sherbet for dessert.' Then I wrote that check. I used Katie's pen. Then I gave it back to her, and she clipped it to the neckline of her T-shirt, the way she'd taken to doing even though we said she'd end up losing it."

"Her pen?" Tom Evers said.

"That's right." My father turned back from the staircase. "A fountain pen like the one Henry Dees carried. Katie admired it, so Henry got her one of her own."

Tom Evers ran his hand through his hair. "What sort of pen did you say it was?"

"A fountain pen," my mother said.

"A Parker," said my father. "A Parker 51."

Tom Evers looked at my father a long time. Then he said, "Junior, would you please come out to my car with me?"

I stepped out onto the front porch and watched them go down the walk to the street. There, in the shade, Tom opened the passenger-side door and stooped over to lean into the car. When he straightened, he had a plastic bag in his hand, and he showed my father what was inside it.

The wind was blowing through the trees, but from the porch I could hear bits of what Tom and my father were saying.

"This pen," Tom said.

"Katie's," said my father.

I couldn't hear enough then to tell that Tom Evers had found the pen in the grave with Katie. My father would tell me that later. All I knew at the time was that the pen in that bag wasn't Katie's. I knew because just before Tom came to show us that library book and the broken hair clip and the check my mother had written, I'd walked into Katie's room, as I'd done countless times that week, and I saw it—her pen, the one Mr. Dees had given her—lying on her dresser.

My father would later claim that he'd genuinely believed that the pen in the bag was Katie's. "How else," he said, "would it have been there with her?" He said it in a way, with just enough bite to his voice, to make me wonder whether he'd been lying to Tom Evers because he knew Tom was on Mr. Dees's trail, and my father was afraid something would come out about what had happened the night before at the glassworks.

That day on the street, Tom leaned in close to my father, and something about the way my father held himself—his shoulders stiffened, and his head went back—told me that Tom was saying something about Raymond R.

The wind died down, and I could hear him say, "Someone posted bond last night, and now I don't know where Raymond Wright's gone."

My father had the nerve to say, "You couldn't find my daughter, and now you don't know where the man who killed her is. Tom, I feel sorry for you when this news gets out."

Tom bowed his head. He stubbed the toe of his boot against the curb. Then he said to my father, "Junior, I hate to do this, but I'm going to have to ask to see your gun, that Colt."

"That Colt?" my father said. "I threw that Colt in the river. Like you said, Tom, I didn't have any business having that thing around. I might have hurt someone with it."

"Who's to say you didn't? Where were you last night?"

"I was home with my family. Ask Patsy. Ask Gilley." He turned and looked at me standing there on the porch. I was thinking how that Colt had gone into the glass furnace along with Raymond R.'s body, how everything had been broken down. "Where else would I have been," my father said, a catch in his voice, "at a time like this but with my family? You've got kids of your own, Tom. Good Christ."

For a good while, neither of them spoke. Finally, Tom said, "If you want the truth, this pen looks sort of beat up." He held the bag up to the sunlight filtering through the tree branches above him. "Sort of worn to be a new pen."

"Well, you know kids," my father said. "They rough things up, don't they?" Tom looked down at the pen. I could see his hand closing into a fist, the plastic bag bunching up in his palm. My father put the question to him again. "You know that, don't you, Tom? Like I said, you've got kids of your own."

Tom's fist relaxed. "Yes, I suppose they do." He opened the bag and took out the pen. He handed it to my father. "I can't say what I'd do if someone did one of my children the way that Raymond Wright did your Katie. I imagine we'll all be hurting for you and Patsy for a good long while. This whole town—I guess I can speak for myself, too—a good many of us, I imagine, wouldn't mind if Raymond Wright turned up dead."

I knew then, with a certainty that didn't make me feel any way at all—didn't make me happy or relieved or sad or full of guilt; it was, as so many things would be in my life from that moment on, a fact—I knew that we would get away with what we'd done.

Mr. Dees

Tom Evers came back to the courthouse, where the fat-fingered policeman had been holding me, and he told me to go home.

"That wasn't your pen," he said.

"Tom, I can tell you the truth about that pen and how it came to be in that grave."

I was prepared to tell him how when I found Katie, I covered her with my shirt and then realized I couldn't be the one to go to the police. So I took the shirt off her and laid her back in that grave and shoved the dirt over her as if I'd been the one who'd done the killing. I'd thought it all out while I waited for Tom to come back to the courthouse, and I was ready to tell the story.

But he held up his hand. He told me again, his voice dead and sad, to go home. I could see how the life had drained right out of him, and I knew he'd barely slept since that Wednesday evening when the call about Katie had come. He'd done everything he could imagine to find her; he'd done everything by the book except the night Clare's snapshot of the Mackeys' house sent him there to do another search and he let it slip to Junior that Raymond R. was in the jail at Georgetown. How much guilt Tom carried with him over that I can't say, but it still pains me to think about what that guilt may have caused him to ignore or the things Junior Mackey somehow forced him to overlook, a good man like Tom Evers, who finally knew the truth—I have no doubt of this—but never had the evidence to bring Junior Mackey or anyone else to answer.

Gilley

HE CAME TO the funeral, Mr. Dees, but he didn't say a word to my mother or father or me, and we didn't speak to him, as if he were a stranger. How could we ever look at him again without thinking of that night at the glassworks when my father killed Raymond Wright?

It broke us; I believe that. Not just the grief we fell into because Katie was dead, but also what my father had done and the way it became something we never spoke of, acting like it hadn't happened while all along knowing it had.

You can pretend that your life is going on when really, all along, you're trapped in a moment you'll never be able to change. For me, it's that Wednesday night at the supper table when I said, *Katie didn't take back her library books.* For my father, it must be the recoil of that Colt Python—six shots, one coming steadily after another. And Mr. Dees? Well, I won't speak for him.

He's the one who found Katie. Even now, when I think of him in the woods that morning, digging with his hands, I don't know how to feel. The only thing I know now is that we're all connected, every one of us, even people we don't know. Raymond Wright saw Katie riding that elephant at the Moonlight Madness Carnival and he said, *Look at that cowgirl.* A few minutes before that, he'd stepped up to me on the sidewalk and said, *Bub, I want to shake your hand.* I didn't know him from Adam. I didn't think he had anything to do with me at all. Not him or even Mr. Dees or the gaunt woman with them in front of the Coach House, sipping coffee from a wax cup— Raymond Wright's wife, Clare, who, when I'm alone at night and I have to admit the truth, is the one I feel sorry for. She was just a woman, plain-faced and simple, who got in the way of trouble.

The day after the funeral, she came to our house. I can still see her on our porch, waiting there when I opened the door. She was wearing a plaid cotton dress, just a cheap wash-and-wear dress, the sort we sold to farmwives at Penney's. The dress had a thin card-board belt covered with fabric, and it was worn and crinkled. The top button, at the vee of her collarbone, was broken in half.

"It's your mama I'd be wanting to see," she said. For a moment, she looked me straight in the eye; then she bowed her head and stared down at her feet.

She was wearing new shoes, a pair of black pumps that were too elegant for the cotton dress. She didn't have on hose, and when she brought her right foot up on her toes, letting her heel slip free from the shoe, I could tell that it had already rubbed a blister.

Even now, when I think of this, it's the memory of those black pumps that breaks my heart. I imagine, as I did that day on the porch, Clare walking all the way from Gooseneck in shoes she hadn't had the chance to break in. I think of her raw heels, and how she must have thought she needed those pumps to make her look re-spectable. By this time, people were already starting to talk about her and how surely she knew what had happened to her husband, the one who had a hand in kidnapping that little girl.

That morning on the porch, I wanted to tell her what we had done that night at the glassworks. I wanted to tell her not to hope too much, not to wait, not to pin her future on the chance that someday she'd hear footsteps and there he'd be, her husband. I wanted to tell her all of this, but, of course, I couldn't.

What I did do was tell her to sit down on our porch swing. I even touched my hand lightly to her elbow and led her over to the swing. I wanted to get her off her feet, maybe even kneel down and help her slip out of those pumps.

"You've had a walk, haven't you?" I said.

She took a handkerchief from a pocket of her dress and used it to dab at the tears that were running down her cheeks. "I have," she said. "Child, I surely have."

"You just sit here then while I get my mother," I said. "It's cool here."

"It is that," she said. "And lands, look at your mama's flowers." She reached a hand out to the pots of petunias. "Don't they smell sweet? I've always thought a front porch about the best place to be on a summer day. You can just swing back and forth and watch the world go by. You can rest a bit."

In the house, my mother was in the living room sorting through the cards from the flowers at Katie's funeral. The church had been full of them, arrangements from people we didn't even know, people in Kentucky and Ohio and Illinois and as far north as Michigan who had heard about what had happened and had sent flowers because, as they said in their notes and cards, it was all they could think to do.

"Who was at the door?" my mother asked me.

"It's Clare Wright," I told her. "She wants to see you."

A jumble of cards slid from my mother's lap. "I couldn't, Gilley, really. What in the world would I say?"

When I stepped back out to the porch, Clare had her shoes off, but when she saw me, she quickly slipped them back on.

"My mother's resting." I sat down on the swing. "But I'll be sure to tell her that you came."

"Yes." Clare's lips pressed together in a tight line, and she gave a sharp nod of her head. "The burden she's carrying. You tell her I understand. You tell her I'll pray for her. I'll pray for all of you." She got up from the swing and she hobbled down the steps. Then she stopped and turned back to me. "I'm sorry," she said. "I'm sorry I didn't know enough soon enough. I'll be hurting a long time because it's all come to this. I'd change it if I could."

Clare

I DIDN'T HOLD it against her, that girl's mama, on account she wouldn't see me. I knew how it was to want to shut the door and not let anyone in. I thought maybe I could tell her something about that. I wish I'd had the chance.

On through that summer, I worked at Brookstone Manor. What else was left to me but what I knew: waking at dawn to the martins singing, spending my day in Brookstone's kitchen or laundry, coming home in the evening to my quiet house.

At first, I'd go by Henry Dees's place, and I'd think about knocking on the door because talk had already started. I heard it around town, folks saying that he knew something about what went on that night of the fifth.

I wanted to ask Henry Dees straight out if he knew anything about Ray and where he'd gone, but maybe, I told myself, it's better not to know. Maybe there's things in a person's life it's best to walk away from. Back in the winter at the Top Hat Inn, Ray kissed my hand; he called me *darlin'*. I still believe he was true. I don't think he meant to hurt me for the world. He built that porch. He said,

Darlin', name your paradise. I think it was this: like most of us, he was carrying a misery in his soul. I don't say it to forgive what he done, only to say it as true as I can. He was a wrong-minded man, but inside—I swear this is true—he was always that little boy eating that fried-egg sandwich in that dark hallway while the steam pipe dripped water on his head. I don't ask you to excuse him, only to understand that there's people who don't have what others do, and sometimes they get hurtful in their hearts, and they puff themselves up and try all sorts of schemes to level the ground—to get the bricks and joints all plumb, Ray used to say. They take wrong turns, hit dead ends, and sometimes they never make their way back.

One evening, he was there—Henry Dees. He had a ladder up to a martin house and he was reaching inside. I was on my way home from work, and this time, I couldn't stop myself. I came into his yard. I stood by the ladder, and I didn't say a word.

"Oh, no," he said. He was mumbling to himself, but the words were floating down to me. "No, no, no," he said. He was pulling the nest from the house, letting twigs and straw and dried-up grass and leaves sift through his fingers.

Finally, he came down the ladder, and when he saw me there, he said, "Clare. Oh, Clare."

I almost came apart then, hearing him say my name like he was saying he was sorry, but I kept my head up and I said to him, "Do you know anything about what happened to Ray?"

"Don't ask me that, Clare."

"Who else am I to know it from?"

He still had one hand on the ladder. He looked back up to the martin house where birds were coming now to roost, squawking because their nest had been messed with.

"Some folks can't hide things. They don't have enough, not enough money or influence or shame." He swung the ladder down, and I had to move back out of the way. "They'll have to answer someday. We'll all have to answer."

"If you've got the answer, you should give it to me."

"I can't do that, Clare. Please."

"Then you're not the man I thought you were," I said. It's still a mystery to me how Ray could just vanish away and no one ever find a trace or call to account the folks who ought to know. "No, sir," I said to Henry Dees. "You're no kind of man at all."

Mr. Dees

THERE'S NO SUCH thing as a perfect crime. You can think you've gotten away clean, but you always leave a clue. If you're Junior Mackey, though—if you have enough money and sway—you can get to the right people. You can make sure they keep their mouths shut or go blind to the truth right there in front of their eyes. But you can never, ever buy back time and the things you should or shouldn't have done.

I never told Tom Evers everything. This last thing I've saved for you.

It was a Wednesday evening, remember? July 5. The temperature was ninety-three degrees. Trans-Ams and GTOs were cruising around the courthouse square. People were starting to slip into the Coach House for supper. The breeze was rattling the leaves on the oak trees, and the sun wouldn't set until 8:33. All that light, and there I was in the truck with Raymond R., and he pointed across the square to the corner where out in front of the J. C. Penney store Katie was crouched down, fiddling with her bicycle chain.

"Yonder she is," said Raymond R. "A little queenie in distress."

He drove over there. He pulled the truck up to the curb.

"Darlin', you need help?" he asked Katie.

"My chain," she said.

He told her, "Oh, that ornery chain. Dang it all, anyway. Hon, we'll give you a ride home."

She reached into her bicycle basket and took out a stack of books. "I have to take these back to the library," she said.

"Sure, we'll take those books back," Raymond R. told her. "Then we'll run you home. We'll throw your bike in the back of the truck, and you can hop up here with us. You can sit right here between us, and we'll take care of you. You live in the Heights, don't you? On Shasta Drive?"

"How do you know where I live?"

"Your friend here told me. Your teacher. You know Mister Dees, don't you?"

Katie climbed up on the running board of Raymond R.'s truck. She curled her fingers over the lip of the window frame and said, "Hello, Mister Dees."

I could barely stand to look at her because I was ashamed of that kiss I had given her on the porch swing. I stared straight ahead at the J. C. Penney display window, where someone had dismantled a mannequin and left it lying in the corner: torso, head, legs, and arms.

"Katie," I said, "this is Ray. Mister Wright. He's my neighbor."

She rose up on her tiptoes and leaned through the open window. Her hair fell across my arm, and I smelled the faint scent of her little-girl sweat—the smell of talcum powder and a towel fresh from the dryer. A breeze had come up from the south, and it was a blessing—that stir of air—after a day of sun and heat.

"Hello, Mister Ray," she said. "I'm Katie."

"K-K-K-Katie," he sang, and she giggled and then smiled at him and said, "I know that song."

"I bet you do, darlin'," he said. "I surely do."

I felt like things were the way they should be. I was out of the picture and it was just the two of them—sweethearts. Oh, it was easy to see. They adored each other, and I thought I might as well have been that mannequin in the J. C. Penney window—a heap of bones snatched and tossed away.

I told Katie to please hop down from the running board, and I started to open the door. All I wanted was to go home. You have to understand: I had no idea then that Raymond R. had any intent of doing her harm. I'm not even sure he knew that himself.

"I'm going to walk," I told him.

The air was cooler now. The leaves rattled on the courthouse lawn's oaks. Cars roared down High Street—sporty cars all jazzed up with cherry-bomb mufflers and lifters and racing stripes. Teenage boys honked their horns—*Shave and a haircut, six bits.* Their tape decks played loud rock-and-roll music. People went into the Rexall, came out of the Coach House. Couples strolled around the square, looking in the store windows. I wished I could be like them: a man with a woman who had known him for years, a man just killing time, comfortable with who he was.

"Take it easy, Teach," Raymond R. said. "I told you I'd give you a lift."

"No. Please," I said. "Just let me go."

"Henry." It was the first time that he had called me by my Christian name, and I couldn't help but face him, look him in the eyes. What I saw amazed me—left me, though I was loathe to admit it, delighted. Raymond R. Wright was afraid—fearful, I imagined, of something torn loose inside him, some howl screaming through nerves and veins. That's how it happens with people at the end of misery. All the torment builds up and then lives explode, and there they are, broken forever. I was happy—oh, I know it was a horrible way to feel—but it was the truth. For a moment I was happy because, when I looked into Raymond R.'s eyes, I knew that he was in trouble. I had given him that money, and it hadn't been enough to buy him peace. Now, as I stood witness to his anguish, it made me believe that things weren't so hopeless for me. I could walk away, join the people strolling around the square, nod and say hello, and then head out Tenth Street to Gooseneck, just a man walking home on a summer evening. "Henry," Raymond R. said again. "Please."

I got out of the truck so Katie could get in. I fetched the three library books from her bicycle basket, got back in the truck, and held the books on my lap while Raymond R. drove away, down Fourteenth Street past the public library.

Katie squirmed around on the seat. She came up on her knees. "Hey, the library," she said.

Raymond R. told her, "Don't worry, darlin'. We'll get there, but first let's just ride around some. Let's enjoy the breeze."

He drove down Fourteenth Street, the library disappearing behind us, until he got to Taylor. He turned left and went a block east to Thirteenth. We were just driving, he said, just lollygagging.

That made Katie laugh. "Did you hear about the fight in the candy store?" she asked. "The lollipop got licked." She giggled and squealed and toppled over until she was leaning against me. "What did the chocolate bar say to the lollipop?" She rattled off the punch line. "Hello, sucker!"

Raymond R. tooted the horn. "That's the ticket," he said. "Now we're cooking." He turned back west on Cherry. "Let's air things out. Let's get up some speed."

He reached into his shirt pocket, fished out a pill, and popped it into his mouth. The truck went south on Tenth and soon we were passing Junior Mackey's glassworks and Gooseneck. The air rushed into the cab. Katie's hair came undone and whipped around her face. I tried to help her brush it away from her eyes, and one of her hair clips came loose. It fell to the floorboard, and when I reached for it, my foot came down on the metal clasp, snapping it. I picked up the thin, gold bar and closed my hand around it, knowing I would keep it for myself.

Katie patted the top of her head. "My hair clip." She crouched down, looking for the clip on the floor of the truck. I moved my feet, nudging away a crescent wrench, chewing gum wrappers, an empty Pepsi bottle. Katie found the metal back of the clip. "My mom will kill me," she said.

"Forget that hair bob." Raymond R. grabbed Katie's arm and jerked her back up onto the seat. "Hey, little doll. Do you know what the snail said while he was riding on the turtle's back?"

"I know that one," she said. "My dad told it to me." She threw her arms up over her head and shouted, "Wheeeeeee!"

I'd turn that moment over in my head a good while after— Katie's voice ringing out so clear and gay. "Wheeeeeee!" she said again, and Raymond R. took his hands from the steering wheel. "Wheeeeeee!" he said. "Come on, Teach. Join the fun."

So for an instant there were the three of us, silly with the air rushing in and Katie's hair flying about and the road stretching out toward the horizon.

Raymond R. put his hands back on the wheel and kept driving, not slowing down until we were a few miles out of Tower Hill. Nothing but farmland, a haze hanging over the fields. For a while, none of us said anything. We'd laughed ourselves silly over those jokes and then gone quiet, and I knew we were at that point where we felt strange to one another, when we knew we couldn't keep driving forever. Soon something had to happen.

Raymond R. turned off the highway and onto a gravel road. He stopped the truck and let it idle. Quail were bunching together in the middle of the road, a sign of rain coming, he said. Then his head lolled back and his eyelids drooped. "I'm give out," he said. "Jesus in a basket. I've been on the move all day."

Katie said, "Mister Ray, you promised you'd take me to the library."

"Shut up about that library," he said. "Jesus shit."

I snaked my arm around behind Katie and snapped my fingers close to his ear. He opened his eyes. He turned his head very slowly and looked at me, his face going hard.

"Please don't talk like that," I said. "She's a little girl."

"She's a sweetheart." Raymond R. took a strand of her hair in his fingers and very gently tucked it behind her ear. "Lordy, Lordy," he said. "Lookit all that pretty hair."

I couldn't bear to watch him touch her hair. I had to look away. I stared straight ahead down the gravel road past where the quail ruffled their wings, taking dirt baths in the dust. I kept my eyes on the point where the road dipped and then began to climb. I stared at the top of the hill where the gravel blanched white in the sunlight and land seemed to meet sky. I thought of the day, back in spring, when I'd been patching the cement steps, and the airplane flew over and I tipped back my head, wondering what I looked like from such a height. It was the moment just before I introduced myself to Raymond R.

Now I took a breath. "Katie," I said, "we're going to get out of the truck. You'll come with me, won't you?"

"But the library," she said, and I could tell she was starting to worry just a little.

"Give me your hand," I told her. "I promise you'll be all right."

That's when Raymond R. put the truck into reverse and started backing up toward the highway. The engine whined. The quail lifted with a riffling of wings, their white tail feathers flaring as they flew. The truck moved back into the dust that its tires kicked up, and I put my handkerchief to my nose and mouth. For a moment I thought about throwing open the door and tumbling out. I'd pull Katie along with me. Together we'd roll down the slope of the ditch. But Raymond R. was having a hard time keeping a straight track. The truck was skating over the gravel, and I couldn't take the chance.

"All right now," Raymond R. said. "We're done playing games."

"Please," I said.

"Stupid man." Raymond R. snapped his fingers in front of my face. "What ever made you think you had any say in this?"

He drove back into town. He drove by the Little Farm Market, and he honked his horn at a woman sitting on a bench. She was wearing a flowery summer dress—all oranges and purples—and nylon stockings rolled down to her ankles. A big woman with a transistor radio held up to her ear. "Him," Emma Short would later say.

"It's funny," Raymond R. said. "There she is, a woman in a tutti-frutti dress, just watching the world go by. She doesn't have a clue, does she?"

"A clue?" I was holding Katie's hair clip in my hand, rubbing my fingers over the smooth metal. "That woman with the radio?"

"She doesn't know there's people in the world." Raymond R. honked his horn again. "People like us."

He drove to the edge of Gooseneck and pulled down a grassy lane that ran along a wheat field. He cut the engine and the truck coasted to a stop.

The wheat field stretched out to the horizon. To the south, a wooded grove rose up. It was quiet there, away from town. Locusts chirred. A combine had cut a few swaths around the edge of the wheat field, and grasshoppers leaped up and stuck to the truck's fenders, its windshield, making faint ticking sounds.

"You're a darlin'." Raymond R. took Katie's bare foot. He cradled it in his hand. "Yes, sir. A real sweet potato."

He let go of her foot, and he reached across her and took my hand. He laid it on her knee, made me touch her like that. "A doll baby," he said. "Just what you've always wanted, right, Teach?"

Katie's skin was hot from the sun. I lifted my hand as if I had stuck it into fire. A noise came from the woods, a hawk taking flight, and I recalled the evening when Raymond R. and I put up the martin house, and the Cooper's hawk hid itself in the catalpa tree, just waiting for its chance at one of the martins.

"You know I'm in the dope, don't you?" Raymond R. was whispering now. "You know that's my story, right? I'm not afraid. People? They stopped meaning anything to me a long time ago. You know that too, don't you?"

I thought about the hawk, filled with hunger and greed, and yet so glorious. It was gliding now, banking and turning in widening circles, and I watched, mesmerized by that gentle float and spin, the hawk lifting higher and higher with each pass until it was a dark speck wheeling through the sky.

"Don't you think about Clare?" I asked Raymond R. "Such a sweet, good woman. Don't you think about how you hurt her? Me? I don't have anyone to be accountable to. But you . . . Clare . . . Ray, she's had enough heartache in her time."

That's when he looked down at his hands, studied them as if they weren't his anymore, belonged to a stranger. He reached into his pocket and took out the Sucrets tin. He opened it and started to fish out a pill. Then he stopped. He closed the tin and tossed it on top of the dashboard. "I never had a woman to love me until her," he said.

There comes a time when you have to believe in the goodness of people. "You don't want to hurt anyone, do you?" I asked him.

"You're right. I'm a lowlife kind of man. Always have been." His voice shriveled up to a puny thing. "You shouldn't be here with me. You shouldn't have anything to do with me at all. You ought to get out of this truck. Take this little doll baby with you. Take her back home. Go on. Take her back to her mama and daddy."

Katie scooted over closer to me, and I heard her sniffling, trying hard to fight back the tears. I felt a panic flare up inside my chest. I tried to imagine taking her home. How would I explain to Junior and Patsy Mackey how she'd come to be with me? I imagined ringing their doorbell and then standing in the glare of the porch light as the front door opened and Junior or Patsy waited for me to explain. How would I tell them the story? What would I say that would ever be enough for them to forgive what I'd done—the kiss, the time we'd spent with Raymond R.? Worse yet, how would I be able to stand it if Katie went running into the arms of her mother or father and I had to listen to her sobbing, telling them how frightened she'd been? How could I, who loved her, ever face something like that?

"I can't," I told Raymond R. "What in the world would I tell them?"

"Tell them, 'Here she is.' Say, 'Here's your little girl.'" He closed his eyes. "Please," he said. "Just take her and do whatever it is you have to do."

In just an instant, it would come to me that maybe Raymond R. was shooting straight. *Take her away from me,* he meant. *See to her. Make sure she gets home. Tell the police what you have to.*

But by the time I thought this, I was already out of the truck, stumbling over the ruts in the grassy lane, wanting to get back to Gooseneck, back to my house where I could hide with my shame, because what I heard when Raymond R. asked me to take Katie, to do whatever I had to, was *You've been wanting this, you've been wanting her. Now's your chance. Go on. Don't worry, I'll keep your secret. I won't tell.*

That's what I'm guilty of: being a coward, too much afraid of my own confused desires.

I turned back once, thinking I'd go back to the truck and I'd take her. Katie. I'd take her back to the courthouse square, and there her bike would be, that Sting-Ray bike with the banana seat and the butterfly handlebars and the silver streamers. I'd put the chain back on the sprocket. I'd buy a screwdriver at the Western Auto Store if I had to. I'd get my hands greasy, maybe even ruin my poplin jacket, but that would be all right. That'd be fine. Then Katie would pedal away, and it'd be like all the time the three of us had been in that truck never happened at all. She'd put her books into the library's after-hours returns bin and then she'd go home, and the next morning she'd wake to another grand summer's day.

Then I'd be able to say at least I did that, and in the morning, when the martins began to sing, I'd think, All right, this is my life, not so bad as I'd feared. Not perfect, but enough, not one to have to answer for.

I turned back to the truck, but it was already moving, driving farther down the lane. I ran a few steps after it, but I was too late. I bent over, put my hands on my knees. There in the grass were two of Katie's library books, *The Long Winter* and *Henry and Beezus*. I picked them up, and then I watched the truck until I couldn't see it anymore. I stood there a long time, hoping I'd see it come back, hoping that Raymond R. would change his mind and I'd be able to do the thing I should have done in the first place, the thing I've spent years wishing I could make happen: if only, when I had the chance, I'd taken Katie by the hand, got her out of that truck. If only I'd had the courage to take her home and tell my story and face the Mackeys, who by that time were surely starting to wonder whether they had any call to worry. I've had the rest of my life to go over it again and again. I'll have the rest of my days to wish I'd been a better man.

Did I think that Raymond R. might hurt Katie? I spent the rest of that evening convincing myself it couldn't be so.

If that night at the glassworks, he got what he deserved—Raymond R.—does that mean I should have gotten the same because I left Katie with him that evening in that grassy lane along the wheat field? Or Clare because she was too simpleminded, too trusting to know that her Ray was a dope fiend? Or Gilley because he tattled on Katie at the supper table and sent her off on her bicycle? Or her mother because she didn't tell her to stop and put on her sandals? Or Junior because Katie had been complaining about her bicycle chain for days, and he'd never done anything about it?

Oh, I heard it all that day at Katie's funeral. I heard the stories they told, the moments they kept going over in their heads. I'm sure, like me, they call them up now. How many times I've thought about that instant on the porch swing when I kissed Katie, or later when I walked away from her down that grassy lane along the wheat field.

And what about the ones that evening who saw us come and go—me and Katie and Raymond R.—and never for an instant thought there might be something wrong?

The problem is this: how many of us were there who could have done something to stop what was going to happen? Where does responsibility start and end?

Sure, some of us were more guilty than others. I'm not a stupid man. Still, there were people moving through our town that night, thinking they didn't have anything to watch out for. Maybe they saw us downtown on the square talking to Katie. Maybe they saw her up on the running board of Raymond R.'s truck, or me opening the door so she could get in and then fetching her library books from her bicycle basket. Maybe they thought, What's that little girl doing with those men?

Maybe you're one of those people. Or maybe you saw us later driving past the public library or heading out Route 59 or turning down that grassy lane at the edge of Gooseneck, and you didn't stop us, didn't follow us, didn't call the police. But what call would you have had? It was just a summer evening. People were everywhere moving through the long light, and we were just two men in a truck, a little girl between us.

If anyone's to blame, it's me. I was the last person who could have saved her. No matter how long I live, I'll know it forever. I'll imagine the two of us walking up that grassy lane, away from that wheat field, away from Raymond R., the last of the daylight fading into dusk but still enough left so we could find our way.

If it's true that I did what you claim, Raymond R. said when the police first questioned him (it's in the court record now; you can find it there), *then you ought to put me someplace where I can get help. I'm not saying I didn't do it. I don't know.*

There's no figuring the sorts of ragtag lives people can live, but if you want to, you can go to the circuit court's office and read the file and try to make more sense of it all, the way I did the one time I slipped back into town, the last time before I was gone forever.

So many years had passed, no one in that office recognized me, but they all knew the case I was talking about. They knew about Raymond R., that construction worker who up and disappeared, and a woman said she remembered that there used to be an old bachelor schoolteacher in town who'd been his friend, but she couldn't recall his name or where he'd gone. The Mackeys? Yes, they were still alive. Junior and Patsy. I asked whether they still lived in the Heights. "Oh no," the woman said. "They moved to New Mexico a good time back, and that boy of theirs, that Gilley, last I heard he was living in Missouri. A banker. That's what he made of himself."

I've thought this many times since then. For all of us, that Wednesday evening in July, there was something in the way the light caught the undersides of the maple leaves and set them to shining, some false promise in the way the river water held the sheen of the sun going down and the way the air cooled. We thought we were all free: free from work, from chores, from one another. The court-house clock chimed the hours and folks could hear it in Gooseneck and the Heights, and for a time there was twilight's grace—that muted light just before the final turn to dark. I think of Patsy Mackey stepping out onto her patio, worried because Katie hadn't come back from the library, and Gilley and Junior retracing her route, up High Street to the courthouse square, where they saw that bicycle, her bicycle, leaning against a parking meter. At the time, I was walking from the grassy lane along the wheat field to my house. I was walking through the fading light, and Raymond R. was driving away with Katie in his truck.

"It's a wonder something like that went on," the woman in the courthouse said when she was telling me what she remembered about "that ugly business with the Mackey girl."

"Henry Dees," I said to her. "That was the schoolteacher's name."

"That's right." She snapped her fingers. "Henry Dees. He always looked like he was carrying the world on his back. I'd see him around town, and my heart would break."

"Did you ever tell him that?" I asked her. "Tell him that you saw him, that you felt something about what it was to have his kind of life?"

"I can't recall ever saying a word."

"He might have liked to have heard it," I told her, and that was the last word I ever said to anyone who lived in Tower Hill.

TOWARD THE END of August that summer, Junior Mackey pulled into my drive. I let him in my house, and he stood in the kitchen just as he'd done the night he'd come to ask me to drive to Georgetown and bring back Raymond R.

"I can hardly bear to look at you," Junior said. He paced around the kitchen. "Every time I see you around town, I think of what you did, the way you watched us. I think about what you know." That was his life now, and always would be—a fearful life. I frightened him because I knew he'd killed Raymond R., and even though I couldn't afford to say anything because of my own part in it—I've barely been able to tell the story to you—he must have wondered whether someday I'd go to Tom Evers and tell him what I knew. "Do you have someplace to go?" He looked at me. "Somewhere away from here?"

I thought to myself then that it didn't matter where I ended up; I'd always be living that summer in that town, wishing that I'd done things differently, tormented by the fact that I hadn't. I'd never go far enough to be able to escape it. Maybe you're happy about that. Or maybe you're not. Maybe you're carrying your own regrets, and you understand how easy it is to let your life get away from you. I wish I could be the hero of this story, but I'm not. I'm just the one to tell it, at least my part in it—this story of Katie Mackey and the people who failed her. It's an old one, this tale of selfish desires and the lament that follows, as ancient as the story of Adam and Eve turned away forever from paradise.

"I guess one place is as good as another," I told Junior Mackey.

He nodded. "Then maybe you could be thinking about going." He took five bills from his wallet. They were thousand-dollar bills, a sight I'd never seen, and he reached them out to me. "To take care of yourself for a while. To get you back on your feet."

I pushed his hand away. "You live with your own regrets," I said. "I'll live with mine."

That was the end of it. He got back in his car and drove away, and a few weeks later, toward the end of summer, I closed the door to my house in Gooseneck for the last time. I left the furnishings there, left the martin houses atop their poles in the backyard. I wouldn't be there in spring when the birds came flying back. They'd sing their dawnsong, but I wouldn't be there to hear it. I got in my Comet, and when I turned onto the Tenth Street spur, I didn't look back.

The day was clear. I remember that, one of those bright days when it's still summer but we've already made the turn toward autumn, and the sky is blue. Here in the flatlands of Indiana you can hit a straight stretch of road, and you can see all the way to the horizon. If it ever happens to you, you might swear, as I did that day, that if you can just keep moving—keep driving long enough, fast enough—you'll come to the edge of the world, that point where land rises up to meet sky, and you'll have no choice; you won't be able to stop. You'll just float out into all that blue—call it Heaven if you want—and just like that, you'll be gone.

Acknowledgments

Many thanks to those who offered advice and encouragement along the way: Phyllis Wender, Sonia Pabley, Susie Cohen, Amy Bloom, Steve Yarbrough, Ladette Randolph, Hilda Raz, Karen Shoemaker, Gerald Shapiro and Judith Slater, Paul and Ellen Eggers, Bart and Melanie Adams, Harry and Mildred Read, Jim and Maria Duncan, Ron Read, Lynda Clemmons, Brenda Boganwright, Amanda Dean, Christine Bonasso, Kathleen Finneran, Doug Johnstone, and Amos Magliocco. The Ohio State University has been generous with its support, as have my colleagues in the English Department and the creative writing program. The fates have blessed me with Sally Kim, an editor of great courage and grace. My eternal gratitude to her and to everyone at Shaye Areheart Books who believed in this novel.

About the Author

LEE MARTIN is the award-winning author of the novel *Quaker-town*; the memoirs *From Our House*, which was a Barnes & Noble Discover Great New Writers selection in 2000, and *Turning Bones*; and the short-story collection *The Least You Need to Know*. He has won a fellowship from the National Endowment for the Arts, the Mary McCarthy Prize in Short Fiction, a Lawrence Foundation Award, and the Glenna Luschei Prize. He lives in Columbus, Ohio, where he teaches in the creative writing program at The Ohio State University.

About the Type

THIS BOOK was set in Adobe Garamond, a typeface designed by Robert Slimbach in 1989. It is based on Claude Garamond's sixteenth-century type samples found at the Plantin-Moretus Museum in Antwerp, Belgium.

Composition by Stratford Publishing Services
Brattleboro, Vermont

Printing and binding by Berryville Graphics
Berryville, Virginia